BEYOND SOLSTICE GATES

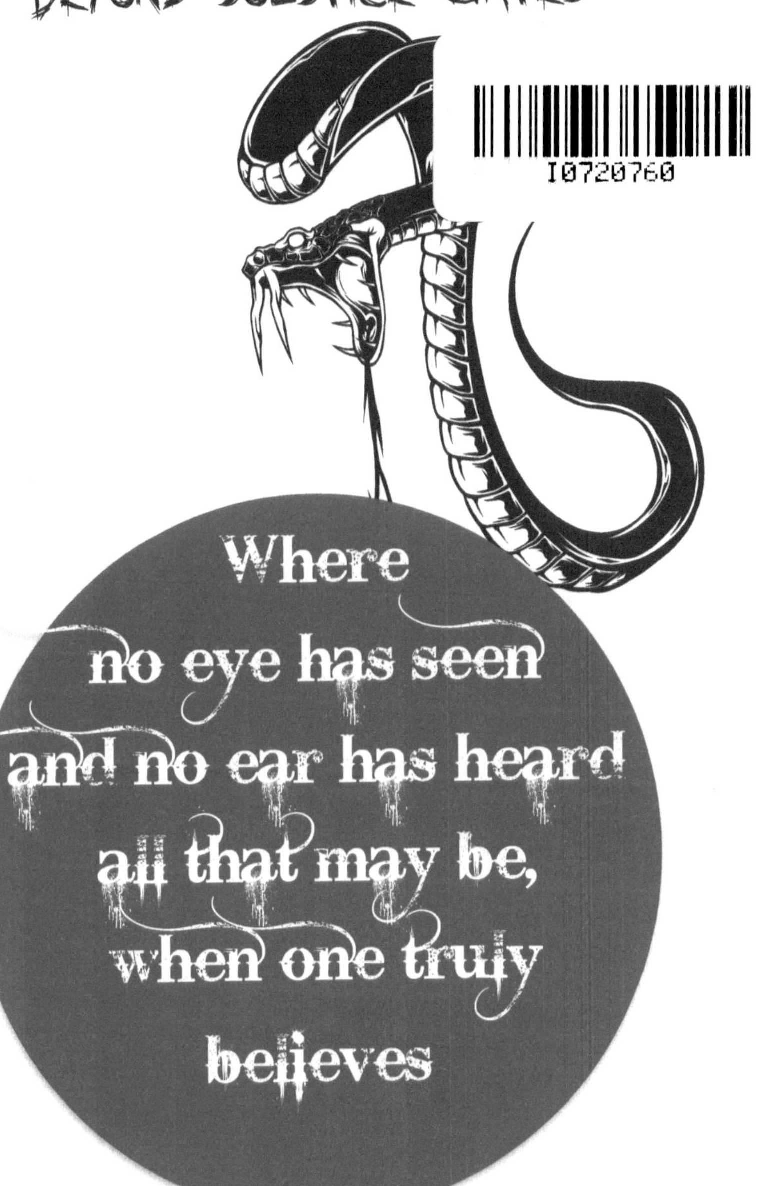

Ahelia Publishing
Helena, Montana

CHASM of ACHERON

By Kimm Reid

BEYOND SOLSTICE GATES

Where
no eye has seen
and no ear has heard
all that may be,
when one truly
believes

Chasm of Acheron

ISBN- 978-1-988001-03-6

1. Supernatural 2. Science Fiction 3. Fiction

Published by Ahelia Publishing, LLC.
Printed in the United States of America

www.aheliapublishing.com
kimm.reid@outlook.com

TABLE of CONTENTS

Chapter One

Cleft in the Rock

"WE NEED TO GET INSIDE!" Judah shouted. The winds were so fierce, so wild, so unpredictable, that the Travelers could barely keep their balance. The winds weren't blowing to the east or coming from the south necessarily; they were swirling. One minute they'd be hitting the Travelers in the face and the very next minute they'd be coming at them from behind. It felt as though the winds were angry and the Travelers were the target of their fury.

Everyone agreed with Judah's command. However, it was going to be difficult—if not impossible—to find any place to get inside of. Jennifer wasn't so sure she wanted to be inside of anything —not with the winds howling so viciously and the land shaking itself as violently as it was. As she glanced over to the pile of rubble that used to be a cave, Jennifer shifted from being unsure to being absolutely certain. She didn't want to be inside of anything that could collapse from either the shaking ground or the pounding winds … or from any other reason for that matter.

Even though it was terribly dangerous and unpredictable out here in the open, she considered that it might be more appealing to be fried by a lightning bolt or knocked over by a falling tree than to be buried alive under a pile of rock and rubble. Jennifer didn't particularly like small spaces to begin with, so being buried alive was definitely the worst choice on the long list of terrible choices.

Sam was doing significantly better now with his arm wrapped tightly. It was probably too tight and cutting off the circulation, but right now, that was the best they could do. At least he was conscious and the bleeding had stopped. A little of his color had come back, but overall, he was still pale and wobbly on his feet.

It's hard to have color in his face when so much of his blood is on the ground, Jennifer thought to herself. Even bloodied, pale, and wounded, she thought Sam looked wonderful, and she wanted to stay near him. She wanted Judah to stay close as well since she trusted her twin brother more than any other, but if Sam stayed close, she would be fine with that.

The boys had brilliantly thought to grab the dead guards' swords, and as Bella watched Matt persuade one to come out of its sheath, she'd noticed each guard also had two flasks of water attached to their belts. She squealed in excitement and jumped up and down.

None of the Travelers had eaten in a couple of days; they were famished. If they had water, though, at least they could keep going a while longer. Hopefully, they'd come upon some berry bushes or fruit trees, but the chances of that were pretty slim since they had yet to see either of those things in all their journeys to the Dark Land.

"LOOK," Bella shouted into the wind. She was pointing and waving frantically because certainly, nobody could hear her words. Matt looked to where she was pointing and noticed the enormous flasks. He'd been so busy trying to wiggle the sword free that he hadn't bothered to see anything else.

Matt ran over and motioned the others to come near as well. There seemed to be less blood to swash through now, although only slightly because what the ground hadn't swallowed up was being scattered by the winds. They unhooked the flasks and dragged them closer to the pile of rubble where they'd been earlier. It seemed to be the only place where the Travelers could get any shelter from the hurricane winds … even that shelter was rather flimsy.

Squeals of delight and glee were sent out and dry lips were moistened as they shared the cool, clear contents of one of the flasks. Oh, never had water tasted so sweet. There were no worries about germs or who drank out of the flask before whom. The Travelers had gone without water for too long so the only thing any of them cared about was getting some of that cool water through their parched lips.

Without a doubt, they could have easily polished off two or more of the flasks, but Matt spoke up loudly, reminding the others they needed to save some for later.

They all knew he was right, but that didn't stop them from wanting to lap up every last drop. They had no idea how long they'd be stuck out here in the dry, trembling, angry land, so rationing the water was a necessity, no matter what they *felt* like.

Every Traveler was desperately begging their Shailma for safety, or direction, or wisdom; anything at all, really. They were horribly afraid, but it was a feeling they were becoming used to. Each of them determined to carry on, no matter what.

"As long as we stay together," Bella had shouted, "we'll be okay."

"That's crap!" Jennifer said. She would have whispered it because she didn't want to annoy Bella, but nobody would hear her anyhow with all the racket and commotion the land was making. All she could think about right now was Pierce. They had all stuck together—he was right with them. Now he was gone, or at least, he hadn't come out of the cave with the rest. She supposed they didn't know for certain what had happened to the boy, and she knew she shouldn't assume but …

Obviously, her auntie's idea of being "okay if they stayed together" was not accurate, for one of them was not okay—he was not okay at all. How could Bella say they'd all be okay? They could only assume that Pierce had been lunch for whatever ravenous beast had been in that cave with them.

It made no difference since the shaking ground had caused the cave to crumble in on itself. If the beasts hadn't ravaged Pierce's flesh for their dinner, the cave had become his grave. Either way, there was no way they'd see him again, so they decided not to stick around and wait. It had to be put out of their minds for now. They could not afford to become emotional, or distracted … not right now.

None of the Travelers had any idea that the cave had been a trap set for them. It hadn't worked nearly as well as the army had hoped. The plan was for all of the Travelers to be lunch for the caged beasts—all except the twins, of course. It didn't matter now … nothing mattered. The Travelers wouldn't get far, and King Shrailzhar knew exactly where they were. He'd be back in no time to take their lives and steal their souls, cursing them for all eternity to his land.

Kaija Mae was the one who finally shouted out a suggestion. It was not her own thought, but one that Shekinah had put into her heart. She was confident it was the right thing to do. The quiet girl always sang when she was talking with Shekinah, not loudly but out loud. The Travelers could always tell, no matter how quiet her songs were, that she was talking to her Shailma.

She stopped singing now and motioned for everyone to come near. Kaija Mae was quiet by nature so screaming and shouting odd, and possibly unacceptable, suggestions were very much out of her comfort zone. Comfort was not an option now, however, and so with every ear turned toward her voice, she shouted with all her might.

"THE HOLLOWS," she yelled. "WE HAVE TO GET TO THE HOLLOWS," she shouted again. She knew everyone had heard her because before the last word had rolled off her tongue they each whipped their heads around to look her in the eye. The looks they had in their own eyes were not welcoming or agreeable. None of them seemed to think returning to where they had just come from was a good idea at all. Nobody had to say it; she could read it in their stares.

It wasn't that going back in that direction was a bad idea all by itself, but rather it was the fear that Asphelia's Hollow had been discovered by the army that was the dreadful thought. If it was even still a standing hollow was questionable, but what was not questionable and what they did know for certain, was that the army had swarmed inside of it. There was no way they'd be safe in their hollow now.

"I DIDN'T SAY ASPHELIA'S HOLLOW," Kaija Mae hollered. "I SAID *THE* HOLLOWS!"

Now they were confused. They'd seen many of the rocks Kaija Mae told had them were hollows, but they'd never been inside any of them, and they didn't know if she had either. Their imaginations couldn't go that far—not right now. The Travelers didn't want to go anywhere, but they knew they couldn't stay here. They had only two choices: stay or go. Neither was acceptable.

It was so hard to hear—communication was almost impossible. Words were getting mixed up or not heard at all, and it was causing crazy confusion and misunderstanding. Kaija Mae wanted to grab them all and drag them to the hollow that she knew well—the hollow which she, Aviel, Tahlia, and the others had used as their home since they'd been here. But she knew they would not follow her easily. Somehow she'd have to make them understand.

Kaija Mae looked around, searching for anywhere that would give them enough shelter from the outrageous winds for her to explain what Shekinah had told her. She found no acceptable place.

Shekinah, she cried, *I need help.* He touched her eyes so she would notice a small gap just to the south of the cave where it looked like the winds wouldn't find them. Kaija Mae tried to run to the spot and trusted the others to follow. The winds would not let her run, however, so she put her head down and with all her might plowed her way to the spot. The others did follow, even though none of them could see the small shelter in the cleft of the rock.

It was an effort to get there, but once they did the shelter opened its arms to the Travelers and welcomed them inside. It was small, so small that they couldn't actually get inside, but it sheltered them enough that they could hear Kaija Mae if she hollered.

She did holler. There were no other options.

"SHEKINAH IS LEADING US TO *OUR* HOLLOW," she bellowed. As she did, her fingers pointed to Aviel, Tahlia, and the others who were still with them. "YOU FORGET THAT *WE* HAD A

HOLLOW FOR MANY YEARS BEFORE *YOU* CAME TO TRILLEAH." She was disappointed in these Travelers who seemed to forget there were some in this Dark Land long before themselves. She was annoyed they didn't seem to want to consider anything other than their own experiences, their own hollow, their own ideas.

"We've been here a long time," she huffed, still shouting. It was unusual to see Kaija Mae upset, so now that she was, everyone else paid attention. They felt sorry that they hadn't given her the proper respect she felt she deserved. Kaija Mae was right, though. She and the others who'd been here since the beginning *did* have a great deal of information about Trilleah, the king, and the army that the others didn't have.

"Sorry, Kaija Mae," Judah shouted.

"Tell us what to do," Bella shrieked.

"What did Shekinah say?" Matt hollered.

"He said to return to *our* hollow—the one he showed us when we were dragged to this Dark Land … it's over that way," she said and pointed to the north. "It's a long way, but not as far as Asphelia's Hollow."

Suddenly their minds began spinning and whirling. The idea of being in a safe hollow sounded acceptable … almost pleasant.

"Is there food?" Jennifer asked, for she was famished. Her stomach ached and she was weak.

"Do you think it's still standing?" Bella asked Matt who, of course, didn't know.

"Are there painkillers in the hollow, Kaija Mae?" Sam asked. He wanted those more than food or shelter or anything else for that matter. He was acting very bravely, but they could tell he was in horrible pain.

Simeon, Jennifer asked, *is this the right thing to do?* She trusted Kaija Mae very much, and she knew Kaija Mae heard accurately from her Shailma many times. But Jennifer had also learned always to double check with her own Shailma before following someone else.

It is, Little One, Simeon whispered. *Follow her, but keep your eyes on me.*

"Let's go," Jennifer shouted. She stood up but wasn't prepared for the powerful gust of wind, and it sent her back down to her knees. She wasn't shaken, though, and got up quickly. This time she grabbed onto the unwounded hand of Sam and also one of Bella's hands. There was no way they were going to be able to make their way back to Kaija Mae's hollow unless they depended on each other.

Together, hand in hand—except for Sam, of course, who had only one had held, and Matt who had the basket of tiles—they hung onto one another and moved away from the little covering that Shekinah had shown Kaija Mae. They stumbled and were tossed around by the winds. Never had they felt such powerful winds ... like the wind had the arms of an octopus that kept wrapping around the Travelers trying to fling them to the ground and keep them from moving ahead.

The ground was not somewhere they wanted to be flung to. It was not too hot, but neither was it cool and since this was the winter, it should have been quite cold. As long as it was not hot enough to boil their skin, they wouldn't complain about it. There were plenty of other things to complain about. The elements in Trilleah were bad … very bad.

Even though the hard ground was not burning them, it was beginning to form cracks … this *was* something worth complaining about. The bubbling orange and red lava they'd seen earlier wasn't boiling over at the moment, but it was shooting up big blasts of smoke and sulfur from countless fusions in the ground. Their noses were burning, but they didn't dare let go of each other to cover their faces.

The Travelers were soon back around to where the pile of rubble was once a cave … back to where the bodies of the gigantic guards lay, lifeless and without their heads.

"THEY ARE SO HUGE," Matt hollered.

As they were about to pass them by, Mishan came to Judah's mind and again, Simeon came to Jennifer. They both seemed to suggest the same thing, and as Judah began to holler the instructions he'd heard, Jennifer's attention rose.

"GO TO THEM," he shouted.

The others looked at him defiantly. Nobody wanted to go anywhere near those dead, smelly, headless corpses.

But Jennifer knew what he was doing and began trying to move toward the guards.

"WHAT FOR?" Matt shouted.

"THEY'RE DISGUSTING," Bella added.

"YES," came the screaming voice of Judah, "BUT THEY MIGHT HAVE SOMETHING WE NEED!"

Like what, was what everyone was thinking, but nobody bothered to ask. Jennifer knew. Judah knew. The others followed, but not without much persuasion. The twins knelt down and began searching the guards thoroughly, completely unsure of what they were looking for but confident they'd know when they found it … at least that's what they were hoping.

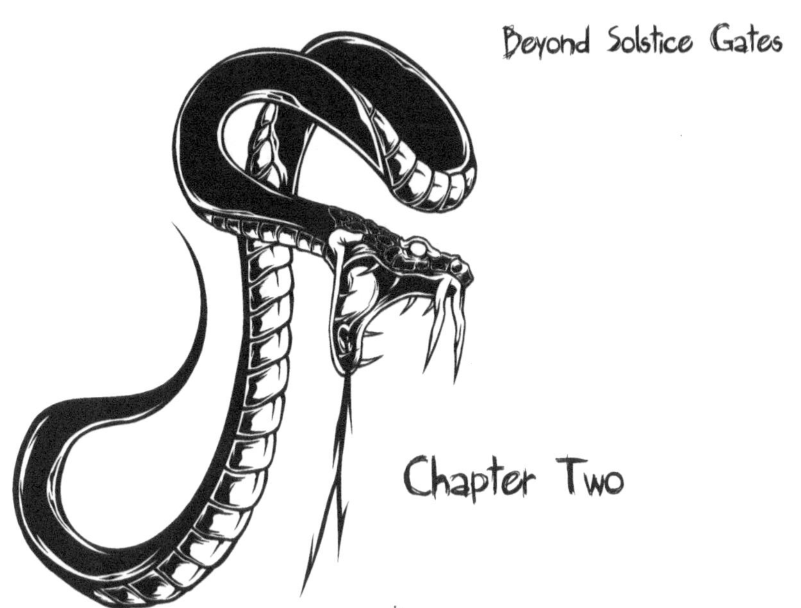

Chapter Two

Fractured

The smell of dead guards and the pool of their blood was so nauseating that Jennifer wanted to throw up. Her stomach knotted and writhed. She held herself together, though, twisting and yanking until finally, she managed to pull off some of the guard's heavy armor. The twins had a feeling that what they needed was underneath, even though neither of them had any idea what it was they were looking for.

They already had the guards' swords—which were much too heavy to carry—but both Judah and Jennifer had heard their Shailmas direct them to search the guards for "needed things," so that was exactly what they were going to do.

Neither of the Shailmas mentioned what those "needed things," might be, but the twins hoped that when they found them, they'd know. They were right. As one enormous piece of armor came off, and then another, and another, and another, there, tucked away in deep hidden pockets were gizmos and gadgets and whatchamacallits and thing-a-ma-jigs and do-dads … a bunch of them.

There were so many things hidden inside those guards' pockets that the twins didn't know what to take and what to leave. Their Shailmas did not give them such information, so they had to choose for themselves. Of course, if they would have asked the Shailmas—and indeed they should have—Judah and Jennifer would have known what to take and what to leave behind.

That's the thing with Shailmas; they always know the answers, but they are neither bossy nor pushy. Often, they will only offer the answers if the questions are asked.

The others who had been standing back curiously watching the twins, finally realized what was going on and joined in the search. Even Sam, when he began to see all that was being discovered inside the armor and pulled out of the hidden pockets of the dead guards, joined in. Even if it was with only one arm and an outrageous amount of pain, Sam wanted to be a part of it.

The winds had picked up even more since they'd begun their search for "needed things," and some of the blood that was still trickling from the guards' headless bodies was splattering here and there. It truly was a sickeningly smelly, detestably disgusting, nauseatingly nasty treasure hunt.

Once the Travelers had dumped out everything they could find from the guards' pockets and stuffed all they thought they could use … or might need … or found interesting … into their own pockets, they continued toward the hollows. They had no idea if they'd find any of the boulders that had covered those hollows still there, or if the army had destroyed them all, or if Shrailzhar's goons were interested in destroying only Asphelia's Hollow. They would have all the answers soon enough.

While Jennifer had been busy transferring items from the guards' pocket into her own, she came across the loveliest of all imaginable things. As she shoved her hand in one of the pockets in her jacket and felt a familiar treasure, she shrieked and did a silly little dance. The others were confused, but when she pulled out her tattered red blanket, Bella and Judah understood completely.

Jennifer thought she'd left the treasured blanket in the hollow when she first arrived. She hadn't even thought about it, but now that it was in her hands again, she realized that she had missed it terribly. It was small and worn-out now, just a piece of cloth really, but regardless, it was her most treasured belonging. She brought it out, rubbed her cheek with it, and smelled it deeply. Maybe this was a sign that everything would be okay.

Yes, that's got to be it, she thought. *It's a sign from Mamma*, she told herself and smiled.

That thought faded and was quickly replaced with other much less happy thoughts. Right there, in another pocket in her jacket, Jennifer's hand bumped the little green jar from her room back in the hollow. She'd completely forgotten about it as well. In fact, when her fingers landed on it, she didn't recognize what it was and certainly didn't remember putting it there.

Now it might seem odd that Jennifer had forgotten about such treasures, especially since she'd had them in her pockets all this time. But then again, she had been busy since leaving the hollow and so maybe her forgetfulness wasn't so odd after all.

I wonder if the stupid green jar is like the cloaks in the hollow? Jennifer let her mind wander to Asphelia's Hollow and remembered her first time in the underground hideout. She'd been given a hideous gray cloak for her birthday and had hung it in the Eating Chamber. But when Bella had taken her to her Sleeping Chamber for a rest, there it was—hanging on a hook behind her door.

Jennifer knew she hadn't brought the cloak with her to her Sleeping Chamber, and decided her auntie must have. When she went back to the Eating Chamber later, though, there it was. Perhaps this little green jar was like that cloak in that it appeared wherever it needed to be. *Some things are, I suppose,* she thought to herself.

As Jennifer held it in her hand now, she had a feeling that indeed it *was* right where it needed to be. Somehow it held information that would be needed soon … very soon. She didn't know the jar kept appearing because she had not heard Simeon say anything to her about it. It seemed as though maybe it was the little green jar itself that had given her the thought. There was no way to know where the thought came from, but there was no denying that it was an interesting thought nonetheless.

Now, some might say there is no way such things happen and others might shrug their shoulders and say, "I dunno, maybe." But anyone who'd seen that little green jar knew it was so. There was no denying this was no ordinary little green jar. There was some sort of unexplainable powers tucked under the lid and the only one to whom the jar would show those powers, now held it in her hands.

Jennifer pressed the lid on tightly and crammed it back into her pocket along with a small knife, a spool of thick black nylon thread, and a couple of other things she wasn't sure about. She wanted to grab a few more things, but her pockets were already packed full and they had no cloaks to carry heavy things.

All of the Travelers took as much as their pockets could hold as well. Some had many things, while others had very few—but they all wished they had their cloaks. Those cloaks would have been so helpful to them for so many reasons, but it made no never mind now.

"This way," Matt motioned. Nothing looked familiar to any of them, but they followed a narrow path, the only path there was to follow. The twins had gone off the path earlier when Simeon had taken them to the shelter, which turned out to be more like a rat hole.

The others, though, had followed this narrow path all the way, so they knew it was the right way to go now.

Still, it was odd that nothing looked familiar. It had only been a day or two since they'd been on this very path so it was concerning why it seemed like a brand new one now. They had no other path to follow, though, and the weeds and brush were too high and too prickly to try and maneuver anywhere else. This seemed the right way —it had to be. Surely Kaija Mae would know the way to her hollow, especially if Shekinah had told her to go there.

Jennifer grabbed hold of Sam's unburned hand in one of her own and Judah's hand in the other.

"Do *not* let me go, no matter what!" she hollered to the boys. They both nodded to her, but neither heard what she'd said.

Simeon came to Jennifer's eyes just then. He didn't say anything … not even a whisper. Her Shailma simply moved alongside them for a few minutes before letting the atmosphere cover him again. Jennifer wondered if the others had seen their own Shailmas as well, or if only Simeon let himself be seen. She wanted to ask, but the winds were howling too loudly for her voice to be heard. She could hardly even hear her own thoughts.

Simeon, she whispered and was suddenly very thankful the Shailmas spoke to their minds and not to their ears. That's all she had to think, and Simeon came to her straightaway.

Little One, this is the reason we communicate to your minds. It's moments like this—moments when the winds are howling so loudly, and all hell seems to be breaking loose around you, that you need to hear the Shailmas. You can hear us in your mind, no matter how loud it gets around you.

Jenny, Simeon continued, *do you recall when I first brought you to this land? You were so afraid and felt so alone. Remember that first time when you knelt in the dirt at the edge of Malleana Forest? I said something to you then, do you remember what it was?*

I do, she replied. For once, Jennifer didn't need to wander back and look for something she'd tucked away in the back of her mind. As soon as Simeon asked her the question, she knew the answer. She might not have remembered the exact words since it was a long time ago, but Jennifer did remember what he'd told her.

You said there are always ears listening to our words and that the Trows especially, listen carefully. They listen for words they can use against us to trap us. You said some things should never be spoken out loud, only thought silently. Suddenly Jennifer was curious why he would be reminding her about that now … years later. Had she said something out loud that she should have kept in her thoughts? Had her words given the Trows secrets to use against her now? Was she in danger?

Her mind whirled and spun until Simeon interrupted and calmed it down with his answer.

No, Jenny, none of that. I was just taking you back to the beginning so you could see how far you've come.

As the Travelers worked to stay on the path, ducking and swerving here and there to miss this and avoid that, Simeon pulled a movie screen out in Jennifer's mind and replayed scenes from the beginning of her journey. Many things she didn't know mattered, and the numerous times when she'd thought she had made irreparable mistakes, Simeon showed her now.

As the moments flashed by on the screen in her mind, Simeon explained them. It wasn't his usual thoughts that he placed in her mind—like sentences and words—it was more like understandings that she would suddenly have about this situation or that circumstance. All at once Jennifer understood many things that she suddenly knew she hadn't understood before now. It was quite the thing, really, and Jennifer wondered—briefly—if all the Shailmas were doing the same for their riders.

She watched the familiar scene flash onto the screen of when the little green jar exploded in her room; when it had told her of dangers that were lurking in the hollow, dangers even Bella didn't know about. Jennifer remembered running to Bella, telling her of what she'd heard and seen. Oh, she cringed at remembering how angry her auntie had become and at that moment, Jennifer learned that she did not need to run to Bella with every little thing or each new discovery.

As she watched the scene and remembered it, Jennifer had a knowing in her belly that one of those dangers the little green jar had warned her about was Pierce, because he would be bringing Miriam into their hollow. One of those dangers—perhaps the biggest danger of all—was Miriam.

Bella should have asked Pierce right at that moment, when she heard him and Miriam arguing in the dark passageway about the girl. She should have confronted them and demanded the truth, but she was afraid—afraid of Pierce, afraid of Miriam, afraid of the words she'd overheard, and afraid of what those words might mean.

Secrets, she heard Simeon whisper to her.

Huh? Jennifer asked.

Secrets are always lurking dangers, ready to bite, he said. *Where there are secrets, there are lies. Where there are lies, there are open doors for the dark voices to enter.*

He went on to explain that it was Pierce's secrets and lies that had let the dark voices into his mind. *Dark voices need a door opened for them*, Simeon explained. *They cannot just barge in anywhere. Pierce let power and ego and jealousy get into his head, and he wanted more than just to free the souls of the Waiting Ones. Pierce wanted the power of what he saw in Trilleah. All those things he'd seen that lived behind the curtains of the air and all their power, or at least the power he thought they had, he wanted for himself.*

Simeon explained much to her. As they wandered down the unfamiliar path and she listened carefully, many things made sense to Jennifer that had never made sense before.

Jennifer was so intent on watching the screen inside of her mind, seeing this scene and hearing that explanation from Simeon, that she didn't see the ground open up right beneath her feet.

A decent-sized quake traveled through the land and caused a part of the ground to split apart. It was Sam who pulled her out of harm's way. Judah dove to grab Kaija Mae, even though Aviel was beside her, and Sam pulled hard on Jennifer's arm. They all tumbled to the ground but sprang up instantly, avoiding the thick orange lava that was lapping from the newly formed chasm in the ground.

"JENNIFER!" Judah screamed.

Of course, she never heard her brother because the wind was getting louder and louder the closer they ventured to the place of the hollows. The Travelers had been split by the wide crack made by the quake. Sam, Jennifer, Bella, and Aviel were on one side, Judah, Kaija Mae, and the rest were on the other.

There was no point in screaming across the land's fracture. No words would be carried across the chasm. Each group looked across to the other group; their eyes all met. Not every face had the same look, though. Some of the faces had looks of fear; desperate questions mirrored in their eyes. The others had looks of confidence and eyes full of hope.

No matter which side of the chasm they were on, the only thing they could do was to keep going toward the hollows and hope— and pray—that at some point the land would join itself up again and the Travelers could all be back together.

Chapter Three

Returning One

Ferocious lightning began to streak its way through the skies, and Jennifer glanced up to watch. Back home she and Judah loved to watch the lightning. That was not the same type of lighting that was going on here, however. These bolts of lightning were so magnificently bright that her eyes felt a sharp sting pierce through them. She had to cover them quickly and turn away.

Many powerful bolts of lightning shot to the ground, pounding their way forcefully into the hard surface. Some would smack the dirt and go straight back up to the sky, like a boomerang. Others went right through. The ones that did pierce the ground left openings to whatever was lurking below.

Some of those craters allowed for the orange bubbling liquid to peek through and taunt the Travelers, lapping at the edges of the dirt and threatening to climb over. Other craters, and thankfully there were not many of these, allowed for peculiar critters to scurry up and scatter across the ground.

Those critters were fast. They were black as a moonless sky. Even their eyes were black—if they had any eyes at all. It was impossible to tell from a distance and thank goodness there *was* a distance between them and the Travelers. They had the bodies of ants, only they were the size of rats. Each one had the face of a fly with lion's teeth and at least ten legs, although they moved much too quickly for anyone to count them.

These critters that were scurrying across the ground were shiny, as though covered with a warrior's armor. They had scales that resembled breastplates of iron, and large wings just behind their heads. The whirring noise made by those wings was like the roar of a great number of horse-drawn chariots going full speed into battle; maybe they were. The Travelers didn't know where they had come from—or where they were going.

They had tails like scorpions, which rattled loudly. At least, the Travelers assumed it was their tails that were rattling. It sounded like a nest of rattlesnakes had been disturbed, but the only thing around were these unusual black creatures. None of them seemed to notice the group of wide-eyed, trembling Travelers though, and they scurried right past.

They're probably trying to get away from whatever is down below, was the thought which lingered in the minds of the ones watching. The Travelers kept on going, trying not to be distracted by these critters that were scrambling this way and that. They all seemed to be heading in a very specific direction. A few would get going in a direction different than the others. but those ones would quickly get picked up and swung around by a crowd of others. Soon they were all heading the same way.

"I WONDER WHY THEY'RE GOING THAT WAY?" Sam shouted over the blustering winds. Jennifer shrugged. She didn't hear him really, but assumed he was talking about the critters that were crawling up from the crevices in the ground.

He's probably wondering the same things I am, was her only thought. She had no answers to any of her own questions, so she doubted she'd have an answer to Sam's and didn't ask him to repeat himself; it made no difference whether she heard him or not.

Jennifer's eyes were wide open, watching; watching the path, watching the critters, watching the crevice that separated them from the others, and watching Sam. She wasn't sure what she would do if he became weak again and was glad Aviel was with them. She'd never paid much attention to Aviel before; there was no need to until now. But now, with only the four of them on this side of the crevice, Jennifer was thankful he was here.

As they journeyed along, the lightning continued to pelt the ground. Some started fires as it hit in the more heavily weeded areas, but the fires didn't last. Well, they didn't rage, anyway. Everywhere lightning hit in those areas, a bright orange fire would explode loudly. Then, after only a few minutes, it would die down and simmer there, like burning ashes at the end of a campfire.

Great billows of smoke and strong sulfur would rise, though, filling the lungs of the Travelers and making them cough terribly. They coughed so hard that before long they were beginning to cough up bits of blood. Most of them were trying to cover their faces, but it didn't help much. They'd already breathed in so much of the sulfur that their lungs ached and burned.

All of them were startled when Kaija Mae screamed so loudly that everyone—even those who were separated by the crevice between them—jumped a little and looked over toward her. It wasn't like her to let out such a wail. Out of all the Travelers, Kaija Mae had always been the quietest.

As they turned their heads toward her, they saw that she was pointing to the sky just in front of them, except higher, of course. They looked at where she was pointing and they, too, let out wails and shrieks and loud screams as their eyes caught what hers had already seen. There above them, an eagle far bigger than an eagle should ever be, was flying toward them.

It wasn't the eagle itself that was concerning, but the size of it which was cause for alarm. It was at least three times the size of a large man, and his eyes blazed with greens richer than emeralds. His wingspan was so large that it could not be entirely seen in just one glance without the Travelers turning their heads from one side of the sky to the other. It did seem to take up the entire sky.

This powerful eagle had the head of a lion. As it glided gracefully throughout the skies, swooping this way to miss lightning and soaring that way to avoid the great Shamar Shailmas—who were becoming more and more visible now—words bellowed from the being.

"I am returning this one to you. He has been cleansed and redeemed; receive him now. He has been given authority over the land and power over the sea."

They watched the Great Eagle as it spoke these outrageous words to them. Of course, they had all stopped moving because they could not believe what was happening. They should have been covering their mouths, but they forgot all about the sulfur. They couldn't look away from what was descending upon them, for there, right there, sitting high on the back of this Great Eagle, was Pierce.

Nobody moved. Nobody could! They were frozen … completely paralyzed with disbelief at what they couldn't deny their eyes were seeing.

The eagle gently set Pierce down about a hundred feet in front of them. And then, something else unbelievable came from this eagle. His enormous wings were still moving so gracefully up and down as he hovered just about the ground. He dug his talons into the dirt, some on one side of the crevice and some on the other side. With strength never before seen or imagined, this powerful and majestic creature pulled the land back into itself.

Once the ground was pulled back together, that magnificent flying creature rose a bit higher, about twenty or thirty feet, perhaps. With only one mighty flap of his wings, he swooshed swiftly over the Travelers. Every eye was on him as he soared above them, and then with another graceful swish of his wings, he rose higher and higher into the sky. Within seconds he was out of sight, but something told them he wasn't gone.

They looked and looked, trying to get a glimpse of this amazing creature of such magnificent beauty, but there was so much commotion and flashes and a blinding mixture of darkness and light above them, that they quickly gave up their search.

One by one their eyes dropped back to the ground where only a short time before, there was a wide chasm separating them. Now only a sliver of a crack remained—small enough for the Travelers on one side to have easily stepped over and joined the Travelers on the other side.

Now, each was perfectly thrilled to be back with the others, but no one took even a second to rejoice because right there, only a hundred feet in front of them, stood Pierce. They'd been so absolutely certain and unquestionably positive that this one in front of them had become the lunch of a hideous creature. They were certain he had been devoured by the starving beasts from the cave. If he had somehow managed to escape, it was doubtful that he had gotten out of the cave before the land quaked and the cave crumbled.

But now, here he was. Not only was he standing there looking at them, he was neither bloody nor bruised or even dirty. He had both of his arms and both of his legs. Of course, that isn't what one would expect anyone who had been crawling on their belly in the dirty cave or taken by a savage beast to look like. He wasn't anything like one might expect, though nothing was what they expected. He was dressed in spotless garments and had an unmistakable glow about him that they could see from a hundred feet away.

The Travelers wanted to run to him and expected him to run to them, but nobody moved for a long time. Nobody was sure what to do so, as is normally the case in such abnormal situations, nobody did anything.

The sky rained down lightning, and hail was starting to be hurled to the ground as well. The air swirled ferocious winds, but for a moment—in one brief unbelievable moment—nobody noticed any of it. It was surprising really, more miraculous actually, that none of them were hit by the lightning or hail or even thrown to the ground by the strong arms of the wind. But nothing touched them. Nothing came near them. Every element that was causing such upheaval in both the sky and on the ground and even that place which was hiding just beneath the ground, moved viciously around them.

"Pierce," Bella whispered. Strangely enough, every ear heard her.

That was all it took to break the silence and shatter the fear. The Travelers moved their feet and ran with all their speed to this one whom they'd thought was gone. Jennifer lunged at Pierce, and he caught her in mid-air. Matt joined, then Bella, and soon they were all on the ground laughing and hugging, stunned about such unbelievable happenings. For a brief time, they forgot to be concerned with the temperature of the ground, but for now, they were safe.

"Pierce," Matt laughed. "We thought you were eaten!"

"I nearly was," Pierce replied. He, too, was laughing, but it was not a nervous laugh like was coming from the others. It was a laugh that sounded so genuinely free and deep that it struck the others as just one more oddity about this man … this one whom their eyes were still trying to take in. Their understanding was lacking; what their eyes were seeing could find no place to settle in their minds.

They helped one another up and then the most unimaginable conversation began.

"What happened to you?" Bella asked.

"You'll never believe it, even if I tell you," Pierce answered. He took her by one hand, Kaija Mae by the other. They began walking, with Pierce leading them toward the hollows. It seemed like he wasn't going to even try to give Bella the answers she was looking for.

How he knew they were heading for the hollows, they'd question later. For now, they wanted answers to what had happened in the cave, and how he got out of there without getting eaten … or buried alive. They wanted to know about the eagle with the lion's face, and how Pierce had become so clean, and where the eagle had come from—and where it had disappeared to. Now that they were close to him, they could see there was not a scratch or a scrape on him anywhere, and he was wearing something that was perfectly white. Even his skin was glowing.

"Tell us, and then we'll decide whether to believe it or not," Jennifer begged of Pierce.

"Okay, but don't say I didn't warn you," he said with a sparkle in his eye that he'd never had before; not just before when they were in the caves or before when they were running from the army, but ever before.

"Here is what happened … *exactly* as it happened," he chuckled.

Chapter Four

Stories Untold

The winds were raging and roaring all around, but it felt like they had been stuffed inside a snow globe or something similar— something unseen. Even though they could see the dust blowing and the trees bending and snapping off all around them, none of the happenings was anywhere near them; not even the smallest breeze touched them. They were sheltered somehow, but their eyes could see nothing between them and the elements of the air.

Of course, they had no idea that when the great eagle had stood Pierce on the ground, there was a purpose in the exact place he had set the boy. He could easily have delivered Pierce right into their midst, but he didn't. The eagle chose to set him down a hundred feet away, so when he rose up again and flew above of the Travelers, he could spread a veil over them, shielding them from whatever may try to come against them … for a time.

They couldn't see it, of course, because the veil was hidden in the atmosphere. But since that was where the war was being waged, that's where the veil would be most useful to the Travelers.

No winds could get beneath the veil, and no lightning could pass through. Consequently, the Travelers could hear one another without yelling. They could listen carefully to the story Pierce was about to tell without having to watch for fireballs or lightning bolts, and without having to strain their ears or try to read his lips.

"That beast in the cave did get ahold of me and he was completely horrible," Pierce began. "I'm sure he must have had fire in his lungs because his breath was so thick with the smell of sulfur, I thought that alone might kill me … I nearly wished it would."

They were listening—really they were—but there was something about the boy that was so different and it was distracting them; it was his eyes. Something had changed in his eyes, or maybe it was his heart that had changed; his soul perhaps. After all, it's been said that the eyes are the windows to the soul and maybe, just maybe, they were seeing into the very soul of this storyteller.

Nonetheless, something had changed in Pierce's eyes, and it was good … very good.

"I was trying desperately to get far enough into the small part of the cave, but with Sam being unconscious and the cave being too small to run, there was no chance for me. I was the one to lead you all into the cave so it only made sense that I would be the one to have to face the beast.

The faces of the listeners looked horrified—like they felt it was their fault for Pierce getting caught by that monster. Pierce knew full well that was not the truth. He'd listened to a dark voice inside of himself—a dark voice he himself had let in. It was no one else's fault.

"Don't worry," he said calmly. "If it's anyone's fault, it's mine. If I had believed in my Shailma, he probably would have rescued me or caused something to happen to that beast or, well, who knows, really. Anyway, it was my fault, not any of yours."

"Yup, something has definitely changed in him," Jennifer whispered to Judah, who nodded but kept his eyes on Pierce.

"Yes, Jenny," Pierce answered her, even though she had no intention of him hearing her whispers. "Something *has* changed in me."

Jennifer's face turned red and she reminded herself to whisper much quieter from now on, or maybe not at all. Pierce watched her pale skin fill with deep crimson, but he merely winked at her with compassion.

"Anyway, that monster got me by the shoulder and dragged me a long way down the tunnel, back through the cave and out through the other end somewhere. Apparently, it had hungry babies that were waiting in a nest for their dinner … and I was the main course." He rubbed his shoulder and pulled his sweater over a little to reveal three large holes. They didn't look fresh, more like scars of something that had happened many years ago.

The others gasped and Bella moved closer to touch the scars. "Oh, Pierce," she whispered. He turned around to show three matching wounds on the back of his shoulder. There was no way he should've gotten out of that mess with his shoulder still intact.

"He dragged me a long way, through some thick bushes that were covered in quills or thorns or something sharp. I knew I wasn't coming back. I knew I'd never see any of you again and then, I did the only thing I knew how to do. I started hollering and screaming for my Shailma."

"I was shouting, anyway," he explained. "I figured I might as well shout something helpful—if there was anything at all that would be helpful, that is. After what seemed like hours of being dragged through the bush, that creature flung me up and over the side of an enormous nest. It was made of those same sharp, thorn bushes, and it was terribly painful, although …" and Pierce paused here for a moment, thinking of what to say next.

"I was in shock I guess, because even though I was in horrible pain and scared nearly to death—literally—I didn't flinch or wiggle or move. I just laid there, motionless. I remember I was conscious and had to keep reminding myself to breathe because I kept forgetting to."

He laughed now, which was odd since every Traveler was looking at him completely horrified by this truly unbelievable story.

"I guess that's what saved my skin because those babies were looking for a living lunch and I was pretty much dead. Maybe I was for a minute … I don't know."

Now the Travelers were sure he was making this stuff up, but just like he said, it was an unbelievable story. The holes in his shoulder were real, and here he was, so it must be true.

BOOOOOM, came a crash of lightning so large that it easily toppled down four or five big trees. The trees landed a few feet in front of the Travelers, causing them all to jump, their eyes to bulge, and their hearts to race. When their eyes had recovered from the bright flash of the lightning, and they saw what it was that had made the loud noise, they all breathed a bit harder and moved a little closer together.

Pierce barely noticed, though and continued right on with his story. He walked with them for a bit, right in the middle of the Travelers, and then when he'd get excited or to a good part of his story, he'd suddenly turn around and jump a step ahead so they could see his face—or he could see theirs.

"The mother—or whatever this beast was—kept swiping at me with these huge claws, trying to get me to move or maybe wanting me to be more tempting for the babies, I don't know. It was clear to me—even though I was in shock and barely conscious—that these babies were disgusted by what their mother had brought them for lunch.

They'd have nothing to do with me and began their squealing and crying all over again. They moved as far to one side of the nest as they could, trying to get away from me."

Pierce was chuckling by this point, maybe remembering the rejection of these hungry babies, but the Travelers couldn't figure out why he was finding his story so amusing when they were so obviously horrified by it all.

"The mamma swatted at me a couple more times until finally I was hurled right out of the nest—and right into the middle of the thorn patch." He held up his hands to show the Travelers his many cuts from that patch. Again, they looked more like old scars from a long-ago battle, than fresh wounds of only a few hours ago.

"How odd," Jennifer said.

"How odd indeed," Pierce replied.

"How many babies were in that nest?" Bella asked.

"Nine," Pierce answered.

"How big was this beast really, because he sounded huge in the darkness of that cave, but was that just from the echoes?" Matt wondered.

"It was huge, all right," Pierce answered waving his hands around trying to show the size of it. "In fact, the babies in that nest were at least as big as me." He lifted his arms high above his head to demonstrate the size of such things. The Travelers stared at him with no more questions to be asked at the moment.

They'd continued walking while Pierce was telling his story but now stopped briefly to look around. Nothing looked familiar, but then again, the rocks to the hollows were just a few hundred feet ahead. It looked like they'd make it after all.

"While I was laying in that field of thorns, I wanted to stay perfectly still so the mamma would think I was dead and go looking for a different lunch for the babies.

"Now," he paused and held his finger up for dramatic effect. "I would love to say that I outsmarted that ferocious beast and dragged myself away to safety."

"You didn't?" Jennifer asked. "How did you get away?"

"And where did that massive eagle come from?" Judah wondered.

"And how was it that he spoke?" Jennifer wanted to know. The questions from the twins went back and forth, with one asking a question and then the other—back and forth like a ping-pong match.

Everyone wanted the answers to every question being asked, but the twins kept asking more and more and more, not stopping for even a moment. Finally, Aviel held his arms out to hush the twins.

"Let him answer," he said.

"Oh, sorry," the twins replied at the same time.

"Let me see here," Pierce said. He was thinking of which question to answer first, or maybe which ones to answer at all since those excited and bewildered twins had asked so many.

"Here is where the story becomes quite unbelievable," Pierce whispered.

"Here?" Bella laughed awkwardly.

"I'd been shouting for my Shailma earlier, and now, laying silently in that horrible patch in great pain and with my shoulder torn apart and bleeding badly, I screamed and hollered for him in my mind."

"He came to me suddenly, and this is what I heard him say. I will never forget it ... EVER ..."

You are a funny kind, you mortals. You say you don't believe, but when you get in trouble or need help, who is the first one you run to? Pierce, my boy, you have been shouting and screaming into the wind for me, and now, you are shouting and screaming in your mind, searching for me. Well, when you search for me with all your heart like you have done here today, I will be found by you—every time.

I will not hide nor will I remain angry because you refused to believe in me earlier. I am here with you. I have always been here with you. Even when you cursed me or said you would not believe unless you saw me, I never left you.

It was I, Pierce, who covered you in that nest. It was not that the babies did not want you for their lunch, for they did. They did indeed. They are hungry, and they eat anything their mamma brings them. They didn't rip you limb from limb and devour you for their lunch because I hid you under my wing until that mamma threw you from her nest.

Now, as Pierce publicly recalled what his Shailma had told him in the privacy of his mind while he laid there wounded and bleeding and in great pain, with sharp thorns cutting deep into his skin, and his shoulder freshly ripped apart, he became emotional. The boy—who'd been so rude and tough and arrogant and miserable just hours earlier—now had to wipe tears from his eyes.

The Travelers kept walking, in a bit of shock themselves at what was coming from this boy; all of it—both the words and the emotion. Nobody knew what to say so they just walked in silence until he settled himself and returned to the story.

The rest of the story would need to wait, though. The Travelers had finally arrived to where the hollows were scattered over the land, and they needed to focus on finding the exact one they were looking for. A bit of a defeated sigh arose as the Travelers looked ahead to where Asphelia's Hollow should be and found that the rock covering it was gone. In its place, one lone tree had been set. There was a sign nailed to the tree just a few feet from the ground.

Judah ran ahead to see what the sign said, but he didn't realize that by doing so he left the covering that he hadn't even known had been set above them. He'd put himself in grave danger indeed. Judah trusted greatly in his own Shailma, however, and he quickly reached the tree, read the sign, and returned to the others.

There was much weaving and ducking and covering his head as large balls of hail were hurled toward him.

Panting and soaked and gasping for air, he looked at Pierce with sad eyes.

"I'm so sorry, Pierce. The sign says, 'here the soul of Miriam shall be chained for all eternity.' "

Pierce sighed a loud sigh but said nothing for a minute. He looked like he wanted to, but then sucked it back in and closed his mouth. When he finally did speak, his words were surprising.

"Well," he said thoughtfully, "it looks like I have two souls to rescue."

"That girl was cursed in her life; I'm sure not going to allow her to remain cursed in her death."

Chapter Five

Nehsher

If there had been any doubt before that something drastic had changed in Pierce, there was no doubt now—no doubt at all. Any one of the Travelers would have thought Pierce would be thrilled with the news of Miriam's soul being added to Malleana Forest. Now the forest had been moved; nevertheless, her soul had been added to it.

Pierce's comment blotted out any doubt that he was different. Something drastic had happened to their friend, but so far they didn't know exactly *why* he had changed or how it had happened. Bella wanted to ask him to continue with his story. She was so confused with the changes in Pierce, and the feelings they stirred up in her, that she had a million questions to ask and no idea which to start with.

"Here it is," Kaija Mae said. They were finally standing in front of the hollow, but now that they were here a nervousness sprang up, and they were afraid to go inside. They couldn't tell if the Army of Shrailzhar had broken into all the hollows or just Asphelia's.

The Travelers stood around wondering such things to one another and then, with either great braveness or much stupidity, Judah finally muttered, "Well, there's only one way to find out."

Before anyone could stop him, he stepped forward and jammed his foot inside the tiniest of openings under the boulder. As quick as a wink the space opened up, and he disappeared inside. The others listened with painstaking focus. They waited, not sure whether to follow him in or wait outside for some sort of signal. They all stood looking down at the hole under the boulder waiting for something, but they didn't know what it was they were waiting for, so they were dumbfounded to know how to find it.

They heard no great shrieks or blood-curdling screams, so that was a good sign they supposed, but nobody knew for sure. Nobody knew anything for sure, so they continued standing out in the open, watching a hole, half-hidden, under a boulder.

"We should have planned this better," Jennifer huffed. She was annoyed that it was Judah who'd gone in, but she was even more annoyed that he didn't discuss it with any of them; he'd just done it and hoped for the best. Now that was all any of them could do—hope for the best, that is.

Nobody put a foot forward.

Nobody took a step toward the rock.

Finally, Jennifer became frustrated and impatient. She'd waited long enough. If her brother was brave enough to go inside, then so was she. Besides, she hoped that if the hollow had been overtaken by the army, Judah would have come straight back out or somehow let the others know not to come in. At least, that was what she told herself as she quickly took a couple of giant steps forward—before she changed her mind, or anyone else could stop her—and stuck her foot into the small space under the rock.

Whooooosh

With one quick motion, she was inside. Jennifer expected to tumble in and land on the floor as was the common practice at Asphelia's Hollow, but she never; it wasn't like that at all. In fact, once Jennifer was inside and was brave enough to open her eyes and look around, she saw that this hollow wasn't anything like Asphelia's Hollow.

This was certainly not an Eating Chamber she was standing in. There was no eating stump and the only thing she did see was a few hooks on the far wall. They held no cloaks, unfortunately.

They held nothing whatsoever. Also, unlike Asphelia's Hollow where there were many passageways to choose from, only two passageways were seen here in this hollow.

"Any sign of the army?" she asked her brother.

"Nope, not yet," Judah answered. "It seems deserted in here … kinda creepy. I wonder if this Chamber was full of things—like in Asphelia's—and somebody has been inside and taken it all," Judah wondered out loud. His sister would have been perfectly happy if he hadn't wondered such things out loud, but it was too late now and she began wondering as well.

None of the other Travelers who would have answers to such wonderings had come inside yet. Jennifer wished they'd hurry up and find some bravery of their own. She turned to head for the entrance to let them know it seemed safe and to hurry them inside.

"Well, nobody's been in here for over a year, I don't think," Jennifer said. "Probably not since Kaija Mae and the others found us … or we found them … or whatever."

Judah looked at his sister with confusion.

"Jennifer, you do know that they never go home, right? All those who we found trapped in the Labyrinth don't leave Trilleah. They've been trapped here for decades!" He couldn't believe his sister was completely aware of so many things that went on in the atmosphere—hidden from their eyes—but knew so little about other things that went on right under her nose.

Sometimes she seemed so naive and gullible that it didn't surprise him how easily she trusted her Shailma. She trusted everybody … it was just the way she was.

"WHAT? What do you mean?" she asked, figuring that he couldn't possibly mean what he was saying … he must have been pulling her leg because he sure couldn't be serious. Jennifer must have somehow been misunderstanding her brother.

Before Judah could answer though, there was a loud commotion behind them as the rest of the Travelers finally came into the hollow. Such a loud ruckus wasn't about to stop Jennifer from finding out what Judah meant, and she asked him again.

"Judah, what do you mean?"

Jennifer saw Aviel out of the corner of her eye and turned to him since Judah was not hurrying to give her the answers she was after.

"Aviel," she asked sweetly. "You go home between Solstices, right? I don't mean this Solstice. Obviously, you didn't go home—none of us did—but other ones. Like when the Shailmas take us all home, you go home too, right?" She asked the question, sure that she already knew the answer, and Jennifer got good and ready to sneer at her brother and rub his nose in the fact that he was an idiot.

"Um," was all Aviel said. He was very shy so when Jennifer began questioning him in front of everyone, he turned red and looked at Kaija Mae. Kaija Mae looked over to Judah, and he shrugged his shoulders and turned his lip up at one side pretending to know nothing of his sister's foolish questions.

Kaija Mae winked at Judah and quickly took over the conversation, rescuing Aviel and letting Judah off the hook.

"No, dear, we don't go home." She waved her arm around at all those in whose hollow they were now standing. "None of us do. We have no homes to go back to, I'm afraid. This hollow has been our home for many, many years."

"Oh," was all Jennifer said. She didn't know what to ask after that because it wasn't the answer she was expecting and to be honest, she was horrified at such a thought. She didn't want to upset anyone and not having a home might be a very good reason to get upset.

Jennifer tried to change the subject but promised herself to ask Judah about it later. Her brother seemed to have information that he wasn't sharing and she wanted to know what else he knew. Maybe they were all pulling a prank on her, but now seemed like a very odd time to prank anyone.

"Can you show us around in here?" Jennifer asked. "What I really mean is, can you take us to the kitchen?" Everyone applauded and jumped around like cats on a hot tin roof. They were immediately reminded of how hungry they were and thought the kitchen would be a most splendid place to begin a tour.

The reaction—or lack of one—from Kaija Mae and the others who'd been living in this hollow for so long told Jennifer and Judah both that there had never been much of anything in this space. If it had been full and was now empty, surely one of the Travelers who'd lived here would have noticed.

"This way," Tahlia said and waved her hand toward the smaller of the two passageways. They all followed, hoping there was food somewhere close and crossing their fingers that there would be plenty of it. They were starving. Sam and a few others had to duck down because the passageway was too low for them.

"I hope you have some medicine of some sort in here, Kaija Mae," Sam whined. Nobody minded his whining, though, because his hand was a terrible, skinless, bloody mess. They were surprised he wasn't more miserable, in fact. Of course, he was still in a great amount of shock; which was keeping most of the pain hidden … for now.

Kaija Mae didn't have a chance to answer the boy. Before they stepped very many steps into the passageway, it started shaking. It was not a gentle shake or a light shake or a "don't worry, this will soon pass," sort of shake. Oh no! The hollow began trembling ferociously! Large rocks were coming loose from above and smacking them on the heads. There was a choir of "Ouches," and "Hey's," and "Watch out's," coming from every Traveler as they covered themselves and ducked, running quickly after Tahlia.

Matt had to cover the tablets, which left his head open to get hit, and it did. One rock after another smashed him on the head. Thank goodness they were only the smaller rocks and the pebbles. He wanted to cover himself, but if the tablets were hit with a big rock, they would be shattered into pieces and useless.

In minutes they stepped out of the passageway and stretched as they stood up straight. They rubbed their heads and moaned. Matt had a little blood just above his right eye, but nothing terribly serious. Most importantly, he'd kept the tablets safe.

There was a pile of rubble and rocks all around this small chamber and it reminded the Travelers of the cave they'd hid in earlier after it came tumbling down.

"Oh no," Kaija Mae sighed.

Some dishes had been shaken from their place on the shelves and now lay broken on the floor. There was one space directly above them where so many rocks had shaken loose that it had made a hole right through to the outside. They couldn't see much because it was a small hole, but flashes of light burst through time and time again. They assumed it was the lightning but were only partially right. The Travelers would find out soon enough what was causing the flashes of light out in the land. For now, not knowing was for the best.

Kaija Mae stepped over the mess of fallen rocks and broken glass that mounded on the floor and whipped open a cupboard to reveal a surprisingly large pantry. Everyone shrieked as they saw it was nearly full of food.

"Oh good, it's all still here," Kaija Mae sighed. She began pulling out cans of this and containers of that, handing them back to the Travelers.

"Do you have an opener?" Bella asked.

"In that rack by the bowls," Aviel said pointing to somewhere Bella couldn't seem to find.

She wiped some dirt and rocks from the counter onto the floor and rifled through a few racks until finally, she came upon an opener. Bella grinned and began opening can after can after can and passing them back to the others. She didn't care what any of it was; nobody did. They didn't mind that it was cold or that it may have tasted a bit better with some spices. Nobody cared.

They hadn't eaten in a couple of days and now ravenously shoved their mouths full of whatever they could get their hands on.

The hollow began to shake again—harder this time. It was getting more difficult to keep their balance and stay standing. Most of the Travelers leaned against shelves or walls just to stay upright. Another chunk came down from up above, making the hole big enough for them to see clearly out into the land. They could see that the Shamar Shailmas had doubled in number; either that or they could just see more of them now.

The Travelers tried to pay as little attention as they could to what was happening outside of the hollow and pretended they were perfectly safe inside the hollow. Matt set the water flasks that they'd guzzled from earlier by the water pipe and began filling them again.

"Can never have too much water," he said and, of course, he was right.

It was quite a commotion in that tiny space. Matt was trying to hold himself up from tumbling over while filling the water flasks, as well as letting Bella shove big chunks of this and little bits of that into his mouth. The water was splashing everywhere and both Matt and Bella were getting soaked.

As the Travelers continued shoving one handful after another into their mouths, Jennifer turned to Pierce, who she'd noticed was not eating all that much.

"Pierce, go on with your story," she said between bites.

"Jennifer," Bella stated, "let him eat first. I'm sure you must be starving," she said to Pierce.

"He's not even eating, Bella," Jennifer said, as bits of food fell from her overstuffed mouth. Just then she thought that was an odd thing and questioned him about it. "Why aren't you eating?" she asked suspiciously.

"Well, I'm not eating because I'm not hungry," he said playfully.

"Why aren't you hungry?" Judah asked.

"Because I ate before Nehsher brought me to you," Pierce answered. He was acting mysterious, raising his eyebrows and not offering any more information than exactly what it would take to appease their suspicions.

Now Jennifer's curiosity was stirring, so much so that she set her food down. The shaking had slowed in the hollow but had not stopped completely, so she continued to lean against the far wall for balance. "Pierce, go on with your story," she asked again. "And who is Nehsher?" she added.

Something was nagging at her that there was more to what had happened to Pierce than just an unbelievable story—something they all needed to know—something necessary and valuable had occurred and she wanted to know every detail of what it was.

"Let's see," he teased, tapping his chin. "Where did I leave off?"

They all began to answer, knowing exactly where he'd left off. With everyone talking at once, nobody could hear anything. Finally, Pierce put his hands up and laughed.

"Oh, yes," he laughed. "I know; I'd just gotten tossed out of that nest."

"Yes!" rang out the overlapping voices of all those waiting impatiently for the rest of the story. If the first bit he'd already told them was the believable part, they couldn't wait to hear the unbelievable part.

Chapter Six

Unseen Realms

"So, I was plunked down in the thorn bushes listening to my Shailma tell me all kinds of things I never knew before. He was spewing a bit of a lecture on how important believing is, and how if I had believed in the power and ability of my Shailma earlier, I would not be face down in the thistles now."

"In fact," Pierce said solemnly, "belief is the most powerful tool we have."

Some of the others already knew that, but none so much as Jennifer. She had tried to tell Pierce so many times, but he would never listen to her. He never listened to anybody, but that seemed to be an entirely different Pierce than this one that stood among them now.

"As I was laying there, trying to keep my cringing and bawling silent, I felt a shadow cover me. I couldn't see anything above because my face was in the dirt, but it suddenly got very dark right above me and I knew something was coming. I was so terrified that I had to force myself to breathe and was literally begging my Shailma to rescue me … or let me die quickly.

"I heard two things right at that moment. I heard something that sounded like a flag flapping in a heavy wind, and I heard my Shailma's voice. It was so calm and so patient and so loving.

" '*I Am*,' was all he said. Two little words, but they changed everything.

"I thought I heard wrong because I didn't know how he was possibly saving me when the shadow that was covering me got bigger and bigger. It covered my entire body by now, but I was still laying there face down. I couldn't see what it was, but I could see the ground around me had gotten dark beneath its shadow."

As Pierce was retelling the story, the Travelers could tell he went right back to that moment in his mind. His arms were flailing and he was covering his head as though the shadow was there right in this moment, which of course, it wasn't. He seemed to be panicking, but they realized he was just trying to make the story fully effective and these dramatic antics were his way of doing that.

The Travelers were mesmerized by Pierce at the moment. After so many trips to the Dark Land, the others had never heard him speak so many words. This was such a different Pierce than any of them knew, and they sincerely wanted to know what had caused the change.

"Before I knew what was happening, Nehsher—that gigantic eagle you saw—swooped down and scooped me up." Pierce's eyes grew bigger as he talked about the eagle he called Nehsher. "I didn't even know what it was at the time," he continued. "I just knew the most gentle being ever, had literally come down from somewhere in the sky and rescued me. I was in the pit of hell, in my mind, and my Shailma sent this thing, this … this outrageously gigantic eagle—with the face of a lion, no less—to rescue me.

"Maybe it was my Shailma." Pierce kept right on talking and the more he said, the more the Travelers were in awe.

"Maybe he turned into Nehsher and came to rescue me, just like he said. I don't know. I can't explain it, nor can I stop thinking about it."

Pierce stopped talking and sniffled. He rubbed his eyes and wiped his nose with the back of his hand. Clearly, he was so moved by the love his Shailma had for him that he had to take a break from the story. It was truly unbelievable.

"Gimme a minute," he said as his eyes again grew damp.

They did give him a few minutes. In fact, they gave him much more than a few minutes, not that anybody wanted to give him even one moment. But when the ground began to shake again, harder this time than the last, they had to run from the chamber they were standing in to avoid getting buried beneath the rubble that was beginning to rain down, pelting them.

Arms were swinging and hands were grabbing whatever could be grabbed. The Travelers didn't know how long they'd be stuck in Trilleah or if they would ever get back to this chamber again. They doubted they would find food anywhere else in the land, so they wanted to take as much of the food from the hollow as they could carry. Judah picked up two of the water flasks; Pierce picked up the others.

"Here," Aviel hollered and threw a couple of large bags to whoever might catch them. Pierce set the flasks down and thrust his hand into the air, grabbing the bags. He tossed one to Matt and scooped whatever was sitting on the ledge into the other. Matt caught the bag and held it open as Bella and Judah threw in cans and containers until the bag refused to hold anything more.

The boys hurried the Travelers out after Kaija Mae, who was leading the way. On the way out, Bella grabbed one of the water flasks, and Aviel grabbed the other. They were barely out of the chamber before the entire roof came crashing down.

"Oh dear!" Bella shrieked. The rubble had blocked most of the door so there was no going back into the room even if they'd wanted to. "I'm glad we grabbed the food," Bella shouted above the racket.

One by one those weary and worn-out Travelers popped out of the small passageway and right back into the open chamber. They looked up immediately, concerned the roof in here may also collapse. It seemed to be steady in this chamber, but they were not trusting of anything now.

"I thought the hollow would be safe," Jennifer cried.

"Me too, J," Bella whimpered.

"Nowhere is safe," Judah replied. "Pierce, do you think we should stay inside or get out of the hollow straightaway?" Pierce scrunched up his face and wondered why Judah had asked him.

"I have no idea," he answered.

Jennifer was asking Simeon the same question since she knew the only answers were going to be found with the Shailmas. They could stand around all day long and wonder and ponder and try to figure it out, or use "common sense," but that would likely lead them to make the wrong choice. Worse yet, spending so much time trying to figure things out might mean that they did nothing at all. They had to make a choice, and they had to make it fast.

The roof could come down and bury them alive while they were busy trying to "figure it out." The best thing to do in this situation—and all other situations that would very likely be presenting themselves soon—was to search for, and ask the Shailmas.

They always knew the answers long before they were ever asked the questions.

Little One, Simeon whispered above the noise. *You needed to come to this hollow only to get the food—it's all you will have now. Trilleah has no more to give you. This hollow is no longer safe for any of you. You cannot remain inside, or anywhere beneath the ground. It will soon crumble, covering everything. Get out now, Jenny, and take the others with you. Go now.*

"We got what we needed from here," Jennifer blurted out. She interrupted the others who were still trying to use common sense and reason to figure out what to do. She didn't care if it was rude or if any of the others got upset with her. Jennifer had heard from Simeon, and that was all she required. He had told her to get the others out of the hollow so that was what she was going to do.

As she hollered orders, the others stopped talking and looked at her like she had three heads and had turned blue. She didn't care; Jennifer never let it distract her. There was a day not so long ago when she would have been hesitant to keep speaking, but those days were long gone.

"Simeon told me that we need to get out, NOW," she said and then turned to step out from the covering of the hollow. The rest thought this was their safety while the War of the Firmament was being fought, but now they were leaving and each one—except for Pierce—was decidedly unhappy about it.

"Make sure you have all the food and the flasks," Jennifer hollered behind her. As soon as she was back out in the openness of Trilleah, she suddenly became very worried that none would follow her. Worse yet was the thought that if nobody followed her, she would have no food and no water and … no friends.

Jennifer sharply spun around to dive back inside but was blocked by Matt, who was the first of all the others to get out of the hollow. He winked and scooted her over, away from the entrance.

"I don't want you to get run over," he said. He was a smart one and knew that Jennifer would feel anxious and afraid. Matt hoped he calmed her fears of being alone—a least a little.

Jennifer smiled and moved away from the entrance.

One by one, the Travelers appeared from the hollow under the ground and one by one they gave Jennifer hugs and words of thanks for knowing how to listen to—and trust—her Shailma. They had all learned how to hear their Shailmas over the past few years, but none had such an ability to trust what was heard like Jennifer did. At this moment, they were each grateful for her presence in Trilleah—and for her boldness.

However, as they stood outside the hollow now, wondering which way they should be heading, they heard a sound. It wasn't a loud *BANG* or a thundering *BOOM* that they'd heard so many times before. No, it was more of a *whoosh* ... *thud*, kind of sound; the kind of sound one might expect to hear when the ground begins to give way.

All at once, those Travelers spun around to find that was exactly what had happened. The ground did give way just behind them and had left a monstrous-sized crater. The hollow was gone. Precisely where that hollow had been, in the exact place they'd been standing only seconds earlier, discussing whether to remain inside or get out, was now nothing more than a gargantuan-sized crater.

Nobody spoke or even whispered. Everyone drew in their breath and held it silently, afraid to let it out as they saw what they saw. Each one looked from the crater to Jennifer and then back to the crater. What they had felt as gratefulness for the girl just seconds earlier exploded within them as they realized that her ability to trust her Shailma just saved them all from a horrific and violent death.

Those hugs from before turned into screaming and chants of "Thank you, Jennifer," and "Oh, dear God!"

Jennifer wanted no credit though, no glory and no attention and no acknowledgment. All she wanted was to get going. She had no idea which way they should be headed or where they would end up. All she wanted was to return to her little yellow house on the corner of Fairview Lane and Mitchell Avenue. Jennifer wanted to scream and run and be swooped up by an eagle and taken somewhere else— anywhere else.

The Travelers were exposed, with no cloaks to cover any of them. But they had water and food, they had all dozen of the clay tablets, they had this and that from the beheaded guards' pockets, and they had the two enormous swords—just in case; just in case of what, nobody wanted to consider. Jennifer had a little green jar and her tattered red blanket. Most importantly, they had each other. They were all here.

It wasn't until now that they had a chance to look around. They wished they didn't but then again, there was no way to avoid it. There was nothing of any good out here in Trilleah and no way the Travelers could imagine, that the land wouldn't be destroyed. It was falling apart and they were smack in the middle of it.

From all of the places in the sky where rips and tears had become visible, all sorts of things were being hurled and thrown down. It was impossible to know if the things were being thrown at the ground or if they were supposed to be going elsewhere. Wherever they were supposed to be directed to, there was no doubt the ground was where they were landing.

Enormous boulders were crashing to the dirt in the distance. Each time the Travelers saw another one flung down, they'd feel the ground shake as it hit. They looked like rocks from a mountain; some looked like a torch had touched it before it was flung down, since many of these boulders were orange inside, like coals from a raging fire. So far, all these things were a good distance away from where they were standing, but not so far away that they didn't cause terrible … powerful … crippling … paralyzing fear.

There were also countless flashes shooting through the air. It wasn't lightning bolts—exactly—but that was the closest thing the Travelers could think of to describe what they were seeing. It was more like the sky was filled with invisible fire-breathers and now, suddenly and all at once, the air began to breathe, spewing out what it had been holding in all this time. There were sudden bursts of flames —some small, some large—here and there. It was altogether indescribable …

Then there was the air itself. High above the Travelers, in the very top parts of the air, it looked as though someone had rolled back the clouds like a scroll and they were allowed, for some reason, to see into the atmosphere. Their eyes were open to all that they'd been closed to … until now. Whether the Shailmas had opened their eyes or whether what they were seeing was simply no longer hidden in the atmosphere, they couldn't tell. Nonetheless, the Travelers could suddenly see all things that they had always wanted to see, but now that they could see them, they desperately wished they couldn't.

All things unseen, everything that had been hidden from their sight for so long by a veil in the atmosphere, had suddenly become visible. The Travelers were about to see things they'd spend the rest of their lives—no matter how long or short that may be—trying to erase from their memories.

Above them, just above the drawn curtains of the sky, were the Shamar Shailmas—thousands upon thousands, row upon row— more than the Travelers' eyes could take in. The army of Warring Shamar Shailmas poured great courage, confidence, and boldness upon these who were looking upon them.

That courage and confidence and boldness lasted only as long as it took for the Travelers' eyes to land on something else entirely; something dark, something terrifying. Circling the army of Shamar Shailmas were thousands of Nakah Warriors. There were four Nakah Warriors that stood much larger than the rest—one in each corner of the firmament. These four were blowing on horns while the rest of those Nakah Warriors were charging madly toward the army of Shamars. An entire indestructible looking ring of the dark Nakahs— four deep—closed in on the army of uncountable Shamar Shailmas.

The Travelers wanted to look away, painfully afraid of what was about to happen right before their eyes, but they couldn't. No matter how hard they tried, they could not turn their eyes from the horrific scene that was unfolding in the air.

All of the Shailmas, whether the Nakah Warriors or the Shamars, had riders securely perched on their backs. Every rider held a sword so large that even an unlimited imagination would be unable to consider the size of them. They were not all the same swords though; not even close.

The riders of the Nakahs had swords that were large indeed, and a dark, silvery gray. They clearly had a sharpness on one side and a bluntness on the other. The handles were black and thick. They looked heavy, like pure iron, and they probably were, for they were forged from iron—or so it looked. Those swords were undoubtedly dangerous and made chills run up and down the Travelers' spines, causing them to tremble.

The riders of the Shamars though, wielded swords that were completely different. Those swords had both edges sharpened. The Travelers could tell because there was a gleam coming from both sides. These swords were also huge but looked weightless. They were nearly clear and looked as though they were made from crystals or diamonds even. The only color to them at all was the bright yellows and oranges glittering around them as light was bouncing off of them.

There was no light, though, no sun and no moon. Maybe the swords themselves were light; it was impossible to tell. All they could see for certain was that there was no light coming from anywhere else, yet the air was well lit. The only thing that made sense was that the swords of the Shamars' riders were somehow providing light in the firmament.

The handles of these brilliantly gleaming swords were red—a deep crimson red. The Travelers had seen this red before … oh yes … in the Chamber of Rest. The crimson walls they'd seen in that space, the very walls they had leaned against only a few days earlier, was the same crimson they saw now on the swords. They glowed brightly and the Travelers wondered deeply about such swords.

They wondered quietly—each to themselves—because with all their eyes were seeing, no words would come to their lips. Surely there were no words in their language to describe such things as these and it seemed pointless to try and find any and so, nobody did.

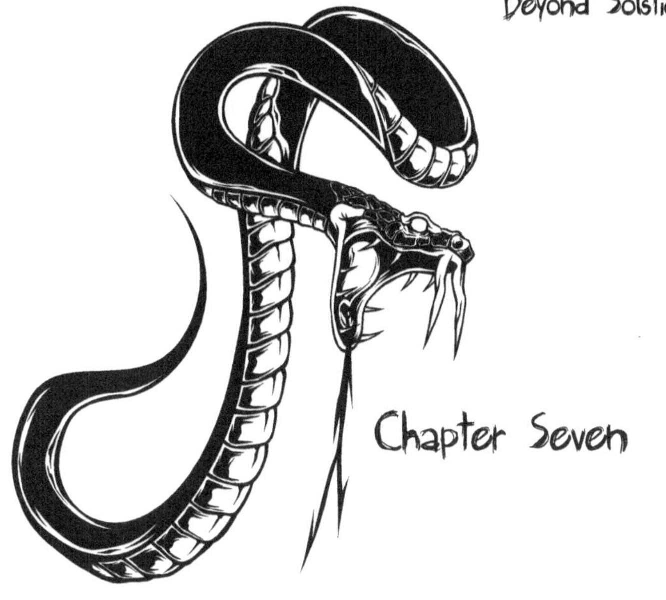

Chapter Seven

Stars for Souls

Time seemed to stand still as the Travelers stood in horror watching the Nakah Warriors rise against the Shamar Shailmas. Even though the fires were still spewing in the air, and the boulder-sized coals continued to be hurled toward the ground, it seemed like it was all a horrible nightmare—one from which they couldn't wake themselves up.

The longer the Travelers stood watching the horrible happenings in the firmament, the more everything else except for the Shailmas and their riders faded behind a thick blanket of fog.

All of the Nakah Warriors were black. *Middle-of-a-moonless-night* kind of black. They were very hard to see behind such a fog; maybe that was their plan. Their riders wore armor that seemed confining. It was all dark gray, allowing them to blend into the Nakahs. It was nearly impossible to tell where the Nakah Warriors ended and their riders began.

Most of the Shamar Shailmas were dark red, but there were some that stood out among the red ones since they were white—pure white. They were a long way from the Travelers' eyes, but from what they could see, the white Shailmas had no marks on them—none whatsoever! There were none with any dark spots or even a small blotch here or there. The white Shamars were uncontaminated and pure, through and through.

The tremendous warriors that sat upon the Shamar Shailmas were of such magnitude that if the Travelers had tried to describe them, they would be unable to. There were no words available for such a description. The Travelers were so stunned at the power of these ones perched on the Shamar Shailmas that they could talk of nothing else for a long few minutes.

"Look at this," one would whisper and point.

"Look at that," would come utterings from another. There was no shortage of things to notice about those magnificent beings of the air, and the Travelers didn't want to miss anything.

Unlike the Nakahs' armor, the Shamars' armor was long and radiant, covering every bit of them. They had helmets without any openings, and what covered them seemed to be one piece—altogether seamless and impenetrable.

"They must be able to see right through it," Kaija Mae pondered. These riders also looked like they were one with the Shamar Shailmas and the Travelers wondered about it, but like everything else they were looking at in the firmament, they couldn't come up with any answers.

Finally, Judah spoke.

"We've got to get out of the middle of this openness," he shouted. Everyone agreed, but nobody could decide which direction to go or where somewhere less open might be since the hollows had all fallen through the ground. None of them were yet aware that Nehsher had spread a veil overtop of them and that nothing crashing or spewing or shooting in the firmament could come near them.

"We could head that way, toward the sea," Jennifer suggested.

"How about over that way back to the gates?" Bella wondered.

No matter how many suggestions were made, none of them seemed to be right. No direction seemed to bring peace. Eventually, it was Pierce who made a decision which seemed to be the right one.

He was listening to his Shailma this time, rather than the dark voice, because in his time away from the other Travelers, he had certainly learned to tell the difference.

Before he had a chance to speak, more of the sky tore open, revealing hundreds of thousands of stars. In all the trips to this Dark Land, never once had the Travelers seen a star. They'd always assumed that Trilleah had none. Jennifer pointed to the sky and squealed.

"LOOK!"

They were already looking, and each was stunned at such a marvelous sight.

"Where did *those* come from?" one asked another.

"I've never seen 'em before," said a third. Kaija Mae finally spoke up after listening to all the chattering about the countless stars and was getting weary from all the mindless jibber-jabber.

"They've been here the entire time," she finally mumbled. "When we first got to Trilleah, the sky was full of them—more than I had ever seen at one time. But then," she paused and looked around at the group, "as the Trows stole more and more souls, the stars became less and less." She looked toward Aviel. "We just sorta figured that for every soul that was stolen and cursed to the Malleana Forest, another star hid behind the veil in the atmosphere."

"Looks like we were right," Aviel sighed softly. "It didn't take long for the number of cursed souls to outnumber the stars, I guess."

Pierce saw a chance to jump in and direct the Travelers, so he wasted no time in doing just that.

"Okay everyone, we've got to get moving." He figured it would be easier to go and trust them to follow than it would be to explain where he was leading them. If they knew where he was going to take them, chances were small they'd be willing to follow.

He waved his hand in the air and shouted, "FOLLOW ME."

None of the Travelers wanted to take their eyes off of those stars; they really couldn't believe they'd been there this whole time. They did finally look away from all that was going on far above them, but not without much grumbling and murmuring.

Even though Pierce seemed as though he'd changed both in his insides and on his outsides, the thought lingered and snapped in the backs of their minds that it was Pierce who'd led them into the cave in the first place—that cave they barely crawled out of—the cave that had crashed and crumbled to a pile of rubble right before their eyes. It made them very nervous to follow him now, but it seemed like they had no other choice. He did, after all, seem to be a very different young man, and they had all seen the giant eagle who had returned him.

Bella and Matt were at the back of the group and were leery and cautious about following Pierce. Bella said to Matt, "I'm not sure about following him. He was the one who led us straight into that ridiculous cave in the first place," she muttered. "We barely got out of that thing, and he was dragged away and nearly ripped to shreds by some hungry beast."

Matt had one reply to her concerns. He listened patiently because, well, that's just the kind of person Matt was. Only one thought lingered in his mind all the while Bella was chattering about her concerns. It only took one remark from Matt for Bella—and everyone else who was within hearing distance of Bella—to hush and confidently follow Pierce.

"That was also the cave which held the last clay tablet," he said. "I'm not sure it was Pierce who led us there at all, but whether it was or it wasn't, we needed to be there to get the tablet."

Yes. Good point. Very good thought. Even though Pierce had listened to the dark voices—the ones the Travelers knew nothing about, it seemed the Shailmas had been on their side the entire time and had led them straight to the tablet, regardless of Pierce's miserable failings.

"Okay," Bella grimaced and walked a bit faster.

It was a bit difficult and a whole lot tiring, keeping up with Pierce. For one thing, he had long legs, so for Jennifer, Bella, and Kaija Mae, keeping up was exhausting. They had to take two steps for every one of his. For another thing, the Travelers couldn't just walk in a straight line from here to there—wherever there was.

Deadly and dangerous objects were being hurled through the air, and the land itself continued to quiver and shake, although, a little less than before. They had to duck behind this bush (and the available bushes were getting fewer and fewer) or jump over that split in the ground (and those splits in the ground were becoming wider and longer) while keeping their eyes on the sky … and on Pierce. They had to dodge those things hurling through the air and weave around all that was erupting from the ground. Yes, the journey had become treacherous although, with the veil of Nehsher, nothing the Travelers were fearing could touch them. They had no awareness of such things though, so the fear of it all remained steadfast.

Besides all of that—as if that wasn't enough—they were carrying so many things, some of them incredibly heavy, it made any weaving and dodging and jumping quite inconvenient. Some of the bigger items—like the swords and the bags of food—were slowing them down, but they needed all those things. The Travelers discussed, more than once, which items they could leave behind, but every time they came up with the same answer—none of them.

They traded off carrying the heavy items and sometimes, two of them would carry something together.

"How far are we going?" Jennifer whined. "I'm so tired."

"It's a far way yet, Jenny," was the only answer that came time and time again. Finally, to pass the moments and keep their minds off of all the happenings that were going on around them, Bella spoke up.

"Can you tell us more of your story while we go?" she asked sweetly. Matt shot her a look of wondering and, of course, he was wondering what Bella was thinking about the new and improved young man who'd suddenly taken over leading the group.

"Okay," he said. Pierce seemed almost intoxicated that they wanted to hear his story; he was excited to tell them about his journey.

"Nehsher scooped me up and I laid motionless across his back," Pierce began. "I was in no shape to hang on or sit up; I was barely breathing," he said. "You can imagine the shock when this extraordinary eagle with the face of a lion began talking to me—I nearly fell right off his back. That's why part of me wonders if Nehsher was my Shailma in a different form, or a different being altogether.

"Does anyone know if the Shailmas can take on the form of something else?" he asked.

Nobody jumped in to answer because nobody had an answer. They'd never thought of such questions before now. As each considered such a thing, they waited for someone else to speak in case one of the others knew about such things. None did.

"I've only ever seen Simeon as Simeon," Jennifer answered, deeply puzzled. The rest nodded and agreed. They'd never seen their Shailmas as eagles or lions or anything other than the six-winged horse-like creatures they had first revealed themselves to be.

Of course, the truth was that the Shailmas could be anything they needed to be. Those Shailmas had been many different beings—

at many different times—but they were always cautious to keep that knowledge from the Travelers.

"So this eagle said to me, *I am Nehsher*. That's all he said for a time, but as I was laying on his back in shock just trying to stay still, I suddenly began wondering if this *Nehsher* was good. Did my Shailma send him to rescue me or had he come from somewhere else to take me to King Shrailzhar? I suddenly realized that I had no idea about any of it. I also realized that I was in no shape to fight off such a beast so it seemed I might be in a terrible spot … again!"

"Either it was a big coincidence, or Nehsher knew what I thought because he immediately told me that my Shailma had called for him to come. Then, he said something I did not understand. He said he was taking me to the One of all Light."

Even though the ground beneath them was shaking, it was hard not to notice the shiver that went through Pierce as he spoke these words. It began at the bottom of his feet and continued up until it left through the top of his head; more like a pulse than a shiver, really.

Nobody wanted to ask, but everyone wanted to know. There was a quietness in the group, but not in the land. Pierce had hushed for a few seconds before he continued. Maybe he was waiting for someone to ask a question—probably about this *One of all Light*, but no one did.

"I wanted to ask him who the *One of all Light* was in case he was someone—or something—I didn't want to meet. But as I thought my thoughts, I suddenly had this peace wash over me. I can't explain it so I won't try, but I'll just say that it was very much like what happened inside the Chamber of Rest, only better."

Everyone understood that, for they'd all experienced the same thing in the Chamber and they knew there was no way to describe such a thing to someone who'd never experienced it. It was just one of those things that a person needs to experience to understand and even then, understanding is far off.

"We went up and up and up," Pierce continued. "Nehsher flew so high that I thought the air might get too thin for me to breathe … I was barely breathing as it was. He assured me that I would be fine, though. I had never heard of this creature before, but he was magnificent, and I believed everything I heard from him. For the first time, I had no doubt about anything; not even a hint of it.

"No voices were whispering to me that he was deceiving me, like those wicked deceivers in the high grasses. Remember them, Jennifer?" Pierce asked.

How could she forget? Those dreadful deceivers had nearly taken her to her death. When those Dark Deceivers had begun whispering their lies to her, back in the tall grasses, it was Pierce who dove to grab her heel just as she was about to step off the path into their web of lies.

"I remember," she muttered. She wished she could forget.

"Watch out!" Bella shrieked.

A large fiery boulder whizzed a couple of feet in front of Pierce and landed with a loud *thud,* causing fistfuls of rock and dirt to fling up. Pierce jumped back and threw his arms up to protect those behind him from what was happening in front of him. For a time, they stood still and waited, stunned that he had thrown himself between them and the dangers ahead.

Jennifer strained her neck and looked up high above her. She gasped loudly and pointed to the sky. Everyone's heads tilted up and looked; they wished they hadn't, but it was too late. Once again they couldn't seem to make themselves look away. Sometimes what an eye sees is so wonderful that it becomes mesmerized with goodness and sticks to the sight; this was not one of those times. This was one of those times when the eye entwines with something so horrific that it dare not look away lest that horrific thing follow too closely. Yes, this one was of those times.

The Shamar Shailmas' riders had raised their swords high and were defending themselves from the Nakah riders. It looked like a fierce battle with many more Nakahs than Shamars. At least, that's what it looked like to the Travelers' eyes. Fear of what they were seeing pulled the Travelers' attention away from Pierce's story and braided it firmly together with terror and trepidation.

"Where are we going?" Jennifer shrieked. "Why can't we just break the curse right here and end all this?" The small girl was overwhelmed with so much going on and she didn't know which way to look. If she looked to the sky, it pierced her soul to see such a battle raging. If she looked ahead, the Dark Land was being destroyed with smoldering coals and flashes of lightning and bursts of fire rising from holes in the ground.

She didn't mind Trilleah being destroyed, none of them did. It truly was a horrible land. They just didn't want it destroyed while they were still inside of it and most definitely not before they could free the souls of the Waiting Ones.

Now, if Jennifer looked behind, her heart would shatter into a million pieces, for that was exactly where the Forest of Malleana had stood for so long. That was where Asphelia's Hollow had hidden them and had been their home while in this horrible land, but now it was gone. All of it that is, except for the one lone tree that held Miriam's soul.

"I can't do this!" she suddenly shrieked. "I want to go home … I'm not strong enough or big enough or wise enough to do any of this … I want to go home!" Jennifer wailed and cried terribly. Bella moved toward her and gently stroked her niece's matted, blood-streaked hair. Judah wanted to say something but had no words to make his sister feel less panicked, so he kept all his words to himself.

It was Pierce who had words to comfort the young girl's troubled soul.

"None of us can do this, Jenny," were his words. Not comforting at all, but what came next comforted them all … sort of.

"It's not us who have done any of this. It wasn't us who found the tablets or escaped the cradle bugs or hid from Shrailzhar. It was the Shailmas. It's always been the Shailmas, and it will always be the Shailmas. They will do what needs to be done and if they need us to do something, then that's how it will be. We will do all that must be done—not in our wisdom—but in theirs. None of it will be with our strength, but with the strength that they give to us. Nothing will be done with our courage or bravery or boldness, but with the courage and bravery and boldness which they pour into our souls.

"No, Jennifer, you cannot do this and neither can I. But if we let the Shailmas work through us then it will get done and the curse will be broken and the Waiting Ones will find their freedom."

Somehow, and with no sense of their own, this seeming rambling nonsense of Pierce found places in their minds and their hearts and felt comfortable there. Jennifer sniffled and wiped her nose on her tattered red blanket.

The small girl sighed a great big sigh.

"Okay," she whimpered.

Chapter Eight

Nowhere to Hide

"UP THERE!" Sam shouted. "What is that?"

They all looked in the direction of where he was pointing, but nobody else caught a glimpse of what had captured Sam's attention. He seemed to be both excited and distraught at the same time; of course, the boy had a horrible fever from the poison his arm was flushing through his body so he may have been seeing things not there, the other supposed.

"Up where?" Kaija Mae asked while straining her eyes to find anything that might be what Sam had seen.

He ignored Kaija Mae's question … for now.

"Pierce, do you see that?" Sam asked instead.

"I do," Pierce answered. "And that's exactly where we are heading."

None of the others noticed yet what was still a bit too far in the distance. As they drew closer, though, a familiar sound was heard. One by one the awareness of where they were going hit each Traveler with a fury. The sounds brought no joy to any of them, but instead overwhelming waves of sadness and despair steamrolled over the Travelers.

"I hear it, but I don't see where it's coming from," Jennifer whined. Her heart sounded broken … like little pieces were chipping off and riding out on her words … being expelled with every breath.

"It can't be so!" Bella shrieked.

But it was so—it was right there sprawled out in front of them. Nobody wanted to believe it, yet it was staring them in the face. They could not deny the painfully familiar sounds of wretched moaning and woeful wailing as they were dragged from the air and stuffed into the Travelers' ears.

It was loud—louder than they'd ever heard those Waiting Ones wail before. It was heavy and sickening … completely dreadful.

There, about thirty feet in front of the Travelers, were trees; hundreds of thousands of trees—maybe even more than that. They were not standing upright like back in Malleana Forest. Oh no! They were thrown in piles, discarded like rubbish. Some of the Travelers fell to their knees, buried faces in their filthy hands, and wailed horrendous wails. Others rushed toward the endless pile of what held the souls of their loved ones, howling and wailing themselves.

They couldn't get much closer, for there, dug all around the endless pile of the discarded forest, was a deep and wide ditch. It circled the entire perimeter of the area that held the trees from Malleana Forest. That ditch was about six feet across and there was no way to even guess how deep it might be. It was filled with the orangey-red bubbling lava the Travelers had seen here and there, just beneath the crust of the land.

Horrible gasps rose from the Travelers, which seemed to cause the fiery lava to bubble up even more, almost laughing at them. It mocked them brutally.

Now, it need not be said that it had been painful enough for the Travelers to experience the wailings of the cursed souls when all these had stood in Malleana Forest, but at least there in the forest, the Travelers could walk among them and touch them. Once in a while it seemed like the presence of the Travelers brought a shred of comfort to the Waiting Ones and they would moan a bit less or wail a bit softer.

When the forest still stood in Malleana, the Travelers could wander and pretend that this one held the twins' mamma's soul or that one ensnared the soul of Sam's sweet baby sister, Justice. No one had ever admitted to the others that they thought such things when they wandered through the forest but the truth was that they'd all thought such thoughts now and again.

There was only that one time, many journeys ago, when Jennifer had been seen by Bella as she gently rubbed her hands on some of the trees and sang lullabies to them, hoping to find her mamma. But they had all done it; they had each wondered and pretended and pondered the same thing.

It was just the way of hope. It was hope that kept them coming back Solstice after Solstice, year after year. Each time the gates opened, whether in winter or summer, it was hope that called their hearts to return.

Seeing all this now, though, they knew like never before that those things they once saw as hollowed out, dead trees imprisoning their loved ones souls were, in fact, the very souls themselves. They could see no roots whatsoever, and the branches had been torn away. These things were now simply gnarled and twisted up bits of death. They'd never been trees; they'd always been prisons.

But now, standing here looking at a discarded pile of death from a forest that no longer existed, their hearts truly and thoroughly broke. Whether the Travelers were still thirty feet back or as close as they could get to the heat of this river of rolling fire, they all did the same thing …

… they wept while the cursed souls wailed. It seemed like in an instant, the souls from both sides—the ones trapped within the curse and the ones working hard to break it—lost hope. In the blink of an eye, all hope was washed away by the Chasm of Acheron, which had been created for the very purpose of separating the dead from the living.

It took a long time before anyone said a word. Finally, Jennifer pulled herself together a little more than anyone else and stood up; she was angry. Not angry at any of the Travelers but angry at the horrific sight. The young girl was overwhelmingly angry that King Shrailzhar and his army had done this great travesty and she was angry that the Trows had stolen so many souls—for the mound of them was great indeed and continued to grow even as they watched. It shocked every one of them that even now the Trows were out stealing souls. Oh, if they'd only known that the king had sent double the Trows out to gather as many souls as possible before the land completed its destruction. But then again, not knowing such a thing was probably for the best.

Jennifer was angry, and she said so.

"Pierce," she demanded sharply. "Why did you bring us here? Why do we have to see such a horror as this?" she wailed. Jennifer wasn't angry at Pierce; not at all. She was angry at everything else, but of course, as anger does, it came out in her words and hit Pierce square in the face.

"Jennifer," Judah said, trying to calm his sister. It didn't work. She stubbornly refused to be calmed. She simply wouldn't have it. But she did apologize to Pierce and reminded him, "I'm not angry with you, Pierce, I'm just angry!"

"I understand," he replied. "I'm angry too. We all are, Jenny. I don't know why I was led here. Nevertheless, I was. I don't want to be here either but I …" Before he could finish his thought, Kaija Mae interrupted. She used her usual quiet voice, but the words she said were full of power.

"It's only here—in this place of such horror—where the clay tablets can be laid out and knit together."

Silence.

There was complete silence from the Travelers and uninterrupted silence from the Waiting Ones. There was even silence in the land as Kaija Mae's words rang out. The rocks and fiery coals that were already hurling through the air fell flat to the ground, but for the time being, no more were thrown. Even the War of the Firmament halted itself and became silent as the secret of Kaija Mae's words was uncovered. The Nakahs froze, knowing that a secret that should never be told had indeed, been told.

The complete silence and lack of motion seemed to last forever but probably was only about six minutes or so. Never before had there been such a silence. Never again would there ever be such a silence.

All was silent for one reason and one reason alone. The truth of freedom had been spoken. Light had been brought into darkness. The light of truth that would forever change everything had dared to be uttered into the atmosphere. Everyone and everything heard it. The land and the sea heard it. The Nakah Warriors and the Shamar

Shailmas heard it. King Shrailzhar and the Trows and all the armies of Trilleah heard it. The souls of the Waiting Ones heard it … and the souls of those still living.

Yes; those words of truth had been heard by every living, and every dead thing, and none dared to argue.

Not one person wanted to speak. Their minds raced with things to say, but with everything silent, nobody wanted to be the one to break the wonder of it all. The cursed souls were not moaning or wailing, and that in itself was the best sound ever to not be heard.

As suddenly as the silence came and hovered, it left.

The War of the Firmament started up again with a fury as the clashing and clanging of sword against sword and shouts of death as both the Nakah Warriors and Shamar Shailmas received death blows rang out more ferociously than before. The Travelers had not yet given time to staring up into the atmosphere to take in any of that war, mostly because none of them wanted to see what might happen.

They all had enormous faith in the Shamar Shailmas to be sure. It was those Shamars who'd escorted them into Trilleah when the king had sent some of his biggest Nakah Warriors to stand guard at their door in Westlock. It was also the Shamar Shailmas who'd rescued Jennifer in the adder's pit when the king's beast refused to come near her.

Time and time again the Shamar Shailmas had rescued or protected the Travelers so now, watching a war take place in the firmament—where the Nakah Warriors far outnumbered the Shamars—was not what the Travelers wanted to see.

They had been able to avoid seeing much of it so far, and now that the silence had tucked itself away, Jennifer asked Pierce to share a bit more of his story. They still hadn't learned what had happened to this young man to change him so drastically. Jennifer had a hunch that his story had much more information woven into it that she very much needed to know about.

"I will tell you more, of course!" he said. "First, let's find a place to lay out the tablets.

The Travelers worked hard to avoid looking at the sky; they did not wish to see even one Shamar meet their death. They worked even harder to keep their eyes from glancing across the Chasm of Acheron, since the souls were louder in their wailing, and more adamant in their groans, now that the silence had gone. The Travelers knew they'd be overcome with emotion if they looked at the mountain of cursed souls, so they worked hard not to look.

Instead, like Pierce had suggested, they looked and searched and searched and looked for a covered place to lay out the tablets. Of course, no such spot would be found. The Shamar Shailmas had made sure of that. The Travelers were unaware that the very moment they laid those tablets out, the ground would open itself up and swallow each and every one of the tablets whole. Trilleah's very existence—and King Shrailzhar's throne—depended entirely on those chunks of clay not relinquishing their secrets or sharing their powers or allowing the Travelers to break their curse.

There was a precise and exact procedure for breaking the curse. The Travelers were enormously mistaken to think all that was needed were those dozen clay tablets. Oh, absolutely they were a *part* of the key that would break the curse and unlock the prison which held the captive souls, indeed. Certainly, though, they were not the only thing required for such a task.

The Travelers wandered, looking around desperately, but were careful to stay close together. As they wandered and looked and questioned and fought to keep from falling apart, Pierce revealed more of what he had experienced.

"I could see that Nehsher was taking me somewhere that none of us had ever been," he began. "I was sure nobody had ever been there or even heard about it, it was so far away.

"As we got closer and closer to somewhere I didn't know, I had to close my eyes and then, soon, that wasn't even good enough." Pierce shook his head as if remembering such a thing made his eyes hurt even now.

"Before long, I had to cover my eyes with my hands even though they were closed tight. The light became so bright that I felt as though I'd been taken into the middle of the sun, although there was no heat. I remember thinking, 'It's going to get hot, it's going to burn me up,' but it never. No heat ever came.

"I felt sick to my stomach and considered throwing myself off the back of the one who called himself Nehsher, because as I was waiting for the heat to destroy me, I kept thinking about Sam and the agony he was going through back in the cave with his burned hand. I have to admit, I thought you might not get out of that cave, but I couldn't worry about that right then. I was terrified out of my mind.

"Nehsher had said he was taking me to the One of all Light, and I began trembling uncontrollably. Nehsher could tell I was, too. I know he could, although he never said another word to me. He was not one to converse with, not at all. Nehsher was one only to speak when he had something of great importance to say—like he was getting words from someone else and had no words of his own."

The Travelers had stopped looking for a covered-over spot by this time and all had turned to watch Pierce as he told a bit more of his unbelievable story. The more of it he told, the more unreal it seemed. The Travelers became mesmerized each time Pierce began speaking about it, like something was drawing them in that they couldn't see and didn't want to avoid.

"Finally ..." Pierce sighed. "Finally, Nehsher came to a place and stopped. He didn't fold his wings in or set his gigantic talons on the ground anywhere because there was no ground. It looked like we were in mid-air and I stretched out the one arm that wasn't wounded and tried to hang on to Nehsher.

"I wondered then if this was a cruel trick and he was going to hurl me off his back and watch me fall to the ground, which I couldn't even see anymore. As I was trying to cling to him, I remembered reading something once about eagles playing with their food or something like that. I'd read a long time ago—and whether it was true or not true made no difference because, at that moment, it terrified me—that eagles catch a field mouse and take it as high in the air as they can and then drop it." Pierce shuttered thinking about this. "Then, just before that field mouse hits the ground, the eagle swoops down and grabs it up again. I did not wish to be the mouse to this eagle."

The Travelers looked at each other, not sure what to think about anything Pierce was telling them. It all seemed ridiculous and so far-fetched, but there was nothing far-fetched about the obvious changes in this one telling the story. There was no way to deny the wounds in his shoulder and on his hands had been healed over.

It was apparent that Nehsher had not thrown him to the ground since he was standing here in front of them. Furthermore, they knew Pierce was speaking truth about this Great Eagle, Nehsher, because it was that very eagle which they'd seen with their own eyes deliver Pierce right back to them.

Then there were the words that Nehsher had spoken as Pierce appeared before them; they'd all heard it. Each and every Traveler heard what this eagle had spoken.

"I am returning this one to you," Nehsher had said loudly. "He has been cleansed and redeemed. Receive him now, for he has been given authority over the land and power over the sea."

What all that meant, none of them knew, and in fact, Pierce himself didn't understand what *authority over the land,* or which *power over the sea,* he'd been given.

He did know, however, and was very clear on one thing. Pierce knew—without a doubt—he'd been cleansed and redeemed.

What happened next, once Nehsher set him down in front of the others, would undoubtedly change every one of the Travelers; it was evident to them all that whatever had happened had already greatly changed Pierce.

Chapter Nine

If You Listen Closely

As Pierce remembered all he had experienced and shared it bit by bit with the others, the War of the Firmament raged on and on above them. Like a wildfire in a wind storm, the battle heated up and spread throughout the skies and across the land. Even the depths of the sea had now joined the battle.

Even though the Travelers were nowhere near the sea now, they'd seen it earlier. They had watched as it had swallowed up

Miriam, and they were so grateful when it had spit out the clay tablet at their feet. It seemed that not every part of Trilleah was against them and from King Shrailzhar's reaction to the Leviathan, it seemed the king as well, knew that part of his kingdom was against him.

The Nakah Warriors and the Shamar Shailmas battled ferociously high above them, just beyond the scroll of the atmosphere. The Travelers wanted to see what was happening since their lives were in the hands of the Shamar Shailmas. They watched for short moments here and there, but then it would become too much to bare and the Travelers would have to look away.

Back and forth, back and forth the war went. As their swords continued to come together in the atmosphere, sparks flew and fires erupted, falling to the ground and burning up whatever was touched. Thankfully, the fires were not spreading too rapidly across the land. It seemed like they would destroy whatever they landed on and then stop burning, or at least fade into embers and ashes and blow away.

Thundering clashes were vibrating from the east to the west, and the north to the south, causing the entire Dark Land to continually quake and quiver. Hail started pelting the ground again, only the ice chunks were much bigger now than before those six minutes of silence that seemed far too long ago. In fact, it was undeniable that everywhere the battle raged was far more vicious and aggressive now than before that silence had momentarily lingered.

The Travelers had to be painstakingly cautious to stay away from this and stand back from that. Their eyes were continually scanning the land to ensure something wasn't coming against them that would take them out. Besides all of that, as if it wasn't enough, the Travelers continued to search for a covered place to duck into but still, they found nothing. None of them were aware of the covering that Nehsher had spread out above them, but it made no difference. They had no need to know about it, although it would have helped their fears be a little less … well … a little less fearful.

Jennifer looked up when she should have kept her eyes on Simeon, and she listened to the battle when her ears needed to be tuned into Pierce. Something caught her eye, though, and she couldn't look away. It distracted her far more than she should ever have allowed herself to be distracted.

The Shamar Shailmas had lost some of their bigger warriors, it seemed. She watched as four of the largest Nakahs she could see cornered one lone Shamar. The Nakah riders held their swords out in front of them and they moved swiftly toward the single Shamar.

Jennifer wanted to cover her eyes or look away. She wanted to scream and warn the one lone Shamar, but she could do nothing. She just stood there and watched as horror embraced her, squeezing the air out of her lungs.

One of those Nakahs let out a blood-curdling shriek as two Shamar riders attacked it from behind, plunging swords deep into the heart of the beast. As that one Nakah Warrior and its rider plummeted to the ground—dead—the two Shamars charged in and joined the other who'd been surrounded.

An outrageous battle ensued between those three Shamars and the three remaining Nakahs.

The swords clashed and thundered. The skies raged all around and the riders battled on and on. Every time the swords would come together, deafening thunder would scream, and waves of fire would streak through the skies.

Jennifer shrieked as she watched one of the Nakah riders thrust his sword deep into a Shamar Shailma. The Shamar stumbled and fell, unable to get up. A second Nakah rider swung his enormous sword, and the Shamar's rider lost his head. He spun and plummeted to the ground below. At the same time, a Shamar rider swung his double-edged sword from behind the Nakah and another head tumbled. Blood-curdling screams were heard throughout the firmament as Shailmas and their riders from both sides were hurled ferociously—and without their heads—to the ground.

The Travelers had seen Jennifer's eyes and the horror that was reflecting on her face. They turned to see what she was looking at and immediately turned away, not willing to watch such a hideous battle. If the Shamar Shailmas could not be victorious in this war … oh … the Travelers couldn't allow their minds to consider what the conclusion would be if the Nakahs overpowered those Shamars.

"Jelly Bean," Judah begged of his terror-stricken sister. "Look away; please stop watching!" Jennifer continued to watch despite Judah's desperate callings, and suddenly let out a blood-stopping shriek of her own.

"LOOK!" she wailed. The others looked, even though they didn't want to. They could not believe their eyes as they saw hundreds of Shamar Shailmas open their mouths, spewing light into the firmament.

At first, Jennifer and the others thought it was swords coming from their mouths since they looked a great deal like the double-edged swords their riders were battling with. However, as the Travelers looked closer and watched carefully, they saw something unbelievable, not that anything they were seeing was at all believable. Some things were just a little more unbelievable than other things.

Nevertheless, as the Shamar Shailmas would open their mouths and blinding beams of light would be sent out like swords, the Nakah Warriors would back off. The stunned Travelers watched closer and saw that as the light traveled farther from the Shamar's mouths, it would explode, filling large chunks of the air with radiant and blinding light.

Any Nakah that got too close and flew into the beam of light or challenged the Shamars who were breathing the light rays would instantly be hurled to the dirt below, dead before they ever hit the ground.

Large areas of the firmament cleared out, allowing the Shamars to spread out and push back the Nakahs who'd been trying to surround them. Very quickly the Shamars were able to take over much of the air.

Deplorable sulfur was quickly filling the sky. It became so thick the Travelers couldn't see into the firmament very well anymore and finally, they looked away. The Nakah Warriors and their riders who continued to be hurled to the ground like rain couldn't be missed, though, and the Travelers watched closely.

They wanted to be sure the Nakahs were indeed dead. Nobody wanted to be taken off guard if these horrible beasts and their riders were not, in fact, dead because surely, they would decide to go after the Travelers. Of course, the Travelers had forgotten that a number of Shamar Shailmas had remained on the ground with them to protect them from the Army of Shrailzhar. Remembering such things was not high on their priority list at the moment.

The wailing of the Waiting Ones grew so much louder as the Nakah Warriors—and their riders—were falling, that it was hard for the Travelers to hear Pierce. Nevertheless, he went right on telling them about his experience with Nehsher and the *One of all Light.*

"With only a couple of flaps of his enormous wings, Nehsher was gone; just like that. The Eagle of immeasurable size just left me there, in the presence of this light. It wasn't just a light, it was … well … I have been thinking and thinking of words to describe it, but all I can come up with is that the light was absolutely, completely, altogether indescribable.

"Without doing anything or saying anything or thinking anything, the power that was coming from that presence was so overwhelming that I couldn't continue to stand. I was in great pain, of course, from the wounds on my shoulder and from being dragged for so long and tossed into thorns, but suddenly at that moment, none of that mattered. Nothing mattered!

"I fell to my knees in the presence of this power—the presence that I couldn't even look at. I had no words. After all, what does one say to such a presence? This light did not *have* power—it *was* power. It didn't *have* light—it *was* light. I can't explain it to you well enough to make you understand," Pierce said. He seemed saddened by that thought. "I can't understand it myself!"

Suddenly, what Nehsher had spoken to Pierce made sense as he retold it to the others. "The *One of all Light*, Nehsher had called him."

KABOOOOM ...

CRASSHH ...

Nakahs and their riders continued to fall, along with some of the Shamars. The more that fell, the deeper the Chasm of Acheron became. The deeper it became, the higher the fires raged. Those fires —liquid fires, in fact—were lapping at the ground now, and the Travelers had to back away a good distance to avoid being overtaken.

"Something stepped out from this light presence and touched my shoulder," Pierce continued, seemingly unbothered by what was going on around them. "In an instant, the bleeding stopped, and the wounds healed themselves." He rubbed his shoulder as he told about it. "The pain was gone! Then, whatever touched my shoulder moved down my arms and my hands, removing all the pain … then it was gone, drawn back into the source of the light.

"I can't explain what it was because I don't know what it was. All I know for sure," he said, "is that in the blink of an eye, my wounds were healed and my pain was gone." He'd shown them his shoulder earlier, so they knew he was telling the truth. Even now he held out his arms for them to see again. If they hadn't seen it with their own eyes, they certainly would not have believed such an outrageous story. They barely believed it even after seeing the proof of it all.

As Jennifer was thinking these exact thoughts, filled with doubt and unbelief, something familiar came to her mind—the conversation she'd had with Pierce just before they were separated a few days before. Pierce had said that unless he saw the army of Shamar Shailmas for himself, he would not believe. She remembered how terrified she'd become because she knew how important believing was, whether he saw or did not see. Now she heard those same words in her own heart—those words of doubt.

Little One, she heard Simeon whisper, *you must believe.*

She immediately decided that even though she had not seen this one that Pierce was speaking about, and even though she had nothing to base her belief on, she needed to believe. She MUST believe. If Simeon told her to believe, then she would believe.

Even though these things were hard to believe, they were not nearly as difficult to believe as what Pierce was about to tell them next.

"As I was on my knees, unable to look at the presence that was before me, I felt no fear. That was odd to me because I think I should have been so terribly afraid … but there was nothing like that.

"In fact," Pierce said and then he seemed to go into his own mind and was quiet for a minute before continuing, "not only was there no fear, but there was the exact opposite. I was covered with complete peace," he uttered in a bit of a calming sigh. "It was like being in the Chamber of Rest except for a thousand times better … a million maybe … if such a thing is even possible.

"I felt that light cover me somehow," he whispered. "Like new skin had been wrapped around me completely, filling me on the inside and swaddling me on the outside."

Jennifer was carefully watching the chasm just behind Pierce because it seemed to be listening to his story as well. She'd noticed that when Pierce was talking about this presence of Light, the liquid fire hushed just a bit, but enough to be noticeable. Her eyes were on the chasm, but her ears were tuned into Pierce. She didn't dare miss even a word or a breath of what he was relaying to the Travelers; neither did she miss anything that was going on around them—either in the atmosphere or in the Chasm.

The War and everything around them was so loud that it was hard to stay focused, but Jennifer and the others finally noticed that there was an unseen force encircling them which allowed Pierce's words to be carried directly to the Travelers' ears. It was as if something unseen by their eyes wanted the power and truth of Pierce's words to get to their ears fully … as though there was something in his story that would empower them as well.

Undeniable … no doubt.

Most bewildering … to be sure.

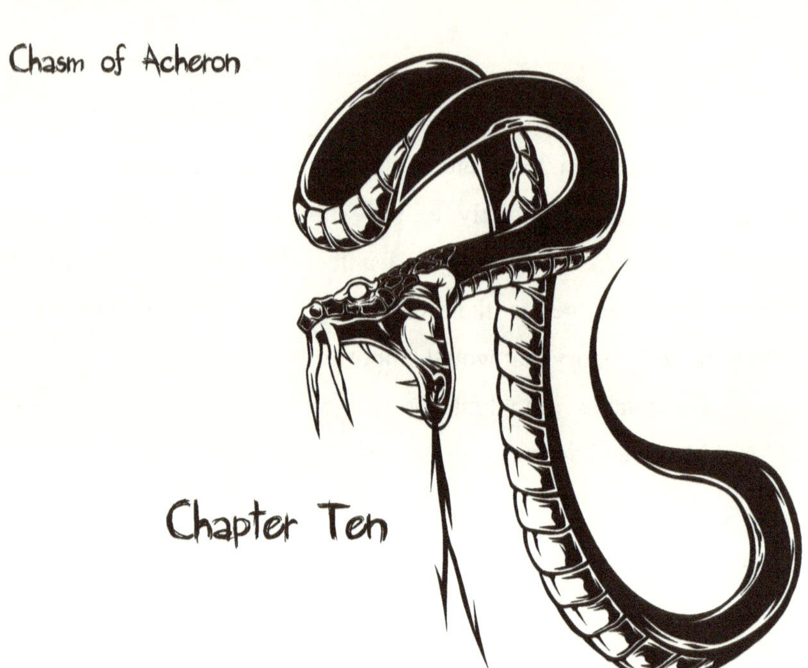

Chapter Ten

Nonsense

Sam, who'd quietly been moaning the entire time, suddenly began wailing loudly. His burned hand was giving him horrible amounts of pain. He could not take one more second of the anguish. "It's shooting up my arm now," he sobbed. Bella looked at it and sure enough, just around his elbow and even a little above that, was turning a horrible shade of green and a most hideous smell was present.

"It looks like it's rotting," she screeched to the others. Bella had to cover her nose because of the smell coming from Sam's dilapidating flesh. "We can't just leave it like this; we have to do something. I just don't know what!"

The others gathered around, and Matt started carefully unwrapping the makeshift bandages. It was truly a horrific wound and the pain was intolerable. As the wrapping came off and the air began to touch Sam's arm, he started screaming uncontrollably. It was more than he could bare—far more pain than he could stand—and he fell to the ground shrieking and gasping and heaving.

Pierce moved close to the boy and put his hand on Sam's head. He was hot with a fever from the infection stirring in his wound.

"Look at me, Sam," Pierce stated firmly. Sam opened his eyes and gritted his teeth. With giant tears stinging his eyes as they pushed through and rushed down his face, Sam did force himself to look at Pierce. He saw something there he'd never seen before.

Sam didn't have any words to describe what he saw in Pierce's eyes, but it didn't matter. It was his words that made all the difference.

"Sam," Pierce stated with deep compassion. "When I was in front of the One of all Light, on my knees with my eyes shielded from the great brilliance and power, I heard something. I didn't know where it came from and figured it came from the light, just as whatever touched my shoulder and closed the wounds had come from the light. I wasn't sure until now," he said, looking right into Sam's pain-filled eyes. "But now I know it was a voice from that Light that had spoken."

Sam continued to grit his teeth as he tried desperately to focus on what Pierce was saying. Even though he hadn't yet said anything helpful about Sam's pain, there was a feeling in the boy's belly that filled him full of expectation and even some shreds of hope.

Hang on, Samuel Collins, he repeated to himself. *Hang on.*

"What I heard made no sense at the time, but it does now. It makes perfect sense. As I looked at you just now, I suddenly knew what the words meant," Pierce sounded rather excited as he rambled on about things that made no sense to anyone else. The other Travelers were listening intently, hanging on every word. But to Sam, it sounded like gibberish, like Pierce was rambling on endlessly about nothing at all.

Still, there was that knowing that continued to flutter in his belly that Pierce had something Sam needed and so, he struggled to listen.

"The One of all Light touched me, and I heard him in my belly somehow, rather than in my ears. *Go and do likewise ... I am in you and all you have seen Me do I now empower you to do.* That's what that One of all Light put into my heart."

Kaija Mae began her singing as Pierce was saying such words. She didn't mean to. It wasn't as if she thought, "I should sing." She just sang. Her mouth opened up and unknown words tumbled out in a melody far more beautiful than had ever been heard before.

"So, Sam, I have no idea about this—I'm only being obedient to the One of all Light who touched me." Of course, Pierce wasn't aware, but he was being directed by his Shailma. It was his Shailma who had suddenly made the words from the One of all Light make sense in the exact moment they were needed.

After saying many nonsensical things, Pierce stuck out his hands and carefully touched Sam's wounded hand. Every eye watched; not even one blinked. They all had the same knowing in their bellies now that Sam had felt in his own belly earlier. The Travelers held their breath expecting something outrageous to occur but not knowing what that outrageous something might be.

As Pierce laid his hand on Sam's arm, skin began to cover the wound. It looked like an invisible hand had come and was stretching the skin from his upper arm, the unwounded part, and was pulling it down over the open and oozing wound. Each Traveler was speechless, including Sam … and Pierce. Kaija Mae continued her singing, but even that was not coming from herself.

Sam's hand wasn't perfect, oh, it was far from perfect. His fingers did not return, and his hand was severely deformed, but the wound closed itself up and the pain was removed. The green color that had begun to spread to his elbow and upper arm was gone, and a healthy pink returned both to his arm and his face.

Everyone's eyes grew ten times their normal size—maybe even a bit bigger than that. Not even one, except for Pierce, could believe what they were seeing. However, as Sam began shrieking again, this time not about the pain but rather about the pain being gone, the hearts of the rest had no choice but to believe what their eyes had seen. Sam leaped to his feet and began dancing and jumping all around. In seconds, the others joined him, forgetting momentarily all that was going on around them.

Pierce had insurmountable difficulty with what he'd just witnessed. But then, it was so similar to what he had experienced with his shoulder that he couldn't deny the power that had come from the One of all Light.

"Where there is light, darkness must flee."

Sam looked to Pierce and said, "I suppose so!"

Pierce looked back to Sam and asked, "What?"

"I guess darkness can't stay where light is, although I'm not sure why you said that," Sam laughed. He hadn't laughed in days—not since he'd fallen to the ground and terribly burned his hand, so now it felt good to chuckle a little … and dance a lot.

"I didn't say anything, Sam," Pierce said.

"Yes, you said where there is light, darkness must flee," Sam insisted. The look on Pierce's face let Sam know that he had certainly said nothing of the sort. He looked around at the others, bewildered. "Didn't you all hear that?" Sam asked.

"Hear what?" Judah asked.

"I heard nothing of the sort," said Bella.

"Me neither," added Jennifer, and on and on it went. Nobody had heard the words except for Sam.

It must've been my Shailma, he supposed but then again, he knew the voice of his Shailma, and he heard these words with his ears, not with his mind.

"What were the words you heard again, Sam?" Pierce asked.

"I very clearly heard someone say, 'Where there is light, darkness must flee,' " he repeated.

"Oh! Yes, okay," Pierce stated as if he knew something nobody else knew and in fact, he did. "Those are the same words that I heard come from the One of all Light when my shoulder was healed up. I had forgotten about them until you said them just now, Sam," Pierce added.

"None of this makes any sense!" Bella stated loudly. She sounded angry, although she wasn't angry exactly, more like confused … or befuddled, even.

"I don't know, Bella, but really … look around," Pierce said. "Does any of this make sense?

"Does it make sense that we're all here, standing in the middle of a war between Nakah Warriors and Shamar Shailmas? A few years ago none of us had ever heard of such things, yet there they are!" He pointed up to the firmament where the Travelers knew the war was going on even though it was fairly hidden behind clouds of sulfur and smoke.

Pierce continued. "Does it make sense that we follow instructions of Shailmas who we rarely have seen and even then, does it make sense that there are beings that surround us at every moment of every day that we cannot see?" Slowly, one by one, and then all at once, the Travelers began listing off things that made no sense but were quite real nonetheless. Sometimes, the things we do see are much harder to believe than the things we don't see.

"Look there!" Kaija Mae shrieked. They looked in the direction she was pointing, and they all gasped and shrieked. The mountain that was formed from what used to be Malleana Forest (which still held the souls of the Waiting Ones, by the way) had begun to shake viciously. It was like the land beneath it had become more disturbed than before, although, the land where the Travelers were standing did not become more disturbed and was not moving any more than it had been only moments earlier.

The entire land had been trembling since the War of the Firmament had begun, except for that six or so minutes when everything was silent. But besides that brief time, the land quivered continuously. It had not gotten any better—nor any worse—but at the same time as the words about light making darkness flee were uttered, the souls of the Waiting Ones began trembling harder. It seemed as though that one statement had set them off somehow and had caused them to be more disturbed than before.

"That makes no sense either!" Bella added. And then, the gurgling of the fire that was being contained in the Chasm of Acheron raged wildly. It stood up somehow, terrifying the Travelers and making them turn and run. They ran a good distance before slowing down, but as anyone who's run anywhere before knows full well, a person can only run so far before their lungs are empty and their legs give way. Finally, it was Matt who turned around and looked back.

"It's good," he panted, for he was quite completely out of breath.

The others turned to look.

They all noticed the raging flames had calmed back down to a rumbling boil and had receded to the chasm—but the mound of gnarled, branchless trees that held the souls of the Waiting Ones continued to quiver and tremble harder than the rest of the land, and harder still than they were earlier.

"Another thing that makes no sense!" Bella said.

Sam looked back down at his arm; he still couldn't believe the pain was gone. If it wasn't his own arm … if he had not remembered the agonizing pain so great that it caused him to lose consciousness earlier in the cave … if he did not feel that absence of pain now … he'd have never believed it to be true.

What he saw was one thing, and maybe he could have convinced himself that his eyes were deceiving him. But what he felt was undeniable … undeniable! As he looked at Pierce—and back to his pain-free arm—then over to the Chasm of Acheron—and finally up to the sky, searching for that Nehsher they had seen earlier, it suddenly dawned on him. All at once, everything made sense even though it still seemed like nonsense to the others.

"What was it that Nehsher said as he brought Pierce back?" Sam asked. He remembered full well but was hoping to stir up the same sudden knowing in the minds of the rest. The others looked at him, confused as to what the eagle had to do with trying to make sense of such things.

"Why?" Judah asked.

"He said something about Pierce having power over the land or something," Sam said. He was trying to get them to remember, but nobody seemed too interested in Nehsher, or what he had said about Pierce.

Just a few minutes ago, they had all remembered and seemed to think it was important. That was before Pierce had touched Sam and watched as the wound was healed over. Since that moment, though, some jealousies rose up and nobody wanted to remember. Or they acted as though they had forgotten.

Finally, Jennifer spoke up; she held no jealousies whatsoever. She remembered word for word what Nehsher has said and told the others because as she considered all these things, it was beginning to make some sense to her as well. Likely, it was Simeon ordering her thoughts to bring some understanding, but of course, Jennifer had no knowledge of Simeon's power to do such things.

"He said, 'I am returning this one to you. He has been cleansed and redeemed. Receive him now for he has been given authority over the land and power over the sea.' "

Each head turned to her and nodded. One by one it seemed to be dawning on them as well. Nobody said anything for a moment or two, and they looked around instead. They looked to the sky which was still covered by the mixture of smoke and sulfur … and to the Chasm of Acheron … and to the souls of the Waiting Ones. Maybe they were looking for Nehsher now.

"What does, 'He has been cleansed and redeemed,' mean?" Judah asked.

Pierce didn't seem to know, although he knew what had happened in him while he knelt before that One of all Light, and so he went on with a bit more of that explanation and hoped somewhere in its words, they would find the answer to Judah's question.

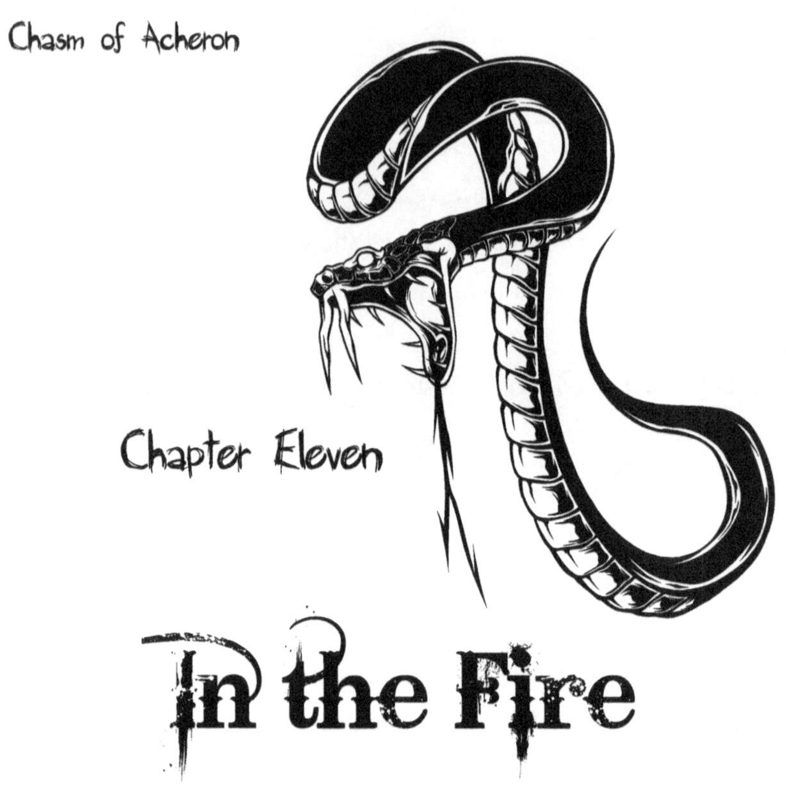

Chapter Eleven

In the Fire

More Shailmas fell to the ground. They fell so hard that they made massive craters where they hit. Each time a new crater was made, hundreds of those rat-sized critters would come scurrying up from below and scatter across the ground. Some that fell were Shamars, but there were many more of the Nakahs that plummeted to the ground.

It seemed like the firmament was beginning to take on a different form now since there were far less Nakah Warriors than at the beginning of this horrible war. Even the stars that had been hiding behind the curtains of the atmosphere were beginning to shine just a little brighter and poke out between rips and tears in the sky—almost as if they wanted to see what was going on.

The fact that the Shamar Shailmas had begun spewing swords of light from their mouths made a noticeable difference. The Nakahs had backed off so much now that the Shamars were taking over much of the firmament. In fact, the Nakah Warriors had been pushed right back to the very edges of Trilleah again, which was the same place from where they had started.

The king was roaring with vengeful anger. He was outraged and had begun screaming things at his army. It seemed that King Shrailzhar thought the army should take the brunt of his wrath for the Nakahs' great failings. They had not lost the War but it wasn't looking good at the moment. Unless the Nakahs started killing way more of those blasted Shamar Shailmas, the king would have to come up with a new plan.

Of course, King Shrailzhar had expected to lose many of his Nakah Warriors in such a battle, but the amount he saw falling to the ground was far more than he had even considered. He hollered and screamed at the general of his army, causing both the army and the land to cower.

"But King Shrailzhar," the army general dared to speak. He immediately fell to his knees, bowing low before speaking any more words to the great Shrailzhar. "The battle is out of our hands. We can do nothing to help in this War of the Firmament; only the Nakah Warriors can fight the Shamars."

"SILENCE, IMBECILE," the king roared.

He was so loud that a great crack echoed across the entire land and a fracture was made in the ground. It started from right where the king sat upon his beast and opened the ground clear to the other side of Trilleah, which was a very great distance indeed.

That fracture went straight through where Malleana Forest used to stand and continued all the way to the sea. It split the sea in two as well, causing much of the bloodied water to drain into a hole made by the fracture. As the water slipped away, bits of Leviathan could be seen poking out of the now shallow water. It was clear that he was dead.

The gaping fracture barely missed the Chasm of Acheron, staying just to the west of it, but ended up crossing it on the back side. This, of course, caused the entire chasm to spread greatly and now, instead of the chasm being only a few feet across, it was terribly wide.

The Travelers watched in silent horror as many of the mangled trees that had been piled high on the other side of the chasm toppled down and landed in Acheron ... what a horror! What a travesty!

Just before the ground split itself open, they had been discussing how to get over the chasm—if such a thing became necessary—and had come up with a bit of a plan. Although it was not a great plan, it may have worked; but not anymore. The Travelers' feeble plan would never work now—not with a chasm of such great size. They hoped as the fracture in the land got bigger and bigger, that the gurgling flames in the chasm would fall into it and become less and less. The Travelers continued to holler and wail and became distraught as the exact opposite of that began to happen.

With each shake of the ground and with each Shailma that was hurled to the ground causing trembling, more of the gnarly, leafless trees tumbled into the chasm and were instantly incinerated by the great heat.

As the fracture grew wider on the ground and caused the chasm to expand its borders, the fires threw their flames even higher. Every time another Waiting One would tumble in, the flames would explode and inhale the soul. It seemed that instead of the fires falling below the ground as they'd hoped, the bubbling lavas from below the ground were being pulled up and thrown higher into the air.

The boiling fires that had been only a narrow creek surrounding the souls of the Waiting Ones had now become a raging river. It didn't appear as though it would be stopping anytime soon.

As the Travelers watched, their horror expanded and exploded as quickly as the flames. Either their imaginations were getting completely out of control or their eyes were seeing sights that eyes should ever see. In the wildest of all imaginations, such things should never ever be considered.

"LOOK ... THERE," screamed Jennifer as she pointed to the thick fires that were now laughing and leaping high into the air—at least seven feet. She knew it was not her imagination when Judah yelled back.

"AND THERE!" he hollered.

Jennifer's stomach ached and she turned around, throwing up whatever leftovers were still in it, which weren't many at all. Her body began sweating terribly and her hands shook uncontrollably.

The others did the same as one by one, and sometimes more than that, the Travelers screamed and wailed and shouted as faces of their loved ones began to appear in the flames. Over and over again, as the fires would leap into the air, faces could be seen in the bright oranges and blazing reds mingling in the flames.

The faces were nightmarish and sickening. It looked as though they were suffering terribly, but seeing the Travelers standing so close somehow made it worse—if such a thing were possible. Then, when the twins and Pierce and Kaija Mae and the others were sure that things could get no worse, things got worse … much worse.

The faces that kept rising out of the flames began screaming out to the Travelers. Now, if there had been any doubt in the Travelers' minds about what they were seeing, it was quickly erased. It became unmistakably obvious that the faces in the flames could see the Travelers as they began calling out to them by name.

"JENNIFER … JUDAH," screamed the face of the twins' mamma. "HELP US!" she wailed. The twins fell to the ground in despairing anguish, burying their faces in the dirt and begging for the ground to swallow them up.

"PIERCE," came the voice of Peter.

"SAMUEL," shrieked the tiny voice of baby Justice.

On and on and on it went. It was unthinkable. Oh, such an unthinkable, unimaginable thing.

"SIMEON!" Jennifer wailed. "I CANNOT DO THIS! PLEASE … PLEASE TAKE ME HOME … THIS IS TOO BIG FOR ME … IT'S TOO MUCH!" The others followed her lead, not caring who heard them crying out to their Shailmas. Within seconds, every Traveler was on their bellies with their faces in the dirt, trying to hide their eyes and plug their ears. They did not want to see anything more or hear anything else. They couldn't bear it; it was too much. They couldn't take any more of this hell that was before them … not one more second.

Simeon did not whisk Jennifer up even though he heard her desperate pleas. Neither did Shemaiah come for Judah. None of the Shailmas snatched up their riders … not even one.

Instead, Kaija Mae began singing at the top of her lungs—screaming almost. She, Aviel, and Tahlia were more horrified than all the other Travelers because they recognized so many of the faces in the fire. It was their entire villages who'd had their souls stolen and so when the twins saw the face of their sweet mama or Sam heard the cries of little Justice, Kaija Mae, Aviel, and Tahlia saw the faces—heard the unbearable cries—of their mammas and daddies. They saw brothers and sisters and aunts and uncles and granddaddies and grand-mammas. Furthermore, there were neighbors and classmates. Everyone they'd known so many years ago was now begging to be released. It was altogether unbearable, and Kaija Mae sang louder than she'd ever sung before.

Shekinah put his words in Kaija Mae's mouth and poured strength into her lungs, so she sang. On and on and on she stood and sang. Even as the tears streamed down her face, that valiant, strong old woman caught in a young lady's body, kept right on singing.

The others looked at her like she had gone mad—as though she'd completely lost her mind. Who could blame her? Who could blame any of the Travelers if they'd lost their minds? All of this was certainly too much for any mind to consider and still function, after all.

But then, as the words left her mouth and danced around in the air cocooning the other Travelers in the power they carried, they too gained some sort of unexplainable and unexpected strength. One by one they stood up and somehow looked straight into the fires and caught the eyes of those calling out to them.

All fear and brokenness that had taken hold of those Travelers were suddenly transformed into strength and determination. They didn't know how it happened—there was no explanation for it. It was completely beyond their understanding, but of course, it was the words that Kaija Mae sang that had done such a thing.

The reason they didn't understand the words—they never had, after all—was because the songs that Kaija Mae had been singing all this time were songs from the One of all Light … the very One known by every Shailma as the "Nameless One."

She did not know it, of course, but it was Shekinah who carried the words from the Nameless One to Kaija Mae, and it was Shekinah who had put those words in her mouth this entire time—from the very beginning. It was her Shailma who wooed her to open her mouth and let the words of the Nameless One roll out into the atmosphere and bring strength to the weary and peace to the broken.

Of course, darkness cannot stay where light is present, and this was the purpose of the unknown words. Those words were light. The Trows could not get to Jennifer's soul when the others had carried her limp body through Malleana Forest because the words of light were coming from Kaija Mae's songs. The Trows hid from the light. They wouldn't survive if the light found them and so they cowered in the shadows when Kaija Mae sang.

That was why wounds would get healed and why now, fear was leaving the Travelers' souls. Fear is darkness and darkness cannot stay where light is brought in. That was exactly what Kaija Mae's songs were. They were light … they were power … they were a weapon of war.

The Travelers began screaming back to the faces in the flames—with outrageous courage, power, and loud voices. They screamed so loud, in fact, that King Shrailzhar heard them. The fierce winds picked up their words and carried them straight back to the king's ears, as though the land itself wanted to make sure that its king was aware of all that was happening.

He was aware, and if he was angry before, then there were no words to describe the rage that stirred in him now. He turned his beast around and screamed to the general of his armies who was still down on his knees.

"GET UP AND GET THOSE CURSE BREAKERS!"

King Shrailzhar knew that if the Travelers learned about the power of light, or if they stumbled upon the Nameless One, he and his Dark Land were finished. Trilleah would have no more power to stand; his kingdom would be no more. His Nakahs would fall to the ground … dead … or be thrown into the Sea of Acheron, chained by the Nameless One Himself.

Shrailzhar could tell from the words the Curse Breakers were screaming now that they had indeed caught at least a little bit of the truth of light and so he hurried. He needed to hurry. King Shrailzhar jammed his razor-sharp speared boots into his beast and screeched at the very top of his lungs.

"HiYah," he wailed. "HiYah!"

The general jumped up and gave a sharp command to the army to move. They moved. Not quickly, for they had no beasts or creatures to carry them, but they moved, nevertheless. As one unit, in complete unison, they raised their swords, marched steadily onward, and chanted, "The Curse Breakers must die."

With every step, they chanted louder and with every chant they got more and more thirsty for the blood of those who were threatening the land of their great King Shrailzhar. They were thoroughly aware that if the king lost his land, he'd have no need for an army and they'd be finished. They would join the others whom the king no longer had any use for and whether they lost their heads or not, they would all be thrown into the Sea of Acheron.

The army marched faster and chanted louder. "The Curse Breakers must die … The Curse Breakers must die … The Curse Breakers must die."

The king was far ahead of them now, even though he was dodging the massive chunks of hail that continue to be hurled down from the broken bits of the sky. It had stretched itself thin—too thin—and had nothing left with which to repair itself. This, of course, only made King Shrailzhar angrier, causing him to kick his beast harder and move faster.

Kaija Mae was still singing, even though the faces that leaped out of the fire and begged the Travelers to free them were getting more and more hideously appalling. They knew that King Shrailzhar was coming. Those souls of the Waiting Ones heard it in the air, and they knew that if he got there before the Travelers could figure out how to break the curse, it would be too late for all of them.

Those who were already in the flames wanting to have their souls freed to Heaven were quite aware that if the Army of Shrailzhar got ahold of the Travelers, their souls would be added to the great Chasm of Acheron, leaving no one to bring freedom.

Worse than all of these things that the souls of the Waiting Ones understood, was one thing that the Travelers had not yet seen—

that one thing that would be too much for them to bear—that eternal Sea of Acheron.

The truth that the Travelers did not yet know was that the Chasm surrounding Acheron was only a tiny river that flowed from a much, much larger place. Directly beneath the ground, covering much of the underbelly of Trilleah, gurgled a sea so large that the human eye couldn't possibly take it all in with one look. It was from that Sea of Acheron that the river flowed, and it would be that sea that every cursed soul would sink into if the Travelers failed to break the curse in time.

The Travelers had no idea of the existence of such a sea. The souls of the Waiting Ones wanted to keep it that way. If it cost them their freedom—if they had to remain in that Sea of Acheron for all of eternity to keep the Travelers from joining them—then that was what they would do.

Unfortunately, the choice was not theirs to make.

With the giant unseen hand of time ticking down … with Trilleah working to destroy itself … with the War of the Firmament carrying on and on … and with the Army of Shrailzhar coming quickly … a battle would soon rise between the king and the Curse Breakers like no war had ever risen before.

The fate of the Waiting Ones, so it seemed, would be determined by that very battle.

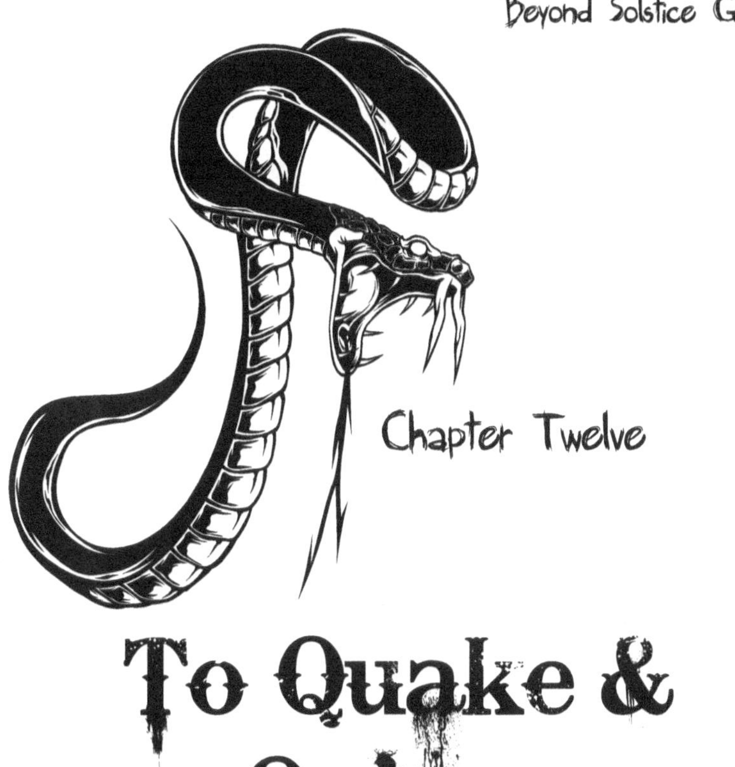

Chapter Twelve

To Quake & Quiver

A deafening explosion erupted in the sky far above the Travelers, but they heard it nonetheless. It was so loud that the entire land quaked hard, driving every Traveler back to their knees. Even a large group of the armies tumbled to the ground. Some of the black critters were shaken back into the craters in the ground and disappeared, and the chasm split even wider apart.

Chunks of rock started tumbling down from the hills in the distance; the land was speeding up its self-destruction. Countless numbers of Waiting Ones rolled and tumbled into the Chasm of Acheron from every direction.

There were still so many of those rat-sized critters with the scorpion tails scurrying along the ground that it was nearly covered by this time. It looked like the ground itself had turned black and was moving, but in fact, it was the great number of critters that made it appear that way. Nevertheless, it was eery and terribly horrifying.

There was no room left on the ground for any more of the critters, but that didn't; they kept crawling up from the craters and cracks being made in the dirt below. Some of the bigger ones took flight and with their wings flapping curiously loud, the Travelers didn't know what to do. If they stood up, it would be difficult to stay that way since the land was quaking furiously and continually. If they stayed on the ground, those critters would crawl right over them and bury them completely; there was no good choice.

Then again, the air was becoming filled with the critters as more and more of them left the ground and began hovering. The only good part about them being in the air—as far as the Travelers could tell—was that their tails didn't rattle as long as their wings were moving. Only those critters that remained on the ground had the rattles in their scorpion-tails furiously buzzing.

Pierce chose to stand—or at least tried to. He wobbled this way and that but finally moved back a few feet to where a couple of large boulders had rolled. He found some balance there, in between them.

"What was that explosion?" he shouted.

Even though the noise going on all around them was tremendous, the Travelers were still able to hear one another. They didn't know it, but the Shailmas were carrying the words from one's lips to the others' ears because their communication was vital for both what was happening now, and what would be happening soon.

Some of the Travelers remained on the ground, but others crawled over to where Pierce was bracing himself. Those ones leaned or stood or sat against the boulders. If either of those boulders began rolling again, they'd all have to jump out of the way, but for now, it seemed the most steady and sheltered place to be.

"I have no idea what that was," Judah replied to Pierce since it seemed nobody else had any answers to give. Whether they remained on the ground or plunked against the boulders, they all cranked their heads toward the sky to try and see what was going on. A little of the smoke and sulfur had cleared and the Travelers could see some—but not much—of the war which continued to rage in the firmament.

They noticed that the Nakah Warriors were spitting fire—perhaps they had been the whole time. With so much happening in the war—in the firmament and on the ground and under the ground—it was hard to tell just what was going on at any time in any location.

It didn't seem to matter, though, at least not for the Shamar Shailmas or their riders. With the swords of light coming from the Shamars, the Nakahs couldn't get close enough to them for their fire-filled spits to reach them. Those spores of fire would instead drop all the way to the ground and most times they were extinguished long before they landed. The ones that did keep a bit of a flame only managed to scatter the black critters and smolder in the dirt.

As the Travelers were scanning the air trying to see what had exploded, a second explosion came … and then a third … and on and on it went. The brightness hurt their eyes and the Travelers were forced to turn away. Still, nobody knew what had caused any of the explosions. They had no idea that the stars—which had hidden away years ago because they couldn't bear to watch what the king was up to—were beginning to explode. The stars were becoming so vexed that they were erupting one by one, causing the entire Dark Land to quake and quiver.

It seemed that everything was self-destructing and the Travelers were trapped … right in the center of it all.

"We have to get out of here," Sam hollered. Fear was getting a good grip on him, despite all he'd seen—even with the healing of his arm—and he shouted louder. "TRILLEAH IS IMPLODING. WE HAVE TO GET OUT!" There was no calming him down. The more they tried, the more upset he got.

Most likely, seeing the face of little Justice and hearing her beg Sam for help was more than he could bear. The poor boy was young, of course, even though it was a fact easily forgotten due to his tallness. Nonetheless, he'd been through much on this very long journey, and it was taking a toll on the poor boy. He had nothing left to give. He was altogether undone; entirely spent.

The others didn't know it, but he was begging his Shailma to take him out of Trilleah. His Shailma would not, of course, for each of these remaining Travelers was needed if the curse was to be broken. Each one of them, however, was having a great amount of doubt now about ever breaking the curse. They all wanted their Shailmas to take them out of Trilleah, but they'd seen the faces of their loved ones—they'd heard their screams. The Travelers couldn't possibly leave without doing all they could to break the curse—no matter what it cost.

They had been so sure that all they needed to do was gather those dozen tablets, which they had done. Hundreds of times they talked about it, both in Trilleah and back home.

"One more tablet," somebody would say.

"Then the curse will be broken," another would reply. On and on the conversations would dance and twirl until the excitement would rise as they mistakenly thought nothing more would be required of them. But something more *was* required; much more. Against all they hoped for or ever wanted, the Travelers were about to find out what that was.

King Shrailzhar continued toward where he knew the Curse Breakers were waiting. They had no idea they were waiting, though.

They assumed they had randomly stumbled upon this Chasm of Acheron all on their own.

The Travelers had no idea this very place was the final destination for the trap the king had set for them. It was the last trap he'd set because the king was convinced that it would be so enticing to the Travelers that they would never escape it. King Shrailzhar was confident this would be the trap that would slam its jaws shut, forcing the very life from those miserable Curse Breakers—dragging their souls away—to the bottom of the Sea of Acheron.

His plan, which he was working on executing right this moment, was to distract the Travelers entirely so that he could skulk through on his beast so quietly and so quickly that he'd be unnoticed until it was too late. On his way through, he'd scoop up Jennifer with one hand and grab Judah with the other. The army would come behind him and make sure every one of the remaining Curse Breakers was tossed into the Chasm of Acheron where their souls would join those already ensnared.

Shrailzhar's perfectly drawn-out plan would end with him taking the twins to a prison he'd made himself because, of course, he was the "only one competent enough to make it," he had told his army.

Those wretched twins would have their hands bound and their feet shackled until the day they died. King Shrailzhar had stored up hundreds of creatures from the Dark Land—such as cradle bugs and vexaturs—to release into the prison of the twins to torment them until their deaths. When that moment finally came, the Trows—who would be waiting impatiently—would happily take the twins' souls and the king would finally celebrate his long-awaited victory. Oh, he was a beastly king indeed.

There was another explosion as another star erupted into the atmosphere and another horridly fearful conversation among the Travelers ensued.

"Judah," Jennifer whispered to her brother as they both focused on holding onto the boulders … and to each other, "I want to go home," she cried.

"I know, Jelly Bean, me too. But we can't go … not yet. We're not finished here."

Bella overheard her niece and nephew and joined their conversation. She was terrified but mustered up all her strength to sound courageous—for the twins' sake.

"Soon," she said. Bella even tried to force a smile to cross her face, but it refused. How she sounded so confident in such a horrible situation neither of the twins could figure out. The truth was that she was not confident—not at all. She was weak and small and broken at all that was happening. Her blood was running cold and her heart was beating twice as fast as it should have been.

However, she felt it was her fault that both her niece and nephew were here in the Dark Land on such a dark day. Bella had promised their mamma that she'd look after the twins and make sure they were safe. But now … now she was despairingly afraid she would fail on her promise.

Bella put on her bravest face and was in constant communication with her Shailma. *Shura, I don't know what to do. I don't know how we can possibly break this curse*, she told him. *We can barely stand ... how are we going to break the curse and get out of Trilleah before it destroys itself? How Shura? How?*

Having Matt stand so near and hold her hand tightly to keep her from tumbling over was helping a little, but then again, not really. Pierce had noticed and surprising to himself, didn't mind. He knew he hadn't been the person Bella would want, and even though he was changed now, he couldn't blame her for wanting to be near Matt.

Kaija Mae wanted to help but didn't know how. She'd seen many things, such as the stars before they'd hidden away behind the veil of the firmament, that none of the others had seen. She, Aviel, and the others who'd been here since the beginning, knew many things they wished they didn't know. She whispered to Tahlia.

"We need to move away from here before all that is beneath the ground comes to the surface here—at the River of Acheron." Tahlia agreed but didn't know how to get anyone to move away from this place of final destruction. Certainly, it wasn't going to be easy to pull the others away from the faces of their loved ones, even though it was so painfully deplorable to witness.

"Pierce, can you tell us more about what happened with the eagle and the Nameless One?" Kaija Mae was hoping to distract the others and then in the middle of his story she'd suggest they go to the backside of the chasm. Hopefully, the question would take everyone off guard because it wouldn't be what anybody was thinking about.

"Sure," Pierce said, satisfied to get his attention off of what was going on around them and happy to be the center of attention rather than Matt. It wasn't that he disliked Matt. Neither was he upset or angry or jealous that Matt had Bella's attention—and her hand. It was more that he was disappointed in himself that he'd acted so poorly his entire time in Trilleah and that he had pushed Bella—and the others—away. He knew he had to apologize for his behavior, but he wasn't quite ready for that yet. It would come.

Pierce took a deep breath and began to share what he could put into words about the Nameless One. Much of it was hard, though, because he didn't know the right words to describe what he had seen … and heard … and felt. He'd thought about it a lot and was certain there were no words to describe such a being.

"I couldn't stand before the Nameless One. He was huge and blinding to my eyes when I tried to look at Him. I say Him, although, it was not a person; then again, it was. I don't know what it was," he said. Pierce sounded delightfully confused and unsure of what to say and was rambling on, making little sense to the others.

"There was no voice really, coming from the Nameless One. But I knew things, in my belly. I somehow and suddenly knew many things. It was like He was implanting thoughts into my belly, bypassing my ears." Pierce wrinkled up his face, aware that his words were senseless and confusing. Nevertheless, he continued.

"I wanted to cover myself. I was so embarrassed by all of the terrible things I'd done in my life that I wanted to hide from Him. I didn't want Him to see me—or to look at me. It felt like He could see right into my soul and there was a lot of no good things in there.

"I'm not talking about the things that everyone else knew either, but the things that nobody knew," Pierce said. The boulders he was holding onto rolled a little now, and they had to step out of the way. After a few seconds, the boulders got caught up on a crevice in the ground and were still again. The Travelers grabbed hold and hung on.

"I mean, those things you think in silence … like how you'd like to kill the teacher when he embarrassed you in front of the class, or the lie you told your mom about why you missed school, or that you didn't have homework when you actually did.

"It was the strangest, most painful thing ever, but the most peaceful at the same time," Pierce continued. He wanted to make all his words come out right—to force them to make sense—but he knew there was no way to do such a thing. At the same time, the others were all thinking about the bad things they had thought of or lies they had told, and wondered if there really was such a being as the Nameless One who knew all such things.

I hope not, was the thought that every one of the Travelers had dancing in their minds. They each had things they wanted to keep hidden … after all, everyone does.

Pierce knew there was such a being because he had stood before Him, weighed down with terribly heavy guilt and shame.

"The guilt and regret and shame were so heavy on me—like weights that I couldn't carry—and at that moment, I would have done anything to get rid of it all. Right then, as I wanted to fade into thin air just so this One couldn't look upon me any longer, the Nameless One spoke and I heard those words with my ears.

" 'Stand,' that One said. Even though it was so loud, the voice was calming. I could feel compassion wash over me like I was standing under a waterfall … literally." Pierce looked around and saw that the expressions of the others were confusion, mixed with disbelief. He could tell they didn't believe him, but then again, it was hard to argue with the healed up holes in his shoulders, so nobody did. They just kept listening.

They listened so closely to Pierce that they failed to hear what was going on around them. Instead of listening so closely to the stories of this one whom they were having such a hard time believing, those Travelers should have been running with all their strength because the longer they stood still, listening to Pierce, the closer King Shrailzhar and his army came.

It would be no time at all before he was upon them, and then no amount of running would save them.

Chapter Thirteen

Fedora

Finally, when most of the Travelers were focused on Pierce's story, Kaija Mae spoke quietly. She had been waiting for just the right moment; now seemed as good a time as any other.

"Let's go around to the other side of the chasm." She began walking with Aviel and Tahlia close behind her. That was their plan, and now they could only hope the others would follow.

Kaija Mae knew the king had himself set this trap and undoubtedly he'd be coming soon for the twins. She knew she had to get the Travelers away from that spot and since there was nowhere safe for them to hide, she, Aviel, and Tahlia decided that behind the gigantic mountain of broken and gnarled trees would be the safest place for them. Besides that small piece of information, nobody—including those who had been here for so many years—knew what lay on the other side of the chasm. Unfortunately, no one paid any attention to the three of them, so Aviel spoke up a little louder.

"Guys," he said. "Let's head around the other side. Let's keep moving."

"The other side?" Jennifer snapped. "The other side of what?"

"Back around Acheron," Kaija Mae spouted. She wasn't sure why that wasn't obvious since there was nothing else that had a "back around" side. Nonetheless, maybe the Travelers were too intrigued by Pierce's story or perhaps all the shaking had rattled their brains a little too much.

"Why?" Bella asked.

"The ground seems far too unstable to be wandering around," Pierce added. That was true; the ground was unstable. But standing here in the open with the king approaching was too dangerous … and downright ludicrous. If they had to choose between unstable and deadly, it seemed obvious which would be the best choice.

Kaija Mae had not wanted to tell them that this was a trap. She didn't think causing more fear was a great idea, but now it seemed they were leaving her no choice. If they wouldn't follow her because she asked them to, then she'd have to tell them the reason why they had to get to the back side of the chasm.

Shekinah, what do I do? Kaija Mae asked her Shailma.

Tell them the truth, came the unwanted reply.

"Ugh," she sighed loudly and rolled her eyes at Tahlia. She and Aviel continued to look at Kaija Mae for direction. "I didn't want to tell you this, but you're all being very stubborn and far too distracted for me not to," she began. In an instant, she had their full attention.

"Tell us what?" Matt asked.

"What are you talking about, Kaija Mae?" Judah questioned.

They each seemed equally perturbed, and she wished she didn't have so much information. Then again, if she didn't know what she was about to tell the others, they'd all be in a very dangerous predicament.

"Well," she began with her fingers crossed and her heart racing … and then she stopped. She didn't know which to tell them first; that this was a trap or that Shrailzhar would be coming soon to capture them. Kaija Mae looked to Judah and tried to read his face to see which information would be less shocking, but she saw nothing helpful there.

"Kaija Mae," he urged her. "Tell us what's going on!"

"King Shrailzhar knows we're here," she finally blurted out. She'd decided there was no good way to say any of it and so blurting it all out as quickly as she could was her best option—and she took it.

"He set up this trap to snare us and we've been here far too long now." She pursed her lips together tightly and waited for the outraged replies that were sure to come quickly.

No replies came. Not a word was uttered … or whispered … or screamed. For a few minutes, everyone was silent even though there was no silence anywhere else in the entire land of Trilleah. Then, a very panicked Jennifer spoke up.

"What do you mean, it's a trap?" she whispered as though talking in whispers would somehow keep them safe. "How?"

"The king was so angry that Leviathan gave up the last tablet to the sea and then, of course, the sea spit it out to you, Jennifer," Kaija Mae began. "I've been in Trilleah just about since the beginning, and I've never seen the king so outraged.

"I don't know for sure, but I think Leviathan was given that tablet to keep from us. When he gave it up, the king was so angry that he slaughtered the beast. I heard him say that none of the traps the Nakah Warriors or his army set up had worked, and he would have to set the last trap himself.

"We overheard him tell his army that since we had all the tablets, the only thing left that would entice us to go where he wanted was if he used the prisons of the Waiting Ones—the trees from Malleana Forest. He commanded the land to let go of their roots and instructed the winds to pick them up and carry them to a place he called, "Inside the arms of Acheron.""

Kaija Mae stopped to see how angry the others were getting, but instead of them asking her a thousand harsh questions as she'd expected, Jennifer urged her, "Go on, Kaija Mae." So she did.

"I heard him tell his army that the Waiting Ones would be the only bait we'd find attractive and, well, it seems he was right because we've been here a long time now, and still nobody is willing to leave this spot.

"But really, we must go," she begged. "Please, let's hurry to the backside of Acheron."

They did; they hurried as fast as one might expect anyone to hurry when the earth is shifting and shaking, and black critters the size of rats are scurrying around the ground and flying about in the air, and the ground is spotted with craters, and fireballs are being hurled from the sky, and stars are exploding in continual succession. None of these things allowed for "as fast as possible" to be all that fast at all.

It felt as if the Travelers' legs were made of jelly and they wobbled to and fro. They made sure to stay as close to the gurgling fires as possible while staying far enough away to be safe; not that *safe* was possible.

The faces that had appeared earlier in the flames, and were screaming for help, had calmed down, but they'd left their marks on the Travelers' minds. If their faces never appeared again, the Travelers would not notice because the tormenting sights and sounds played over and over in their minds … constantly … as if it was still happening.

The Travelers held on tightly to one another so that when one would stumble, the others could hold them up. Kaija Mae was in the front and she begged Shekinah to give her keen eyes to see all things that were hidden. She wanted to make sure to lead everyone to safety, not into a pit. Her Shailma heard her well, and he opened her eyes to see clearly into all things that were trying to stay hidden in the atmosphere.

Right in front of them was a tall, dark shadow. That shadow was wearing a trench coat and an odd looking hat—a fedora. It wasn't causing Kaija Mae fear but rather seemed to be trying to detour her around where she needed to go. He looked like a traffic cop with one arm out to stop them and the other waving them around to the left.

Kaija Mae slowed a little. She knew she was the only one who could see him and didn't want to concern the others. She turned her head slightly to the left and saw there was a very thin layer of ground ready to give way the moment the Travelers put their weight on it. Kaija Mae could see right through the ground and noticed that beneath that weak spot was the same gurgling liquid fire that was raging in the chasm to their right.

She drew her breath in a little, suddenly realizing that beneath them was a sea and that what they'd seen of Acheron was merely a small river that ran to the sea. The only thing between that Sea of Acheron and their feet was a very thin crust of ground.

Shemaiah, she cried silently. *Where do I go?*

Follow me; keep your eyes on me. Don't put your eyes on Fedora, but recognize he is there so you can avoid him but keep your eyes on me, Shemaiah said. *Do not set your eyes on things above you or things below you or things around you. Keep your eyes on me, Kaija Mae, and follow me. You'll find safety in that.*

She tried. Oh, how the girl tried to keep her eyes on Shemaiah, but she was having much difficulty with it. The further she led the Travelers, the more of these dark, shadowy fedora-wearing beings became visible to her. Finally, when her insides were trembling far more than the ground beneath her feet, she called the only other one whom she knew could help.

"JENNIFER," she shouted. "COME UP HERE WITH ME … PLEASE!"

Jennifer didn't need to be asked twice, nor did she need to ask why. Jennifer had seen all that Kaija Mae had seen and even far more because Jennifer always saw such things. Since that morning in her room when she'd had dreams of the dark shadows and woke up to find them hovering above her door, Jennifer had seen all such things. This was no different and now she scooted up to where Kaija Mae stood still, too afraid to go on.

"Do you see the dark shadows?" Jennifer whispered to Kaija Mae, cautious to keep her words away from the others.

"Yes, and the thin ground and the fire beneath it …" Kaija Mae replied with a shaky voice. She was listing all those things she was seeing, quite aware that none of the others were seeing any of it, but confident that Jennifer saw it all. "You see them too, right?" she asked.

"I do," was all Jennifer said. She remained calm despite all the havoc going on in the atmosphere. It was not these things that caused Jennifer to be anxious or worried; it was the things that were going on in the land—those things that everyone could see.

Simeon had taught Jennifer so well to trust him to look after all the unseen things—whether she could see them or not—that it had become easy for her to keep her eyes on Simeon. But as the lot of them stumbled and tripped and were shaken to their knees only to be pulled up by the others, her fears of all such seen things grew large.

If the ground gave way, they'd crash through to the Sea of Acheron. If a fireball crashed anywhere near them, it would puncture the ground and fire from below would crawl up and lash out at them. There were so many things that could take their breath away that could be seen, that it left little room to be fearful of what could not be seen.

Jennifer grabbed Kaija Mae's hand and they kept right on going. Kaija Mae was astonished when Jennifer easily bolted straight through that shadowy being in the fedora and overcoat.

"You did see him, right?" she asked.

"Of course!" Jennifer whispered. "Just ignore them, like they're not even there. If you don't let them cause you fear, their power is diminished greatly. I'm convinced that fear is the only weapon they have. If we don't let them intimidate us, we can disarm them entirely."

Kaija Mae laughed, not because she thought anything was particularly funny, but because she thought Jennifer must either be completely crazy or the bravest person alive.

Neither was true, of course. It was just that Jennifer had learned to trust Simeon and keep her eyes on him, instead of on whatever may surround her and try to distract or get her eyes off of her Shailma.

The rest continued to follow, unaware of anything that either of the girls was seeing or talking about. Each was far too preoccupied with the River of Acheron and all that was going on in the firmament. They could see a little clearer from this side, or maybe a bit more of the sulfur had cleared. They really couldn't tell which it was; it didn't matter either way.

A few more stars continued to explode, but only a few so far.

From what the Travelers could see, the Shamars were outnumbering the Nakahs by quite a few now. The Nakahs were continuing to fight; here and there a large number of them would come together and attack a small number of Shamars. Most of the Nakahs would have to sacrifice themselves in order to allow two or three of the others to get through and take the heads off the Shamars.

It was a terrible war to watch so the Travelers tried very hard to keep their eyes on the ground rather than in the firmament. There was nothing good to see there. Nothing at all.

CRAAAACKKKK went the ground again, causing another space to split into a wide gap. Jennifer and Kaija Mae were on one side of the fractured ground when they heard the crack, while the others were on the opposite side. The girls looked down and jumped to the right just before the ground split itself wide open. Jennifer screamed when she saw that Kaija Mae didn't jump quite far enough and one foot landed on the side of the gap.

She kicked up some dirt and Jennifer managed to grab her and pull her away from it just before the fire bubbled up. The color drained from Kaija Mae's face and she turned as white as a ghost.

"You're okay," Jennifer whispered. "You're okay, keep going."

She kept going, much faster than before. Kaija Mae, Aviel, and the others who'd been trapped in Trilleah for so long had been here a couple of times before, just before the king had set up and baited this trap. She knew they had to go faster.

As Kaija Mae was holding tightly to Jennifer's hand, Jennifer was holding tightly to hers. One knew how to maneuver the land, the other knew how to deal with the unseen powers of the atmosphere. They each needed the other.

"There it is," Kaija Mae screamed when a covering where they could hide came into view. The others looked at her with a hope that she knew something the rest of them did not.

Kaija Mae heard Shekinah whisper to her right at that moment.

This is the place where you will lay out the tablets and see them be knit together.

But how? We don't know what they say, Kaija Mae whined.

I will give you the keys as you need them, she heard Shekinah with deep assurance in his whisperings. *Trust me.*

Chapter Fourteen

Repentance

So many of the stars were falling by now that the sky looked a bit like an overdone and burned out fireworks display. There were no beautiful colors or "oohs" and "aahs;" just screams and cries from the Travelers along with one deafening explosion after another after another.

The entire sky looked like one continual cloud of fire as the stars erupted and the hiding place of the sun moved out of the way. It was too bright to look at, forcing the Travelers to shield their eyes.

It was horribly difficult to make their way to the place on the far side of the chasm, and they had to slow down to a painstaking speed—sometimes to barely more than a crawl. If they could have looked up, if their eyes would not have been burned out by the brightness of it all, they'd have become aware that the Nakahs could no longer look, either. It seemed the excruciating brightness was too much even for them, and the Nakahs searched for cover but found none.

The brilliant light didn't seem to bother the Shamars in the least, though, and they carried right on pushing the Nakah Warriors back until there was nowhere else for them to go. If there was a dim spot anywhere, any places where the stars' explosions did not illuminate the space entirely, all the Shamars needed to do was open their mouths and let the swords of light burst forth.

Hundreds of Nakahs were dropping to the ground now, smashing through into whatever was just below. The Travelers couldn't see them because it was too bright to watch all the goings on, but they could hear them. The sounds the Nakahs and their riders were making as they plummeted to the land was hideous. They shrieked and wailed loudly until they were silenced by the impact of the ground.

It was altogether, completely and thoroughly, dreadful. It was by far and without a doubt, the most deplorable thing any of the Travelers had ever witnessed—and since coming to Trilleah, they'd witnessed many deplorable things. With every Nakah Warrior that broke through the ground, thousands more of the black rat-sized critters would climb out and scurry away. There seemed to be no end to the critters.

Kaija Mae and Jennifer tried to move faster. They were desperate to get into the shelter since so much of what had been held above them in the firmament was suddenly crashing all around them. There were not enough words to explain how terribly afraid they were and nobody shared their fears; after all, they each carried the same ones.

The Travelers wondered if all their work—all the time it had taken them to collect the dozen clay tablets—would end up as nothing more than a waste. If they couldn't find a safe place to lay them out and figure out how to break the curse, it would all have been for nothing.

"IN HERE!" Kaija Mae finally screamed as she disappeared into a tiny hole in the side of a hill. It was an odd hill just in the fact that it was still standing. It was not damaged or shaken at all but looked as though it was the safest place in all the dark and crumbling land.

"It looks like Trilleah forgot about this hill," Jennifer cried out to Kaija Mae. They were running now, or at least they were trying to run and still stay upright.

Both the inside and the outside of the hill looked untouched by everything that was going on around it. Kaija Mae yanked Jennifer inside, and everyone else quickly followed. They pushed and shoved and stepped over each other as they each hurried to get inside. All that was going on around them in the openness of the land—all the destruction—was far too dangerous for them to remain in the center of it any longer. Of course, they were still in the center of it, but they wrongly believed that because they could no longer see all the happenings, that they were no longer impacted by it.

That was simply not so.

It was only a few seconds between when the last of the Travelers ducked inside and Kaija Mae pointed to a pile of small rocks beside the opening.

"Quick," she screamed. "Pile those up in front of the hole."

"Hurry … Shrailzhar is coming!" Judah shrieked in terror.

Without thinking, everyone did exactly as they'd been told and in only a few moments, any light that was in the little cavern faded to darkness as the opening was closed off.

"Oh great," Judah commented.

"Not again," Sam whined.

Suddenly, the space was filled with light, and everyone looked to Kaija Mae, who was holding a lantern.

"Where did that come from?" Pierce asked her.

"It was one of the things I took from the guards' pockets," she said, seemingly quite pleased with herself. The others began pulling this and that out of their own pockets, nearly forgetting that they had any pockets at all. They'd forgotten that they had shoved them full of "necessary things."

"You had a lantern in your pocket?" Pierce asked. Seemed a bit strange to him … and to everyone else.

"It was an odd thing," she replied. "I didn't know what it was when I grabbed it. It opens up into a lantern," she explained. Obviously, Kaija Mae was quite pleased with herself about bringing such an item and about knowing what it was at the very moment it was needed. As they looked at it, a couple of others realized they had similar objects in their own pockets and began pulling out all the things they'd been carrying. In very short order there was a mound of items—some known and some unknown—on the cave floor.

"Some of these could have come in handy," Sam said, but the truth was that it was for this very moment in time that every one of these objects had been carried. It was their Shailmas who'd directed them to this item or that object, and now, they would learn the importance of each one.

As they were pulling things from their pockets, Jennifer's fingers fell on the little green jar and she sheepishly withdrew it. Judah noticed it; so did Pierce. Both boys stepped forward and held their hands toward it.

"Jennifer, you brought the jar?" Pierce said.

This struck Matt and Judah both as an odd question coming from Pierce. He was the only one who had not been in Jennifer's Chamber of Rest when Miriam had been caught with this very jar in her fingers. They remembered because they had noticed it odd that he was the only one missing from the room that night.

"How do you know about the jar?" Matt asked. The others waited for his answer.

Now, Pierce knew that since he had stood in front of the Nameless One of all Light, there would come a time when he would have to explain his behavior and ask for forgiveness from the others. He didn't plan on this being the time, however, but it seemed it had presented itself to him. He took a deep breath and began to share a bit more of his story.

He didn't know exactly where to begin since there was so much he'd done that the others knew nothing about. Pierce quickly asked his Shailma who directed him to, *blurt it out.*

He did. Pierce opened his mouth and let the words come tumbling out.

"I know about the jar because I was there when Miriam opened it," he said matter-of-factly as if he had nothing to hide which, after meeting with the One of all Light, was the truth. The others were surprised to hear him say he was there. All at once, and only in their innermost being, each Traveler questioned anything Pierce had said up until this moment. They were in Jennifer's Chamber—Pierce was not. If he was lying about such an unimportant thing, he was probably also lying about all the other not so "little things," he'd been telling them all along.

"No … you weren't," Judah said. "We wondered where you were, but you certainly were not there."

"Judah, I was there. Matt nearly saw me when the lid rolled over to the shadows and he moved to pick it up." The Travelers thought for a minute and remembered that the lid had, in fact, rolled into a dark corner.

"Were you hiding?" Sam asked. Suspicions started rising.

"I was," he said sadly. "This is one of those things I was telling you about earlier, those things that caused me to feel such a heavy weight of guilt when I stood in front of the Nameless One," Pierce admitted. "I knew that none of you had seen me or had any idea I was there. Miriam was the only one who knew of my presence in Jennifer's Chamber, and she wouldn't be telling anybody.

"But the Nameless One knew. I didn't tell Him, He just knew. He knows all things." Pierce said quietly but without shame.

"Okay," Bella said. "But *why* were you hiding?"

"And why were you there?" Jennifer asked. "Why were you and Miriam in my Sleeping Chamber at all? You had no business there!"

"We were looking for that green jar," he answered immediately, pointing to the jar that Jennifer still clutched in her hands.

They all noticed that Pierce had an attitude about him that he hadn't had before. He was not trying to come up with stupid excuses to justify his behavior, nor was he trying to blame Miriam or anyone else. That was something they hadn't noticed in him before, so they listened hard now.

"You see," he began, "Miriam had been here for long enough to know that there were secrets and keys that some had, like that little green jar. She knew that Jennifer's Sleeping Chamber was filled with such things as that and she wanted them for herself. What she didn't know—until that little green jar told her—was that those keys and secrets were only for you, Jennifer. They wouldn't be given to anyone else."

Now everyone looked at Jennifer who had put the little green jar back into her pocket. She didn't like everyone looking at her. It made her wonder if they thought she knew things that she'd kept secret. Of course, she had no secrets at all—at least, none she was willing to share with anyone else. Even when the cloud of smoke and fire had burst out of the green jar, she'd tried to tell Bella about it because she had no idea about such things.

"But why were you with her, Pierce?" Jennifer asked. She wanted all the eyes that were now staring at her, to look back to the one they were listening to. They did.

"Because I was jealous of you, Jennifer," he blurted out. "I was angry that I had been here for so many of the journeys, yet I had no secrets or keys or tools at all. I was angry that you just came in not knowing anything about the land. You didn't want to be here; you were tiny and timid and asked a million questions that I already knew the answers to."

Pierce went on and on about how he was jealous and angry at Jennifer and how unfair it was that he'd sacrificed and been to

Trilleah so many more times than her, but for some reason, it was her who was given such privileges. He wanted them, but not enough to steal them.

"However," he concluded, "if Miriam wanted to steal them I would help her just so you couldn't have them."

As he told of his jealousies and what he'd done, there was no anger or jealousy in his voice now. All that remained was truth and repentance.

"I'm sorry, Pierce," Jennifer whined. "I didn't ask for any of this!" she stated, growing a bit teary. "I didn't want to come—I didn't even know Trilleah existed until I found myself alone and crying in the dirt of Malleana Forest." Now she was a bit more teary and had to wipe her eyes and sniffle a bunch as well.

"I know," Pierce said. He moved closer to her and put his arm around her, giving her shoulders a hard squeeze. "It had nothing to do with you; it was my own jealousies. They were stupid, and I got so carried away with wanting to be the leader and be the most important one here that I lost sight of why any of us were here in the first place."

He took her dirty face in his clean hands and looked the small, crying girl straight in her eyes. "Jennifer, I am so sorry. Please, please forgive me. I acted like a fool and could have jeopardized the freedom of all those souls just because I was a selfish idiot."

"Okay," was all Jennifer said.

What was she supposed to say? To find out that someone had been so angry with you for so long—and you had no idea about any of it—was hard to swallow. She knew that she'd not been comfortable around Pierce from her very first trip to Trilleah and now she knew why. Jennifer had always figured it was because Pierce was a miserable louse, but now that she knew the truth it made a wisp of sense, she supposed.

Jennifer also knew, without any doubt, that he had changed—completely changed. Jennifer liked this new version of Pierce and told him so.

"Pierce," she began, "I don't know what happened to you, and I don't know what keys or favors Trilleah has given me. I don't consider this green jar anything good at all and I'm not even sure why I have it with me now. I just grabbed it and jammed it in my pocket. Believe me when I say that whatever things you consider favors are certainly not. In fact, I'd switch roles with you in a second, if such a thing were allowed.

"But this I do know," she continued. "I know that you have changed." She heard the others agreeing with her and she continued. "Whatever you've done in the past is in the past and forgotten about. Whatever happened to you with that Nameless One, I don't know … but I know it's changed you.

"You are forgiven," she mumbled—a little embarrassed by everyone looking at her.

Every other Traveler *mhm'd* and agreed and nodded and moved toward Pierce. He stepped back and continued his story.

"Thank you, Jennifer. Thank you, everyone. But there's more you need to know—more about the Nameless One that I must tell you," he said.

There was no time right now, though. The Travelers heard a familiar sound on the other side of the pile of rocks they'd moved in order to close off the opening.

It was Shrailzhar, and he was angry. Again, his trap didn't seem to be working and he was outraged to find the Travelers were not here, in the one place where he expected to find them.

"FIND THOSE CURSE BREAKERS!" he was screaming at his army. He was shrieking and hollering and the Travelers knew he was outraged. They shuddered in their skin, afraid to breathe or open their eyes or have even a thought.

"Turn off the lantern," Pierce whispered. Kaija Mae turned it off. There were a couple of small holes where the rocks had left gaps, and both Pierce and Bella closed one eye and peeked through the holes with the other eye. What they saw made Bella shiver uncontrollably. Pierce put his arm gently around Bella to give her some of his courage. Both wished they hadn't peeked out.

Explosions were everywhere now, but somehow they were not feeling them in this shelter. In fact, the ground wasn't shaking inside the shelter—not even slightly. There was no way to tell if the shaking in the entire land had stopped, or if somehow in this shelter, whatever was happening on the outside couldn't get in.

It didn't matter, though. Pierce and Bella continued to watch as the king got off of his beast and stood on the other side of where the Travelers were hiding. Bella thought that if she stuck her finger through the hole, she could touch him. She sure wasn't going to try, though. Oh, the terror that gripped Bella was overwhelming. No breath would come to her and she began to feel woozy. Nevertheless, she kept right on peering through the small gap, believing it was necessary to know the king's next move.

Bella was already afraid that the rocks weren't secure enough and if the king kept pounding his feet into the dirt or kicking things around, he could easily stuff his big boot right through the pile of rocks, exposing their hideout. She didn't know what to do.

There was nowhere else for the Travelers to go, so they stayed where they were and sought their Shailmas ferociously.

It turned out that King Shrailzhar didn't need to put his foot through their covering to find them. He had picked up a fist full of dirt and was rolling it between his fingers. Bella watched in dreadful horror—she knew what he was up to. If he threw that dirt up and the wind caught it, there would only be a couple of minutes until it would blow through the cracks in their rock door and find them on the other side.

King Shrailzhar would know they were there and surely finish them off in an instant.

Chapter Fifteen

Symbolic Words

While the king was ferociously rolling the dirt into clay balls with his fingers, and Bella and Pierce were watching closely through tiny holes between the rocks, Judah and Jennifer were busily searching in the shelter for another way out—or at least somewhere else to hide. If even one of those clay balls found its way through the holes, the king would know they were inside and easily crash right through.

It was a bit of a daunting task, trying to see what was inside the dark shelter. While Kaija Mae had a lantern, it was useless to them as long as King Shrailzhar was so close. There was no way anybody wanted to use it and chance giving away their hiding place.

It reminded them of being stuck in the last cave and trying to run away from whatever hungry beast had grabbed Pierce. It had been so dark that they had to form a line and feel with their hands. Now, once again, their hands were all they had to see with. So far, they'd found nothing.

"Anything over there?" Judah whispered to his sister.

"Nope, nothing," she whispered back.

"How about on your side?" she asked.

"Nothing here either," he sighed. There were not too many places to look because unlike the last cave they found themselves in, this shelter was small. There was barely enough room for them all to cram inside and close off the entrance, so any passageways that would lead them out another side was quite unlikely and highly doubtful. They kept looking for one nevertheless.

"Who has the tablets?" Kaija Mae whispered.

"I do," Matt whispered.

"Hand them here," she instructed him although, of course, Matt had no idea where "here" was.

"I don't know where you are," he said.

Kaija Mae and Matt were both waving their arms around, but it wasn't working. Nobody was finding anybody. Matt's arms banged into Jennifer and then into Sam, but so far, he hadn't found the one for when he was searching. Now, it must be said that all their whisperings were so quiet that even to call them whisperings would be a great exaggeration. Regardless, some found the words still to be too loud and wasted no time in saying so.

"Hush," Bella turned around and whispered rather loudly. The king had just thrown the clay balls up into the air and Bella was terrified—so terrified in fact, that even to this day there hasn't been a word thought of that would describe the fullness of her terror. Bella didn't know how those clay balls worked. If they listened for the sound of the Travelers, then she'd make sure they made none—not even a peep.

Bella's hushes weren't working, however, because in just a matter of a few seconds there *was* a peep to be heard. Kaija Mae's peep. Softly, Matt heard her singing. He followed the soft tune and quickly located the singer. He found her ear and put his lips right up to it.

"What should I do with the tablets?" he whispered. Kaija Mae was still waving her arms around and smacked her hand on the basket that was holding them.

"Ouch," she mumbled.

"Here," Kaija Mae whispered and took the basket. "Help me lay these out." They were so close to one another that they could whisper almost silently. There was no way the clay balls would find them because of any noise they were making; that was for sure.

They could have sat in the darkness and been completely silent, of course. However, those desperate Travelers wanted to try and get the tablets into place and break the curse before the clay balls had any chance to find them. The race was on, and silence was just not going to work right now.

"It's pitch black in here, Kaija Mae. How are we going to lay them out?" Judah and the others who'd been listening to their conversation were confused but waited for an explanation—they were sure she'd have one. After all, it wasn't like Kaija Mae to be silly or not know what she was doing so naturally, they all figured that she did know what she was doing.

She did not. Kaija Mae was only following her Shailma's directions and he was never keen on giving more than one direction at a time. None of the Shailmas were.

"I don't know," was her deplorable reply. "I just know that Shekinah is telling me to lay them out. Three rows of four tiles," she said. "Hurry, Matt, help me." For a reason that even Kaija Mae didn't know, there seemed to be a sudden rush to get them laid out in the pattern Kaija Mae had already described to Matt.

After so many times of one or another of the Travelers catching Miriam trying to lay them out on the eating stump or the floor, the time to lay them out had finally arrived and now that it had, they were nervous. What if nothing happened?

Not even one of the Travelers knew what to expect. They'd dreamed of this moment a million times, but now that the moment was here—now that they'd stepped right into the middle of the moment—they wanted it to pass quickly.

None of them knew what the strange symbols or unknown letters meant. Were they supposed to know? Did the Shailmas think that one of the Travelers spoke a different language? Anxious thoughts plagued every one of the Travelers now as they listened to Kaija Mae's instructions from Shekinah, and they began picking up the tablets carefully.

There was not much room to lay them out. With Bella and Pierce against the pile of rocks at the front of the shelter trying to block any holes that might be visible, and the rest of them pushed back against the sides, there was a small (very small indeed) opening in the center. Nobody knew how big or how small that space was because of the dark, but it didn't matter. Matt picked a handful of tablets from the basket, and Kaija Mae felt around doing the same.

Very slowly, and with as much precision as can be expected in the belly of darkness, the two of them laid the tablets out. By feeling the ground and using their fingers, they were able to set down three rows with four tiles in each row. It was painstakingly tricky at first since two of the tablets had been broken. Finding which broken left tablet went with each broken right tablet was time-consuming. Also, they were very careful because they didn't want to bang any more of the tiles together and risk breaking—or even chipping them.

Soon, it became easier and easier to lay the tablets out because as each tablet touched the ground, the words or symbols on them began to glow, illuminating the space. It wasn't like a light stick's glow or light bulb's glow, but more like what they'd seen glowing in the River of Acheron. The words and symbols glowed like hot embers. It seemed almost like the insides of the tablets were filled with a liquid fire, and the flames were trying to escape through the symbols and letters.

It was outrageous.

The Travelers had carried these tablets around for days, and they'd seemed like nothing more than squares of clay with foreign writings on them. Oh, but they were wrong.

Now, as the clay squares were laying out on the ground, the tablets reminded them of the ground of Trilleah and the River of Acheron. Jennifer and Judah both crossed their fingers and held onto one another. They each desperately pleaded with Shemaiah and Simeon to keep the tablets from igniting and burning up, especially while they were trapped inside this shelter with the king and much of his army so close.

As first, Matt and Kaija Mae became concerned … concerned that they had done the wrong thing and the tablets were going to burn up right before their eyes. Maybe they had a self-destruct feature in case Miriam laid them out or the king got ahold of them. Of course, that made no sense because the king would never have laid them out. He would have destroyed them, no doubt, without waiting for even a moment or giving it a second thought. Those tablets would have been crushed to dust and thrown into the sea.

Nevertheless, they worried. None of the Travelers were taking time to think reasonably, and so many unreasonable thoughts danced around in their heads. It's just such unreasonable and unrestrained thoughts that cause a paralyzingly, consuming fear, but of course, none of the Travelers knew such things and so they failed to restrain the unreasonableness and allowed it to keep right on dancing.

As fear gripped … and thoughts danced … and eyes watched the king … and the tiles laid on the ground, something else happened. Something incredibly outrageously out of the ordinary—something surprising and baffling and bewildering and unexplainable.

As each tablet began glowing brighter and brighter from what looked like embers trapped inside the letters and symbols, they began flipping themselves over. One at a time, and in the order they were laid down, those clay tablets flipped over and fell back into place. It was like popcorn popping as the heat touched it. The brighter the embers burned, the quicker the tablets flipped themselves over.

On the backs of each tablet were more words, but not in any sensical order, or so it seemed. They were still not in recognizable words that anyone could read, so they were all still very much confused—that is, until Kaija Mae began singing one of her songs. This song was similar to the other songs she had sung, but there was something different about it at the same time. The words on the backs of the tablets (or maybe it was the fronts of the tablets and they'd just been looking at them wrong this whole time) began blazing with a fire that was ten times brighter than before.

The Travelers had never noticed anything on the other sides of the tablets before, but now, it was unarguably evident that this was not the backs at all, but rather, the fronts. They'd been looking at the tablets wrong this whole time, and now as they all realized such a truth, gasps, and sighs, and muffled cries echoed off the walls. Bella wanted again to hush them all, but as she'd stopped looking at the king and had begun watching the tablets, all sounds and words and bossiness left her. She—like the others—stared in mind-boggling amazement.

Like Kaija Mae, the clay tablets also began humming. At least that's what it sounded like, but then again, maybe it was more of a cracking type sound than a humming sound. It was like when something is in a terribly hot fire, it cracks and snaps. Yes, that was the sound the tablets were making, but there was no heat coming from around them, so it seemed that any amount of heat that was making them pop and crack and hum was coming from inside of them.

As the tablets cracked and snapped and hummed—and Kaija Mae sang her unrecognizable song—the tablets turned a bright blue color and smoothed themselves out like glass. They ran their edges into one another and melded themselves together into one large tablet. The Travelers could see it very well because of the light it was giving off. Kaija Mae reached her fingers out and touched it quickly, expecting to burn herself.

She didn't.

Instead, it was cool to the touch. Kaija Mae rubbed her fingers along it, and Matt joined her and did the same. Soon everyone except for Pierce and Bella were touching the tablet, surprised by its cool smoothness. The one large tablet was now glowing dimly with the most beautiful blue hue. It reminded them of a color they'd seen in the Chamber of Rest. It filled both the Travelers and the air with a similar peace as they'd found in that Chamber many times before.

They each breathed in deeply, for they'd been holding their breath for the longest time. The air was so peaceful that it nearly had a sweet taste to it. Unlike earlier moments when the Travelers held their breath in, they now breathed purposefully and deeply. The peace filled their bellies … their minds … their souls.

The words that had been chiseled into the clay were now scurrying around on the smooth blue surface, jumping from one side of the tablet to the other and back again, rearranging themselves into something that looked like readable sentences. Where symbols had been etched on one side, words now appeared on the other side. It seemed like those symbols were carriers of a whole bunch of messages. It looked as though the lids had been peeled back from those symbols, sending lines and lines of words marching out. They arranged themselves with the others already written.

A story was forming before their eyes. The smooth blue tablet held a story of words that continued to burn with bright oranges and reds. It was the most beautiful thing any of them had seen in Trilleah.

In fact, it was the most beautifully outrageous thing any of them had seen … ever.

Even though Bella knew she should be keeping watch of the king and what was going on just past the rock wall, she was far too awestruck and completely unable to turn back and keep watch on what was happening on the other side of the little holes. Pierce was there, though, still watching … still waiting.

He turned quickly and pulled Bella close to him. Pierce had kept a hand on her arm just in case he needed her and didn't have the time to call out for her—that moment was now. She leaned into him and heard him whisper, "Throw something over that tablet, NOW."

"Why?" she asked.

Now, Bella wouldn't normally have asked him why because she trusted Pierce. Even before this obvious change he'd had, she trusted him … mostly. However, after hearing him explain how he'd known about the little green jar from hiding out and trying to steal it, she realized that she should not have trusted him at all.

Nonetheless, she did trust him now but was afraid that throwing something over the tablet would destroy it or make it stop doing whatever it was that it was doing. She didn't want to risk such a thing unless Pierce had a very good reason.

He did.

"The clay balls have searched the area and are now either on their way back to the king or straight here, to this shelter." He squeezed her arm gently but firm. "Bella, please," he begged.

Just days ago, Pierce would have become outraged that he had to explain his request, but now he was more patient than all the others put together. He'd learned to believe in things he could not see and to listen to what his Shailma was telling him—always—without question or doubt or second-guessing.

Gone were those days when he questioned everything or refused to believe until he saw. Such things had nearly cost him his life, but his Shailma had rescued him and taught him—in a very short amount of time—the immediate importance of trusting him whether or not Pierce could see him.

Bella took off her jacket and tossed it over the glowing tablet. "Shhh," she hushed the others who immediately wanted her to explain her actions.

They didn't know if the glowing tablet would react to being hidden or not, and Bella half-expected her jacket to catch fire or the tablet to throw it off of itself. She hadn't touched the glowing tablet as the others had, so she didn't realize that it wasn't burning hot.

Of course, it wasn't, and her jacket didn't catch fire. Those little clay balls that had been hovering in the sky for so long, however, were now speeding back down.

It seemed, to the carefully watching eye of Pierce, that they were heading straight toward the shelter.

Chapter Sixteen

To Fully Believe

The race was on.

King Shrailzhar could see that the War of the Firmament was not going the way he had hoped it would. Far too many of his Nakah Warriors were falling or being hurled, headless, to the ground. It was raining down Nakahs—like a firestorm. The king was dreadfully outraged!

The crust beneath his feet was getting thinner and thinner as the Sea of Acheron was stirring and bubbling and raging, destroying the ground from below. It was demanding to be released from its borders and was beginning to break loose, erupting here and there. Large portions of the ground were being hurled into the air as the sea forced its way through. It had waited long enough, and now, its rabid appetite was demanding to be filled.

Gigantic hail was pelting against the ground and millions of the black critters—with the rattling scorpion tails—were now completely covering the ground. Thousands more had taken to the air by now, and it too was thick with the critters. The hail wasn't seeming to disturb the critters at all, rather, they were doing a perfect dance together, falling and shifting and scooting out of each other's way— like each was rather fond of the other and neither wanted to disrupt or be disrupted.

Pierce could still see out, but barely. Only the short space directly in front of the holes between the rock pile was visible to his eyes, which was probably a very good thing. If he—or any of the others—could have seen what was going on just outside of their shelter, they would have surely died from fright. None of them would have stopped even briefly to consider that inside the shelter there was a blanket of peace.

Pierce couldn't see anything outside, though, other than King Shrailzhar's boots which were fearfully close to the shelter, and a very small portion of the army. If he strained his eyes and his neck and looked way up, he could see a few of the clay balls that had been tossed from the king's hand. Those clay balls were what Pierce was watching now, even though it stung his eyes greatly to keep such a close watch on them. It was those very balls of clay, something the Travelers had never understood, that could give away the Travelers' location now.

Bella had been unable to turn away from what she'd seen happening with the tablets, but Pierce had kept his hand on her arm just in case he needed her attention quickly.

"They're coming down … coming down … coming down," Pierce whispered to himself about the little dirt balls. Suddenly, he was startled by something behind him, and he spun his head around to look. He was horrified at what his eyes caught sight of.

A large fire was hovering in a cloud of smoke directly above the glowing blue tablet.

Pierce wanted to shout out; they all did—especially Jennifer. Of course, they could not shout, and whispering seemed useless, so they never bothered to do either. Pierce tried to put his body between the cloud of fire and the pile of rocks to keep any light or smoke from being noticed on the other side.

It was anything but dark in the shelter now. The Travelers could see one other plainly, and the look on everyone's face was the same; shock and confusion and terror. Nobody even looked down to the blue tablet they'd hidden under Bella's jacket. For the moment, they forgot it was there.

Pierce puffed up his shoulders and held out his hands as if to say, "What's going on?" Jennifer read his look perfectly and pointed to the little green jar that was sitting, without its lid, at her feet.

Everybody wanted to ask why she'd take the lid off … now … in the middle of such a crisis and with the king not more than three feet away. Of course, they couldn't and instead a few of the Travelers moved to where Pierce was making an effort to become a human shield to keep anything that was inside this shelter from finding its way out.

It required a perfect balance of give-and-take. If even one of the Travelers leaned too hard against the pile of rocks, they would surely give way and the Travelers would spill out right at the feet of King Shrailzhar and his army.

However, if they didn't stay close enough to the pile of rocks, it would leave space for the smoke to sneak out and give away their hiding spot. Either situation would most assuredly result in their immediate deaths, so balancing perfectly between the two became their focus if they wanted to keep their heads which, of course, they did. Keeping the smoke inside the very small space wasn't a good idea either, and as one and then another and another began stifling coughs, they realized what a horrifically gripping predicament they were in.

Judah had stayed close to Jennifer, and now he leaned in toward her face. "Why did you take the lid off?" he asked. "Why now?"

"I didn't, Judah!" she cried. Jennifer was so upset, that Judah threw his arms around her and tucked her under his grip. They both knew how loud the voice in the cloud of smoke was and they waited, on pins and needles, for it to boom out and shake the shelter they were hiding in.

"Judah," she whispered through her muffled tears, "that stupid thing jumped out of my pocket and pulled its own lid off! My hands weren't even in my pockets!" she wailed. Judah believed her, sort of, but he was sure the others would never believe such a seemingly sordid tale.

He moved her a little behind him just in case one of the others wanted to get at her. It was clear by the looks they were wearing that they were angry.

Both of the twins were begging their Shailmas to keep that fiery cloud from speaking, or at the very least to keep it to a hushed whisper. Neither of those things would happen, of course, and as Simeon spoke to Jennifer's heart she became a bit less afraid, but only a small bit. In fact, her fear subsided so minimally that she didn't even notice.

What Simeon was telling her seemed to be the most far-fetched and unlikely tale ever to be told. Even if she were to write the ending to this great disaster herself, she would not have had the imagination to think up such a wild finale.

Little One, Simeon began. *Do not be afraid for I am with you. All the Seraphic Shailmas are with their riders inside of this cave.* That did not help Jennifer much, and she told her Shailma so.

Have you forgotten that I said some of the Shamars would remain with you as well? Simeon asked.

Well yes, as a matter of fact, she had forgotten.

Jenny, there are precisely 120 of the Shamar Shailmas right on the other side of this shelter. They are surrounding it on every side.

It was the Shailmas who put this shelter here for you, and Kaija Mae's Shailma who led her here. This is your safety. This is your safe place. Nothing will harm you as long as you remain inside.

But, Simeon warned, *if you leave this shelter, danger will be on every side, and your safety will be in your own hands.*

Then I shall not leave it, Jennifer promptly told Simeon and made up her mind firmly to do exactly that. Jennifer would stay put.

My dear one, the mighty Shamar Shailmas are surrounding this shelter. The king cannot even see it. You think he can see all that you can see, but have you ever considered that while the Shailmas can open your eyes to see what is hidden in the atmosphere, the Shailmas can also close the eyes of the king and hide what is in plain sight in that same atmosphere?

Well no. Of course, I have not considered that, Simeon. Why would I consider such a thing that makes no sense? Why would I consider those things that you have not told me to consider? Jennifer felt a bit angry with Simeon, and quite embarrassed that she hadn't considered such things. As she wondered about them now, they seemed far-fetched and downright ridiculous.

She had never even questioned the idea that if Simeon could open her eyes, he could also close them. Neither did she consider that if he could surround her with a circle of one dozen Shamar Shailmas in the adder's pit, that he could also surround this entire shelter with those same Shamars.

Of course, it was not Simeon who was doing the commanding or calling of any of the other Shailmas at all, for there was one much greater than the Shailmas who did all the ordering and commanding. The Shailmas, both the Seraphic Shailmas and the Shamar Shailmas, had a King of their own—a King far greater than Shrailzhar; one with unmatched power and unending authority. It was this King who gave all orders and the necessary power to carry out those orders. For now, though, neither Jennifer nor any of the Travelers, except for Pierce, knew anything of such important matters.

Indeed, the more Jennifer thought about and considered what Simeon was telling her now, the more she became less angry with him and more frustrated with herself. Of course, all these things could be so. Why she'd never considered any of them before now was beyond her understanding.

Jenny, Simeon continued. *Whatever you ask of me, if it's in your best interest and you are asking for the right reasons, I will do it for you. Do you not know? Have you never heard? I am on your side. I have been with you in the past, and I will be with you in the future. There is not a moment that has passed when I have not been with you. Never has a second of time ticked by when I was not by your side. If only you mortals would understand the place you have, the value and importance you hold with the Shailmas, you would never worry again. But you do not know. You refuse to believe such things, and so you face trouble—shrouded in fear—and see problems through the eyes of pain.*

Jennifer, trust me. Trust that I see what you don't, for I am not limited to the seen realm as you are, Little One. I see all the things that surround you, and I have at my very disposal all that is required to look after you perfectly. You do see much of what is unseen, far more than the others, but there is still so much you do not see and that is for your own good. Trust me.

Little One, Simeon added, *I work for the Nameless One. Every bit of my power and knowledge and authority of the air comes from Him. He works for none! He is the highest, the greatest, the most powerful. He is everywhere at all times. He sees everything at once and knows all things that have happened, that happen now, and that are still to happen because He is there, in all those places, at one time. There is no time with Him. Therefore He exists in all time at the same time. There is none more powerful, not even one.*

Jennifer was listening intently but still concerned about the fire that was hovering, sure to burst forth with a booming voice at any second. So far, it was just hanging in the air directly above the tablets.

She heard all the words that Simeon was speaking to her soul, every one of them. Still, because they did not find a place to settle, she continued to be worried and had much doubt rattling inside of her mind.

Simeon, what about King Shrailzhar? He has the power to destroy us! He has so much power that he has held the souls of the

Waiting Ones in that stupid, dreadful forest for so long. Unless we can figure out this curse and break it, Shrailzhar will hold those souls for eternity ... AND OURS AS WELL!

Oh, Little One, Simeon replied, *you have not heard me ... even still your ears are closed to my words.*

I did hear you, Simeon! she screamed inside of her mind. Jennifer was so agitated and fearful that while she had heard his words, she had not understood them for if she had, her fears would have faded into a weightless cloud and been blown away by the mere breeze of belief.

Yes; it was clear that even still, after all that she'd seen and done, and after the many times Simeon had rescued her from this dreadful situation or that deadly trap, even still she failed to trust him fully.

Perhaps the voice in the cloud of fire would finally persuade Jennifer to trust—fully and completely—her Shailma. Complete and full belief was the only thing that would rescue the Travelers and free the souls of the Waiting Ones.

Still, she could not find that belief.

Chapter Seventeen

Voice in the Fire

Suddenly, something that Simeon had said just a few minutes earlier found a place in Jennifer's mind and now boldly demanded her attention. She returned to the conversation, hoping she'd find Simeon still in the talking mood.

What do you mean, you work for the Nameless One? she asked him. Now the Shailma was quiet.

Simeon, she called, *what do you mean by that? Who is this Nameless One I keep hearing about all of a sudden? Where does He dwell and how can I find Him? It would seem He is the One we need.*

Simeon would not answer her at the moment, but it was this very moment that the voice in the cloud decided to speak. It spoke only to Jennifer. However, everyone else was fully able to hear what it had to say.

"I am giving this information to the one to whom I was given," it bellowed loudly. "You know who you are, so listen to me … I do not repeat myself as you have learned well in the past."

Jennifer did not *want* to listen. She *wanted* to plug her ears and tune out whatever words this one would speak. It had said nothing useful in the past, and she expected it to ramble on about nothing useful now. The other Travelers would not let her ignore it, though, and so she listened.

"This is the end for you, the last stop. It is here, behind the veil, where you will break the curse of the Waiting Ones, but the souls will not yet be free."

"See?" Jennifer whispered. "I told you. This thing is crazy!" She kicked the jar and it flew across the shelter, narrowly missing her auntie's head. Bella had to duck to miss getting smacked by it. That little green jar thumped hard into the wall and while everyone expected it to smash into a thousand bits and a million pieces … it did not.

Instead, it fell to the floor with a thud. The voice in the cloud raged even louder now. "You cannot destroy me," it said, mocking her. "It makes no difference if you like what my words are or not. These words were not made for your liking, but for your direction. These words are true, and after all, true is true, through and through. Truth needs no one to believe it to make it so."

"That's it!" Jennifer squealed and jumped around wildly. She wanted to explain and she was about to, except it seemed that the voice from the fiery cloud was not finished and cut her off sharply.

"Jennifer Lillian Elliot, under this veil the curse will be broken. There is one among you who knows the words and will sing them loudly and with perfect precision. You are not that one. However, there will be a sacrifice required from you that only you can make."

Everyone looked at each other and then they all looked to Jennifer. A sacrifice? What in the world did that mean? A sacrifice of what? They thought this clouded fire was indeed crazy and wanted to stuff it right back inside the little green jar.

Now Jennifer was ragingly angry. She forgot that the king and all those little clay balls were looking for them and in her forgetfulness, she shouted … loudly.

"WHAT ARE YOU TALKING ABOUT?" she demanded. "WHAT VEIL? WE ARE IN A SHELTER, NOT UNDER A VEIL, AND WHAT SACRIFICE? I DEMAND YOU EXPLAIN YOURSELF RIGHT NOW!!!!"

"You think this is a shelter?" the voice asked. Then it laughed. Oh, a hard, deep chuckle came from out of that cloud which only made Jennifer angrier. The others looked back and forth between Jennifer and the fiery orange cloud, watching carefully, listening intently, and understanding nothing of any of it.

"Oh, Jennifer, have you learned nothing?" the voice asked, still laughing as though it was mocking her. "Do you think that in the middle of Trilleah—on such a day as this day—that you all just happened to stumble upon a shelter as perfect as this one? Do you not think that if *you* saw the shelter, King Shrailzhar could not see it also? Do you suppose that your silly pile of rocks could fool an entire army?"

The voice in the cloud laughed again—louder. It did seem a bit odd now that the Travelers thought about it. Of course, Kaija Mae had seen this place before, but then again, maybe not. Maybe it was one of many other shelters that they had seen over their many journeys that the girl had seen and only thought it was this same one.

"So you're going to convince me that *you* put this shelter here, I suppose," Jennifer wailed. She was disgusted by this stupid nonsensical voice—especially since it had mentioned something about a sacrifice that would be required of her. Had she not already sacrificed more than her share?

"Of course, I did not put this shelter here for you; I can do nothing of the sort. I am only the voice in the wilderness crying for the freedom of the Waiting Ones. I am nothing more than a voice, with necessary information."

Now Jennifer was downright flabbergasted.

Nothing was making sense, but yet somehow in her belly, all of it was. She couldn't explain it. But maybe … if she asked the right questions … this voice in the wilderness could explain at least some things. It was worth a try.

"If this is not a shelter that Kaija Mae found, then what is it?" Jennifer asked.

"Why, it's a veil, of course!"

"A veil of what? What does that mean?" she questioned.

The rest of the Travelers were in such shock at what was happening before their very eyes that they just stood with their mouths hanging open and their eyes opened wide, listening, watching, barely breathing.

They couldn't believe that Jennifer was arguing with this voice that was coming from a fiery dark cloud. But she didn't seem even to notice with whom, or what, she was arguing. Jennifer had put right out of her mind the fact that this voice … the one giving her such ridiculous information … was coming from the center of a dark cloud which was housing a miserable fire.

"Do you not know what a veil is, Jennifer?" the voice said. It had turned away from its shrewd mockery and menacing laughter and had suddenly become very serious.

Jennifer didn't notice, and if she had noticed, she certainly wouldn't have cared.

"Of course, I know what a veil is," she fumed. But, in fact, she didn't know the purpose of a veil. The fiery voice boomed again from the cloud that continued to hover just in front of her.

"A veil is to hide something … for its protection. There is a veil over this place where you are now standing, perfectly hiding you and the others from the king and his brutish army."

Of course, the 120 Shamar Shailmas the Nameless One had posted around the veiled shelter remained exactly where they were told to be. They were ready and fully prepared to protect the Travelers if, for some ridiculous reason of all such human reasoning, one or all of those Travelers wandered out of the shelter, out from the security of the veil.

"They cannot see this place, or the rocks you so carefully piled in front of the opening, or the small cracks between the rocks, because it has been veiled for your protection," the voice boomed and thundered.

"That must be why the clay balls haven't found us … we aren't all that well hidden," Bella whispered to Judah.

"There's no need for whispering here," the cloud again mocked. "No sound can get through the veil. No light or sound or smell or smoke can break through because the veil is perfect. I can't keep you from leaving the safety of it—that is your choice—but I advise against such silliness."

"Where did the veil come from?" asked one.

"Why can't we see it?" wondered another.

"Who put it here?" demanded a third.

But the voice in the cloud would answer none of their questions—only those that came from Jennifer and so, Jennifer repeated the questions and demanded a response.

"Who put the veil here?" she asked again.

"The Great Eagle."

"What eagle?" she wondered, now more intrigued than angry and more curious than annoyed.

"Why, Nehsher, of course. You have seen him. He returned that boy to you—the redeemed one."

The more this voice from the fire explained things, the more explaining was required. It seemed that for each answer the voice gave, two more questions were thought of. This was never going to end it seemed, and the explanations were causing more confusion.

Jennifer opened her mouth yet again to ask about the redeemed one, but as she did, Pierce opened his and gave the answer.

"I am that boy who is the redeemed one, Jennifer," he whispered. Now everyone else was stirring. Bella was the first to respond to Pierce, cutting everyone off the others.

"What … or who … is the *redeemed one?* I mean, what does that mean, Pierce? Why have you not told us this before now? Before that … that voice in the cloud mentioned it?" Bella sounded perturbed and who could blame her, for indeed they all felt similarly annoyed.

Pierce wanted to explain but wasn't sure if this was the proper time. He knew he couldn't compete with the booming voice coming from the fiery cloud and wasn't sure if that voice would be quiet long enough for him to explain much of anything. He also knew that the Travelers were waiting for information and explanations about the veil and the eagle, so he waited for a few moments.

He was glad he did because, in just a handful of seconds, the voice began speaking again.

"The Great Eagle was sent from the Nameless One to veil this very place," the voice explained. "It laid the veil perfectly upon this ground so that you would be safe while laying out the clay tablets. The curse must be broken before anything else can be done … before any sacrifices or exchanges can be made. The tablets hold the keys to the curse. Now remove that covering from them at once," the voice bellowed.

Bella reached down painstakingly slowly and carefully, not wanting to annoy this loud voice or upset the cloud of fire. She kept her eyes on it while feeling around on the ground for her jacket. Once her fingers found the itchy, stiff material, she slowly lifted it up, revealing the most unusual sight.

The tablets had finally finished their moving and shuffling and flip-flopping around. There were no symbols left, but many, many words had been put into some order that looked as though it might make sense—if anyone could figure out how to read it, that was.

But then, the voice from the flame had said that one among them did know the language, didn't it?

Of course, this was the same language that Kaija Mae had been singing the entire time, yet she was unaware of it, even still.

"The Great Eagle," thundered the voice again, "is that one who works for the Nameless One. The Great Eagle is that one who brings all those who are lost, all those who are broken, all those who are deceived, and all those who need new life, to the Nameless One for redemption."

Now they looked back to Pierce who was just nodding and grinning as the words that nobody else understood sat with him perfectly. Not only did he understand the words, but he had also experienced them! He took this as his cue to explain all that the voice in the clouds was talking about and if he was interrupted, well, the voice would just have to wait.

Pierce was so excited about what he had to say that he didn't care much about the voice in the clouds right now.

"When Nehsher took me to the Nameless One, I already told you I'd felt so much guilt on me, like a thick, wet, winter coat. The Nameless One did not say anything to my ears, but instead, he spoke so much into my heart. Deep things He planted in my soul and deep things He pulled out of my soul.

"I heard Him say that I could make an exchange."

"Huh?" Sam asked, echoing what everyone else was thinking. "What kind of exchange?"

"It was the most unreal and unbelievable thing, and we have seen some very unbelievable things," Pierce laughed. "But it was real; it really did happen."

"What happened?" Bella demanded.

Pierce was bouncing from one thing to another and back again in his explanations, and the others could see that he was very excited about it all. They wanted to be excited too, but he was making it hard with such a lack of any good explanation.

"Pierce," Matt said calmly. He put his hands on Pierce's shoulders and spoke firmly. "Please, we want to understand, but you're all over the place. Calm down and tell us what happened with this Nameless One."

Pierce tried. Oh, how he tried, but the excitement was like waves rolling over him. One then another and another and another with no end in sight just crashed over the boy, taking him into the deep places where only such things that are good can reside.

"Okay," he finally said. Pierce took a big breath and let it out slowly before he tried again to explain the unexplainable. "I was kneeling before the Nameless One because I simply could not stand. I knew this light that I could not look upon was pure love and complete power; it overwhelmed me.

"All the things that were held within the light were good; there was no darkness in it anywhere," he said. "No shadows or dim corners. The voice that came to me told me to stand, so I did. It was hard, though, because I felt like the mud of a pigpen standing beside a mountain of the whitest snow.

"All at once I felt disgusting and disgraceful and covered in filth … yet fully and incomprehensibly loved and accepted by this One who was before me. It was so overwhelming that it took all of my strength not to fall back to my knees."

The others could tell that even as Pierce was retelling what had happened to him, he was reliving it. They could see in his eyes that he was feeling everything all over again and hearing the words and seeing the sights again. It made it difficult to retell the story, but nevertheless, Pierce continued.

"This Nameless One burned brighter as I stood, and a voice came from inside of it and went straight to my belly," he explained. "Not even my belly—more like that voice filled every place in me— my skin, my eyes, my thoughts … every place!

"Do you want to give me all that darkness?" it asked of me. "All those things that you are carrying … the weight of the guilt, the heaviness of the hate, the darkness, the sadness, the shame, the regret … give it to me."

"I didn't want to," Pierce cried. "I didn't want to keep it any longer for myself, but at the same time, I couldn't give it all to this One. I would dirty him with my filth. I couldn't do it. I imagined taking a bucket of mud and throwing it all over this mountain of fresh, perfectly spotless, white snow. I couldn't do such a thing," he moaned.

" 'No,' I said, 'I cannot.'

"Then, that Nameless One said something I shall never forget in all my life" Pierce cried out. The others waited with anticipation high but patience low. Even the fire in the cloud was quiet while Pierce reflected on the story and repeated the unforgettable words of the One of all Light—that Nameless One.

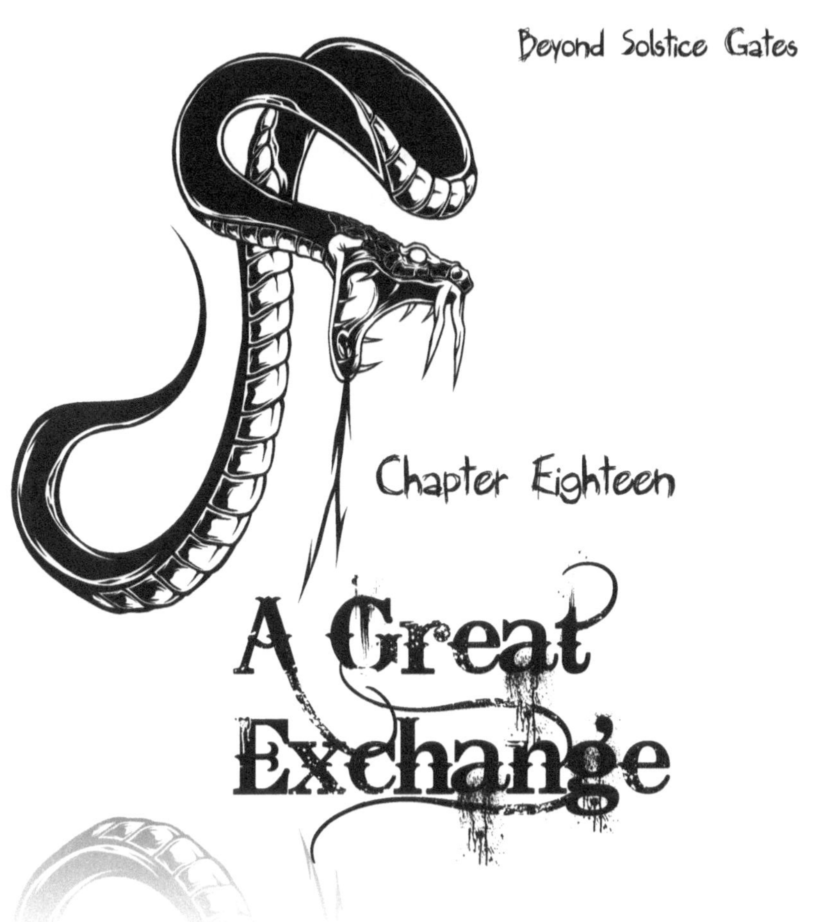

Chapter Eighteen

A Great Exchange

"I'll make an exchange with you," the Nameless One said to me. "I will give you everything that I am in exchange for everything that you are," Pierce recalled. His face was beaming as the words poured from his mouth. His eyes teared up, and he used the back of his hand to wipe them dry before the others could notice. They noticed anyway.

None of the others had any idea what such words as these meant, but neither did Pierce at the time he'd heard them. However, being right there in the middle of that situation, and hearing the words from the Nameless One, it did mean something to Pierce. Even though he did not realize the perfectness and completeness of it at the time, he realized it now.

"You don't see?" he asked the confused onlookers. Some shook their heads while others stared and shrugged their shoulders.

"This presence—this indescribable being—was not just a figure that was before me. It was without limits. Light cannot be contained and neither could this One. His presence surrounded me on every side, but His voice came out of the center of the light and went straight into my soul." The Travelers continued looking at him with blank stares and confused expressions. They could not comprehend what he was trying to explain.

"Picture it," he said and closed his own eyes to do just that. "You're standing before One who is completely perfect, One that is pure and fully light with no darkness. Nobody has to tell you these things; you know it just by being in His presence. In Him, there was no sadness or brokenness or anger or hatred or shame or disappointment or guilt … none … not even a thought of any such things. The light that surrounded Him was unending; He wore it like the robe of a King. Who wears light? WHO?? This One did."

Pierce hushed for a moment, letting that picture sink deep into everyone's imaginations before he continued.

"Then, look at yourself as I had to look at myself. We are filthy," Pierce continued. "We're dressed in disgusting rags that should be burned because they are so filthy and stained and they smell putrid. We are clothed in darkness, while the Nameless One is clothed in unimaginable, uncontainable, unrestrained light. We are filled with sadness and broken hearts and anger and rubbish and worry and fear." Pierce went on and on describing the perfectly pure light of the Nameless One and the disgustingly dark consuming filth of the Travelers.

By the time he'd finished, the Travelers knew just how wretched and broken up they were. They suddenly felt a great need to find this Nameless One and do whatever it was that Pierce had done —to make whatever exchange he had made. There was no doubt that he had been greatly changed.

All the pain from losing their loved ones and all the broken dreams those deaths had left in their souls now poured into their hearts. Every memory of the twins with Mamma and Daddy flooded in and mingled with all the sadness and broken dreams. The rage toward the one who'd caused such an accident, that one who had robbed them of their parents, suddenly filled their bellies, stirring up the poison they'd worked so hard to hide.

"And now that you've got all that in your minds," Pierce said, bringing the thoughts of the twins and the others back to this moment, "hear the words of the Nameless One again. Listen!" he said and slowly repeated the words of the Nameless One—one more time.

"I will exchange all that I am ... for all that you are."

Nobody said a word because there were no more words that could be spoken that would be better, or even comparable to those that were lingering, echoing, hovering in the air right at that moment.

Unfortunately, the voice in the cloud interrupted those thoughts because time was ticking by and had nearly run out. There was still much to be done if the souls of the Waiting Ones were going to be freed before Trilleah destroyed itself. It seemed quite certain now that the destruction would be irreversible because far too much of the Dark Land was already destroyed.

The cloud turned darker, and the flames burst higher. "There will be time for such understandings later but do not forget the words that this redeemed one has repeated from the Nameless One. You will have the opportunity to make your own exchange soon enough," were the words spewing from the fire.

"Look to the tablets," it said three times in a row. "Look to the tablets … look to the tablets."

Kaija Mae had been watching the tablets the entire time. She wasn't concerned about being distracted from what Pierce was saying —even though she listened carefully—for she knew perfectly well what he was talking about. She, too, had come to stand before the Nameless One a long, long time ago. The same offer of exchange had been given to her, and, like Pierce, she grabbed it immediately.

Where Kaija Mae had come from, what had gone on in her village, and all that she'd seen and experienced during the overtaking of her people, would have been far too heavy of a burden to bear if she had not made the great exchange with the Nameless One.

It seemed that the cloud of fire was finished giving whatever information it had to give, at least for now. In one breath, it was drawn back into the little green jar which remained tipped over against the wall where Jennifer had kicked it earlier.

Jennifer picked it up quickly and jammed the lid back on tightly, giving it one hard twist before shoving it into her pocket. What Jennifer really wanted to do was throw that jar into a fire. She wanted to smash it into a thousand pieces or toss it into the River of Acheron.

If Miriam wanted that stupid jar, she could have it. She and that little green jar could sink to the bottom of the sea together, Jennifer thought.

However, Jennifer also wanted to keep it safe because she had a feeling that the voice beneath the lid had more information that she would need very soon. Jennifer loved and hated that stupid little green jar all at one time, and for now, she'd hold onto it and keep it safe.

While she shoved the jar deep into one pocket, she pulled her tattered red blanket from another pocket. It brought a bit of comfort to her soul, albeit not very much. Bella smiled silently as she watched her niece feel the satin edge and wind the frayed bits of the fringe around her fingers.

Nobody knew what to do since it was suddenly eerily quiet inside the shelter. Pierce moved back over to the pile of rocks and peered out again. Now that the voice from the flame had told them they were under a veil and completely unseen by the king and his army, they felt a slight bit safer. Since they had no reasonable proof to believe anything that came from that voice, they remained quiet and cautious.

It was not as though its earlier warnings had proven to be untruthful or inaccurate in the past. As the Travelers discussed it and thought back to what it had originally said in Jennifer's Sleeping Chamber so many journeys earlier, they wondered if perhaps it had spoken some truth. Maybe there were things they could look back upon and see that indeed the voice that shot from the little green jar was one of truth, after all.

"Didn't it tell you that there were dangers in Asphelia's Hollow?" Bella asked. "Dangers that I knew nothing about?"

"Yes," Jennifer pouted. She didn't like remembering those times because it was in those first few journeys to the Dark Land where she'd suffered so much pain. Not physical pain—even though there had been much of that—such as what she'd endured in the adder's pit when her ankles and wrists were bleeding terribly from being chained so tightly by the vines.

It was more the unbearable pain of hearing Mamma's soul groan and cry for the first time. Those were the pains that were so heavy to her soul … even still. That was what made going back in her mind so difficult.

That was the pain that she wanted to forget; she'd do anything to forget those things.

Or, when Bella was angry with her for asking too many questions … or when they all mocked her for mixing the poisonous drink … or when she was learning to trust Simeon.

Those were most difficult times indeed—when she was trusting her Shailma even though nobody else knew it. Those times when the other Travelers, including Bella and Judah, were angry with her because they didn't understand what she was doing. It was those days, those early days of learning to trust Simeon, that caused her the most painful memories.

Unfortunately, it seemed like those were the days they had to look back at now to figure out just how trustworthy the voice from this little green jar was.

"What could it have been talking about?" Jennifer asked. She was truly oblivious to the dangers it was referring to, although she remembered the red eyes and the hands that were on her shoulders when she thought it was Judah in that dark passage and wondered about that now. However, Judah was the only one to know such a secret.

The other Travelers looked at her like she must be joking around. Surely, she must know that the most evident danger lurking inside Asphelia's Hollow was Miriam. Everyone else knew it immediately; not back then, of course, but now.

Bella had never been comfortable around Miriam and certainly hadn't trusted her, but she'd had no idea how very dangerous Miriam was. Bella had thought it was petty jealousies that had caused her so much grief over the girl. Now she knew fully that it was her Shailma giving her uneasiness in her soul over the dangerous traitor.

It was Miriam's job, given to her by King Shrailzhar himself, to steal and destroy the tablets. She was to destroy those tablets and trick Jennifer into following her straight to the king so that Shrailzhar could lock her up and throw away the key.

At least three times, one of the Travelers had come upon Miriam as she had the basket of tablets, either laying them out or sneaking them from their place in the Eating Chamber. Then there was the time that wretched girl had taken the entire basket and threatened to throw them into the sea of Leviathan.

"So Miriam was the danger that you knew nothing about, Auntie Bella?" Jennifer asked. She was certain that was the right answer which meant the little green jar did, in fact, tell them the truth.

"I'd say so, J, yes," Bella replied, dumbfounded that her niece seemed, even still, so naive.

"It doesn't matter now, does it," Sam whined. He was tired of this whole thing. He just wanted to go home and said exactly that. He was whining and pouting and shoved his hands deep into his jacket pockets to wait for something … but he had no idea what. His eyes got large, and he pulled his hands right back out of the pockets. In one hand he had the Book of Truths and in the other, the Book of Lies.

"Look," he shouted. "I forgot all about these," he squealed. Sam squatted down beside the blue tablet with the smoldering words and opened the Book of Lies to the spot he'd been reading so long ago when they had begun this journey. He'd been reading in the dimness and trying to remember as much as he could.

All that he had really accomplished was nothing at all.

Sam had read so much, that as more truths or lies went into his mind, the ones he'd already read were squeezed right out the other side. Instead of looking for what was important, he'd crammed his mind full of unimportant things, leaving no room for anything else. Of course, poor Sam had no idea way back then what might be important information and what was useless gibberish.

When they had to leave the cave quickly, he'd tucked a leaf inside where he was reading and shoved the books into his pockets. He'd completely forgotten anything was in his jacket pockets until just now, when he'd begun his little pity-party and jammed his hands into those pockets.

"Sam," Matt cried. "That's fantastic!"

"I'm sure those will come in very handy as we try to break the curse," Pierce added.

"Sam," Jennifer said softly, "you said it made no difference now whether Miriam was the danger or not, but that's not right." Everyone looked at her oddly, but of course, she had gotten quite used to such looks coming her way. "It does matter," she whispered. "It matters a lot."

"How so,?" Bella asked, curious as to what her niece was thinking.

"If Miriam was the danger that you didn't know about, Auntie Bella, then it means that the voice in the fire was telling the truth, which means that it is probably telling the truth now," Jennifer said. She was quite pleased with herself. The others nodded and grinned and agreed that Jennifer was right.

"I think it was Miriam who stole the Book of Truth and Lies," Sam blurted out.

"What?" Bella questioned.

"Really?" Matt added.

"Why do you think it was her?" Bella asked.

Sam went on to explain how he'd been reading the books at the eating stump when Pierce had made some comment about the Living Maps. "So I went—just for a minute—to see what Pierce was getting so excited about and when I went back to get the books, they were gone.

"Miriam was the only other person in the Eating Chamber," Sam whispered. "I was sure it was her, but at the time nobody was too sure about her, so I didn't want any of you to think I was blaming her for something that was my fault."

"I'm sure it was Miriam who stole the basket of tablets as well, Sam," Matt said. "I didn't see her do it, but she was looking through them and the next thing I knew, they were gone."

Thank goodness the boys had found them in that dark passageway. They'd startled Miriam, and she hadn't had a chance to hide them—or destroy them. Even though a couple of the tablets had broken in half, it didn't seem to make any difference now as they looked down and saw how perfectly they'd all melded together into one big tablet.

Speaking of the tablets …

Chapter Nineteen

Sacrifices Made

"I've been looking at these tablets, and I have no idea how we're ever going to break the curse from this confusion," Kaija Mae whined. "It's completely unreadable!"

You will know what to do ... when the time is right, she heard Shekinah whisper to her heart.

"I've been looking out into Trilleah. If we don't break the curse soon, there will be no need to," Matt replied. "Even if this little shelter is veiled, it's only to keep Shrailzhar and his army from finding us, I think," he continued although truthfully, he had no idea. "If Trilleah self-destructs, or if the ground gives way and everything falls into the Sea of Acheron, then I can only suppose that it will be too late for any curse breaking … or Curse Breakers." He finished his rant with a horrible look smeared across his face.

The others' eyes grew large. They hadn't considered such things because inside this shelter, under the veil, it was calm. Nothing was shaking or moving or smashing or exploding, so for a brief time, they'd forgotten about what was happening in Trilleah—on the other side of the veil.

Also, to make matters just a bit worse—if such a thing were possible—they had all wrongly assumed that the veil protected them from every danger. Of course, that was ridiculous. The veil, as Matt had now pointed out, only kept them from the king and his army's sight. Nothing more … nothing less.

The king was so close to the shelter that Matt was flabbergasted he couldn't see it. It was obvious his eyes had been blinded. Matt could also see that Trilleah was shaking hard and was surprised they couldn't feel any of it inside the little shelter; not even a quiver or a whippet.

Some of the Travelers were hunched down around the tablet. The words, even though unreadable, were smoldering viciously. Oranges and blues and reds continued to simmer, but the words had stopped moving around.

"Tell us how to read you," Kaija Mae whispered.

"Give us a hint," Jennifer begged. It seemed silly to be talking to the tablet, but then again, it was hard not to. They still had a hard time believing that what they were looking at now used to be twelve clay tablets. The Travelers' minds whirled with trying to make sense of anything.

They were not expecting the tablet to speak back to them, of course, which was a good thing because it most certainly was not about to. The Travelers were asking these questions of their Shailmas, not the tablet, and from them, they were expecting answers. If their Shailmas had gotten them this far, surely they would not abandon them now. How absurd.

The Shailmas knew the answers—they must. For some reason with the ways of the Shailmas, the timing always had to be just so. They never seemed to give any information before it was absolutely necessary. To the Travelers, it often seemed to come much too late.

Trust in the timing, Simeon had said to Jennifer many times in the past when she was questioning this or demanding that. Jennifer thought she heard him whisper that same thing to her now. *Trust in the timing, Little One ... always trust in the timing.*

Trusting in the timing of anything is difficult. With everything falling apart from above the ground, and everything gurgling and bubbling from below the ground, it was nearly impossible to trust in anything at all. Jennifer, as well as the others, could not understand why the timing for breaking the curse, freeing the souls of the Waiting Ones, and getting out of Trilleah, was not right now! Immediate! Instant! Straightaway! Tout de suite!

Simeon, Jennifer searched in her mind. She said very little because she didn't need to. Simeon knew her thoughts and read her heart. So now when proper words were hard to find, she didn't bother looking.

All at once Jennifer was interrupted from her searching for Simeon … and Matt was pulled away from his watching the king … and the others were called from their own searchings and wonderings, with just one word from Sam.

"LISTEN," he hollered.

They listened.

"Everybody, listen to this," he repeated himself. Something had the boy excited, so each once turned to look at him and listen to whatever it was he had to say. Kaija Mae had given him the lantern earlier since they no longer had concerns about the king spotting light through the rocks, and Sam had been hunched down scouring the Book of Lies and the Book of Truths.

"I was scanning through the Book of Lies," he said. "Listen to this."

"You are each your own god. Nothing can truly harm you because in your own hearts you are your own kings, your own gods. None has a need for any other god. There is no need to hide or fight because each king, each god, is responsible only for themselves and to themselves. Each one must leave the other to himself and trust only

themselves for indeed, that is the only trustworthy being. No god has the power to bring harm—or good—upon another god."

"And this," he continued, so excited, that his words were becoming a high-pitched screech and a little hard to understand. *"Believe only what you see with your eye for there is nothing more. Nothing exists beyond your sight."*

"Well, that's all a big pile of rubbish," Pierce said. "I have seen things much bigger than myself, and I believe them because I have seen them." He chuckled a bit before continuing. "On the other hand, I have experienced things that I have not seen, and I believe those things just as much—maybe even more."

"Like what?" Jennifer asked. She had seen many—but certainly not all—things because Simeon had opened her eyes a long time ago. Jennifer always assumed the others saw the same things that she did and so was curious as to what Pierce was talking about.

"Like when I was thrown into that nest by the savage beast from the cave. The one who nearly ripped my shoulder off," he squealed. "Those babies were hungry, Jennifer. They didn't rip me apart or gobble me up. They didn't even come near me.

"I didn't see, nor did I know, of course, that my Shailma had spread his wings open wide, covering me. The reason those hungry babies moved as far back as possible and the reason they screeched so loudly was NOT that they didn't like what their mamma had brought them for lunch, but because they saw something I couldn't see."

"Oh, yes I suppose so," Jennifer said. The others had all been listening closely, and they too, were well aware that what Sam had just read were lies. So if they were lies, then the opposite must be the truth. The opposite of such things would be to "believe in the things we cannot see and trust in each other," Kaija Mae whispered. They all agreed.

"But wait," Sam said. "There's so much more here, you guys … listen to this; listen to what I found in the Book of Truths."

They all listened intently while Sam read from the Book of Truths that lay open on the ground in front of him.

"There is One, greater than the rest. This One holds all power and has authority over all things. He sees you. He knows your name. Even the greatest among the Shailmas obey His every command."

"What?" asked Pierce. "That has to be the Nameless One! I have met this One, and I know, I can tell you, this must be Him."

"Wait, Pierce, there's more!" Sam shrieked. He was filled with excitement as he continued reading. *"He alone knows unknowable languages, and He alone will give you the keys to the Kingdom in which He dwells. This One, the All-Powerful, Uncreated Being, longs to have you sit at His table and eat the food He offers, for in it dwells the fullness of all life."*

Again, Pierce cut Sam off.

"Whoa," Pierce shouted. "Yes, that's Him … that's the One I've seen … that's the One who redeemed me!"

"I want to know that One, too," Matt shouted. The Travelers went on and on, rambling about how great this One must be and if it was in the Book of Truths, then it must be so.

Of course, having seen the changes in Pierce and having heard his stories and seeing what he'd done to Sam's burned flesh, there was no doubt left in any of them that this One was real and His power was life-giving. That was exactly what it had given Pierce. They'd seen the undeniable changes in him themselves; with their very own eyes.

"Wait," Jennifer said. She was as excited as the rest but had heard something the others must have missed hearing.

"If He is the only One who knows the unknowable language —and surely this must be the language of the tablets—then how can we possibly decipher it?" Her question put a pause on the excitement that had been bubbling among the group. They had forgotten they were already told that the language would be given to Kaija Mae since she'd been singing in that unknown language all this time.

"That's true," Judah said. He had remained quiet for much of the time, but nobody had noticed. He was in deep conversations with his Shailma, so he hadn't been paying much attention to what had been going on inside the shelter. He did listen, though, as Sam had read from the Book of Truths and this seemed to help with his difficult conversation with Shemaiah.

Judah, Shemaiah had been instructing him, *a time is coming quickly when you will need to let go of all that you have been holding.*

Everything you've been thinking was your responsibility, your duty, your obligation, will become mine. I have let you carry it for a little while but only because you were not ready to let it go. But soon, Judah, soon you will need to release Jennifer into my hands.

Judah argued furiously with Shemaiah because he wrongly believed that he was the only one who could protect his sister. Judah would give up his very life for that one with whom he shared his DNA if the time ever came. He wouldn't like it, and he would fight it with everything within himself, but if that moment came where it was either Jennifer or Judah, he would step forward.

That moment would come sooner than Judah thought, but he would not be nearly as brave or as tough in it as he was sure he would be. Judah would be required to sacrifice greatly indeed, but not what he thought would be required of him.

Someone was calling his name. He heard it slightly but ignored it until it came to him again.

"Judah," he heard. The boy shook himself into the moment, not realizing how deep he'd gotten into the conversation with Shemaiah. He looked around and saw it was his sister who'd been calling to him.

Judah moved closer to her.

"What is it?" he asked quietly. There was a look of deep concern on her face, and Judah wasn't sure if his sister wanted everyone's attention … or just his. "What's wrong, Jelly Bean?" he asked again.

"Judah, I feel like something is shaking in my belly. I can't explain it—I can't even try—but it's like something is warning me of some sort of horrible approaching danger. Like doom," she whispered to him. Judah was right; she only wanted her brother's attention, and so he whispered back softly.

"Is that all you can figure out?" he asked. "Is Simeon telling you anything?" Judah asked. He reached his hand out and took hold of his sister's. The more he looked into her eyes, the more anxious concern he saw stirring up. She squeezed his hand tightly.

"I have been asking Simeon, begging him to let me know what this is about, but all he keeps saying is, 'all things are as they must be,' and then he asks me to trust him more than ever before," she whispered. "I don't know, Judah, I don't know." There was fear in her eyes and dread in her heart. Her brother could hear it, but he didn't know how to help her … not this time.

The twins chattered quietly back and forth in the corner of the shelter and for a long time, nobody noticed. Everyone else was preoccupied with their own things. Kaija Mae, Bella, and Pierce were busily studying the tablet and begging their Shailmas for an interpretation of the thing … or any help whatsoever.

Sam was continuing to page through the Book of Truths, for the Book of Lies seemed useless at the moment. Matt and Aviel were busy with their faces pushed up against the rocks watching every move of both the king and his army. Tahlia and the others were wandering this way and that, helping out where they could, adding some wisdom here and some thoughts there.

Yes, everyone was far too busy with their own things to notice the whispering, anxious twins. It seemed that both of their Shailmas were packing them full of information and trying to persuade them to be braver than they'd ever been before.

There was a key that the two of them held. Neither Jennifer nor Judah held it on their own, but both Simeon and Shemaiah were telling the twins the same thing. Together they held the final keys to opening the prison that had held the souls of the Waiting Ones for so long.

The tablet would break the curse indeed, but after that time—after the curse was broken—the twins held those final keys that would open the lock. The prison doors would be open and every soul that had been locked behind its gates for so long would be released into freedom.

The question remained, though, what those keys were, and if the two of them together would have the courage in their hearts—and the faith in their Shailmas—to use them. They would find out shortly that to use each of their keys, it would be more difficult than they could image, take more courage than they could find, and cost them more than they could afford.

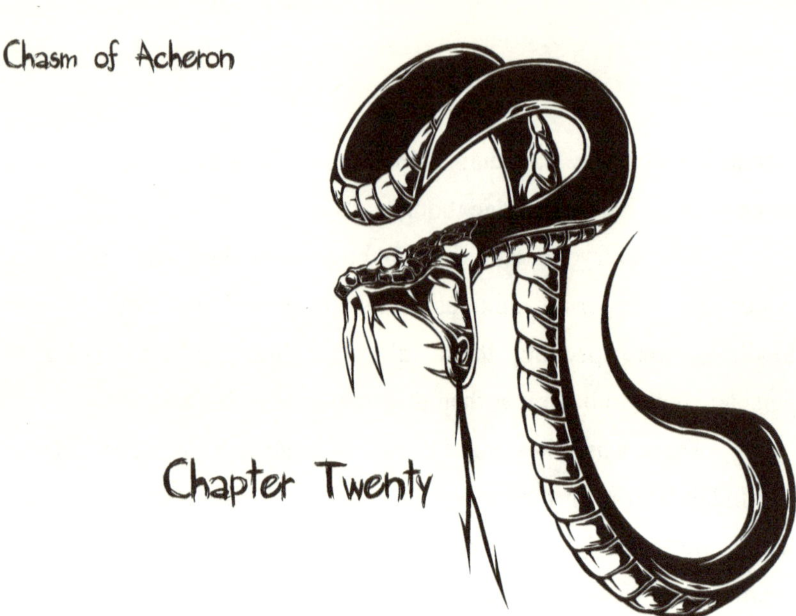

Chapter Twenty

Time to Go

"Shrailzhar is leaving," Matt shouted.

"And his army is following right behind him," added Aviel. The two boys popped up and turned around but then, giving it a second thought, Matt went right back to peeking through the holes in the pile of rocks. He thought it might be another trick of the king, and wanted to see if they were actually leaving.

"Where are they going?" Jennifer asked.

"I have no idea, but they are definitely leaving here," Matt replied.

"He was raging—screaming and shouting at the army about another failed trap and useless dungeons … or something like that," Aviel told the others.

The Travelers didn't know what to do. Were they to remain inside this shelter or was there somewhere else they should be heading? For right now, they decided to remain inside, at least until they knew for certain that they were supposed to leave. This shelter was calm and reasonably safe under the veil, and they were happy to stay put.

That wasn't to be the case for long. With none of the Travelers anywhere near the pile of rocks now, it was a surprise when the pile that had stood perfectly sturdy for so long, suddenly gave way and tumbled every which way. Some rocks rolled this way and others rolled that way, but whichever way the rocks rolled, one thing was sure. The door had been reopened.

"What in the world …" Matt stammered.

"But how did …" Aviel added. Pierce got down on his knees and peeked his head through the door. He looked carefully out into the land but quickly yanked his head right back inside.

"It's purely dreadful out there," he cried. "I cannot believe we have to go back … out … THERE!"

None of the Travelers wanted to leave the safety of this shelter, but when the Shailmas began speaking loudly and clearly to each one of their riders, it was perfectly obvious that this was no longer where they should be. If this was no longer where they were supposed to be, then chances were good that it wouldn't be safe for long.

The veil has been removed, Kaija Mae, Shekinah whispered to her heart.

Without the veil covering the shelter, it's no longer a place of safety for you, Shura uttered to Bella's mind.

Time to leave this spot, Matt heard from Mishan.

One after another, the Shailmas let their riders know that the shelter was no longer safe and they were to leave it straightaway.

Pierce picked up the large blue tablet—very carefully—and ducked as he stepped from the shelter back out into the Dark Land where the hurricane winds encircled him immediately. He tucked the tablet under his jacket and held it tightly.

One by one the Travelers ducked out from the shelter and back into the land. They hadn't realized how peaceful and calm it was inside the shelter until they were returned to the openness of Trilleah. They were out now and wondering which way to go, when Sam screamed. They all spun to look at the boy.

"The books!" he shouted and turned back to rush in and retrieve them. "Oh no!" he wailed.

The Travelers turned back toward the shelter to keep an eye on Sam. Before he could duck inside, an enormous spiral of wind came out of the sky and picked up the entire shelter. Matt grabbed Sam and pulled him back just as the shelter was being yanked up into the middle of the wind. Judah jumped forward and grabbed Sam's leg.

Between him and Matt, they were able to pull Sam back down to the ground. He fell with a hard *thud*.

"THE BOOKS," he bellowed. "I'VE LOST THE BOOKS!" Sam laid on the ground wailing and pointing his arms up toward where the shelter had been inhaled. Matt shouted at him to get up, but when Sam didn't move, he reached down and pulled the boy up by his britches.

"Here," Pierce hollered, as he ran toward a cluster of large trees. They moved quickly, following Pierce, and were glad they did. Before they got very far at all, but thankfully far enough, the powerful winds opened her hands and the shelter came crashing back down from high above. It smashed hard into the ground, completely leveling every rock, pebble, and stick that had only moments ago been their veiled refuge of safety. It was evident that something had kept that fortress safe for as long as they were inside. It was also evident—probably even more so—that the Shailmas were leading them, and a strong knowing filled each one of them, a knowing of how intricately important it was to listen to—and follow—the directions of the Shailmas. It was a matter of life and death.

The Travelers couldn't believe what they were watching. Everyone ran as fast as they could, although, where they were running to none of them knew. They wanted to get away from where they were and didn't care where they went. Nobody considered that King Shrailzhar might not be as far away as they had thought. In fact, nobody thought about it at all. Perhaps they should have … yes, they definitely should have considered such a thing.

Unfortunately, the king and his army were not far away at all and heard the crashing of the shelter. King Shrailzhar's boots went hard into his beast's sides, causing him to turn around sharply.

"HiYah!" he shrieked, and the beast took off running.

The Travelers heard him before they saw him.

"RUN," Judah wailed.

They ran.

Some ran in this direction and others ran in that direction. They were scattered now, all over the place. There was no time to stop, though, and maybe their best chance of escaping was to scatter.

Of course, King Shrailzhar was only interested in two of the Curse Breakers anyway, and so, those were the ones he chased now. His army could get the others, but that wasn't of any priority at the moment.

Judah and Jennifer stayed together, mostly because they hadn't let go of each other's hands since they were in the shelter. Judah had a feeling that what Shemaiah had been speaking to him about earlier, this thing that he was soon going to be required to let go of, was Jennifer. Because of this, he was even more determined to hold on to her.

Now, once again, Judah heard Shemaiah loud and clear. He refused to believe what he heard, though, for surely … SURELY … this could not be right!!!!!

Judah, he heard loudly. *You must let go of her. You must trust that Simeon will keep her ... that Simeon will look after her. Jennifer is his responsibility, not yours. Let her go. She was never your responsibility.*

Judah held on tighter. There was no way he was about to let go of his sister.

He couldn't!

He wouldn't!

"I WILL NOT!" he screamed.

Jennifer would have turned to look at him, but there was no time. The twins were running as fast as they could possibly run. In fact, Judah was running a bit faster and so it was only every few steps that Jennifer's feet even touched the ground. They had to keep their eyes steadily in front of them since the ground had so many open cracks and crevices, which were releasing fountains of gurgling fires.

That bright orange, bubbling hot liquid was reaching out and swiping at the twins' feet as though trying to grab them or trip them up. It all seemed more focused on Jennifer's feet than Judah's, but nonetheless, it was essential they watched where they were going. She could ask him about it later—assuming there would be a later for the twins to ask anything whatsoever.

Jumping over cracks, ducking from the embers and hail that was plummeting the ground, weaving to avoid the flying critters, and trampling overtop of the ones that covered the ground, the twins moved as fast as they could.

They could hear King Shrailzhar laughing behind them as he was quickly gaining ground on the twins.

"JUDAH," Jennifer screamed.

Let her go, Judah, spoke Shemaiah firmly to his mind. Oh, but how could he do such a thing?

Judah knew, without any doubt, that if he let go of his sister, the king would swoop by and scoop her up. He couldn't think … he couldn't breathe. There was nothing in his mind, but every emotion ever felt by any breathing creature ever before was suddenly fighting for space in his heart. Judah's mind became consumed and overwhelmed by too many thoughts to think any of them. So, rather than try, he pushed them all out and began screaming at his Shailma. After all, Shemaiah was asking something far too great for him to accomplish. He just couldn't do such a thing. He just could not!

Take me, he wanted to scream. *Please leave her, but take me!* Judah begged Shemaiah to let him take Jennifer's place, but he knew that was not going to happen. From the very first moment that his naive twin sister had stepped foot in this dreadful land, Judah knew that this moment would eventually come.

He didn't realize it until right now, but as they were running, Judah pulling his sister and keeping her on her feet, he suddenly knew in his heart that everything right up to this very moment was to prepare him to release Jennifer and trust Simeon with her.

He thought it had come before—when he had to use Jennifer's blood to defeat Choshek in the cave, but Simeon had rescued her then. Kaija Mae had sung sweet songs over her as they carried her through the Forest of Waiting Ones. Even now, as he recalled the incident, Judah could see in his memory all those Trows sitting like vultures in the trees waiting for Jennifer to take her last breath so they could steal her soul. Kaija Mae's songs had covered her though, and the Trows were denied his sister's soul.

And again, Judah's mind blew back to that moment when he'd been holding his sister's hand in the vineyard—when she had been ensnared by the vines and taken down to the adder's pit. That time too, he thought he had lost her. That day as she was ripped from his grasp, Judah's hands had been unable to hold her. He'd seen the look of defeat and terror on her face as the ground covered over her. That look would haunt Judah forever. Of course, he had no idea the look that was about to be displayed on his sister's face would be innumerable times worse than the one currently playing in his mind.

Jennifer had told him the story about how the king was in that adder's pit—since it was his temporary kingdom while he waited for Trilleah to be set up for eternity. She had recollected to him how the king stared her in the eyes, but his beast would come nowhere near because of the ring of Shamar Shailmas that Simeon had called to surround her.

Judah thought then, too, that he'd lost his sister forever but again, Simeon had been with her and had rescued her. This memory and that recollection rolled through Judah's mind, and every time, he recalled how it was Simeon who had rescued Jennifer. As he pondered it ever so briefly now, Judah realized it had never been him who'd kept her safe … not even once. It was the Shailmas who kept her safe and had brought her back every time.

Judah had never been asked to make the decision to release his sister. Every time he could remember, it was not an option given to him. He'd hung on and fought hard every time, but each time Jennifer had been ripped from his grip—against his will.

It had never been his choice. But now he had to make the choice himself. Maybe all those other times, those times the choice had been made for Judah, was to teach him about trusting the Shailmas and to give him the courage to do so when the time came. Perhaps every other time was to prepare him for this time.

Shemaiah was continuing to beg Judah to let Jennifer go, but he just couldn't do it. If Shemaiah wanted Judah to release his sister, then the Shailma would have to make it happen. Surely Judah would never have the strength to make such a choice on his own.

Every other Traveler had stopped running. After all, there was no need for them to continue. Nobody was chasing them. Instead, they had all turned to see what was happening with the twins. There was no doubt that Jennifer held keys to the freedom of the cursed souls that none of the others held. Of course, unlike the little green jar, nobody wanted those particular keys.

Pierce watched, reasonably calm, while the others were screaming and yelling and panicking thoroughly. There was nothing any of them could do now, and they knew it. Matt moved to be beside

Bella, who was weeping wildly. She refused to be consoled, though, and all Matt could do was hold her tightly and try to shield her eyes from seeing the certain doom of her niece and nephew.

They all huddled closely together under a clump of dead trees that miraculously, were still standing. Their roots had come up from the ground so it was doubtful they'd be standing long. For now, it was the best place for the Travelers to be—just so long as when the trees did tumble over, the Travelers were quick enough to get out of the way.

The king was gaining on the twins—nearly about to run them right over—but he wasn't slowing down even slightly. The onlooking Travelers wondered if the twins were under a veil even now because it looked to them like the king may go right past them. The twins knew differently, though, because they could hear Shrailzhar screaming at them.

The army was close behind him, and for some reason, King Shrailzhar was shouting at them and waving his arms back toward the rest of the Travelers. Matt was trying to calm Bella, and Pierce was focusing on keeping the tablet safe. The others had their eyes—and their ears—focused sharply on King Shrailzhar and the army.

As they watched in absolute horror, begging the Shailmas for another veil to cover them and the twins, the army slowed, with about half of them turning back while half kept following the king. The half that turned back was now heading straight for the Travelers who were huddled together under the clump of trees.

"Oh, I wish we had our cloaks," Tahlia cried. They would have come in handy right about now, but those cloaks were long gone, and the Travelers worried that the army would come right for them. They felt only slightly hidden within the clump of trees, but as the army came closer and closer, the Travelers could hear them yelling and chanting loudly.

Even though the king was nearly upon the twins, the Travelers who were huddling together could no longer worry about them. The army was heading straight for the trees in which they were hiding, but there was nowhere else to go.

They'd been spotted.

They were trapped.

Their fate was sealed.

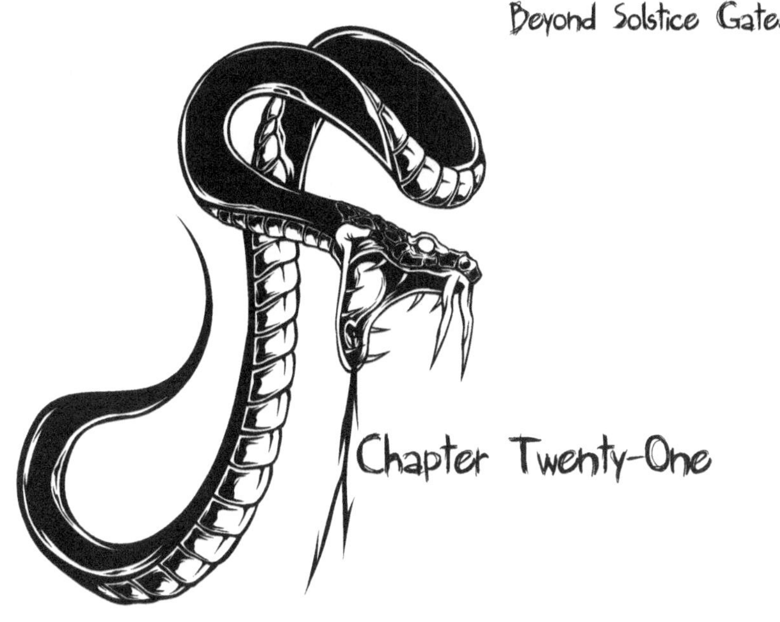

Chapter Twenty-One

Scooped

The lightning was flashing so brightly that it was hard to see much else during those times when it was striking furiously at the ground. There was getting to be less and less of the ground that was still holding together. Nobody could run any longer. Instead, everyone had to jump and step carefully to go around this way and dart quickly over that way.

There was so much to avoid now, between the gurgling fires spitting up from beneath the ground and the critters that covered the undisrupted bits of it. The Travelers could not understand how those black critters were able to ride upon the waves of the roaring fires without getting burned up. It didn't matter; they trampled right on top of those critters since there were far too many of them to step over. The critters who'd taken to the air didn't seem to be concerned with the Travelers, but the Travelers were certainly concerned with them.

Then there was the hail that continued to pelt down from the sky, and the Shailmas—both the Nakahs and the Shamars—that were randomly hurled from the same place. On and on it went; things coming up from below—things coming down from above.

The stars continued exploding, and now, the bloody moon began peeking through a broken bit in the atmosphere. Great drops of blood rained down and splashed onto the land. Those drops that missed the land and fell into the sea of fire sizzled and popped, making the Travelers cover their ears.

Thankfully, all of these horrendous happenings were also slowing the army significantly. The ground was breaking apart for them as well as the Travelers, so in those areas where the Travelers had to move slowly and cautiously, so did the army. This worked against the army more than it interrupted the Travelers because the army was much bigger and heavier.

More than once, and to the Travelers' delight (if any delight in such a deplorable disaster were to be found), when groups of the army would leap over a crack in the ground, it would often give way, pulling many of them into the ferocious, gurgling pit below.

Now, no longer able to hide amongst the uprooted trees, none of the Travelers knew where to look or where to go. They wanted to close their eyes and pretend it was a nightmare, praying that when they opened them again, they'd find themselves back in their homes, tucked safely in their beds.

Of course, they knew differently.

As much as they wanted to look nowhere and see nothing, the happenings all around them demanded they keep their eyes open and pay close attention.

Now it need not be explained that none of them wanted to look toward the twins, yet somehow, the alternative choice was no good either. Looking at the army bearing down on them made their hearts race. Fear replaced the blood that should have been scurrying through their veins. If ever there was a greatness of fear, one that could kill a man, it would be the one that ceased the flowing of blood and replaced it with terror. This was the occurrence happening now to all those watching the army move toward them.

The Travelers could not possibly have seen the twins if they did want to look in that direction. The one-half of the army which the king had sent to retrieve the Travelers was blocking them from seeing beyond their marching. The one-half who had remained with King Shrailzhar was blocking the twins from that side, and so, there was no way the Travelers would be able to find the twins even if they dared to try and look.

After running in circles, this way and that, searching for anywhere else to hide and finding none, the Travelers ended up right back in the group of trees. There was nowhere else to go.

None who huddled closely together under the uprooted trees wanted to look at each other either because the looks on their faces were only mirroring the same fear that was bubbling in their own hearts. It was best not to see such a thing.

There was no escape.

The trees they'd run under to hide in were now blown to and fro by the brawny winds. Those same trees had been shoved so close together that they'd become a prison—there was no way out of their hiding place except straight ahead, which would lead them right into the hands of the approaching army. It seemed as if Trilleah had caused those very trees to become a prison of which the only escape was straight into the hands of the army.

They huddled closer together … if such a thing were possible.

Pierce held the tablet so close to himself that he was nervous he might break it. Nonetheless, if they could not avoid the army, and the king was able to grab the twins, Pierce presumed the tablet would be useless to them anyway; he gripped it tighter.

The army spread out now, forming a semi-circle as they hurried over the last two hundred feet between themselves and the Travelers. They continued to spread outward, likely to surround the trees that were poorly attempting to hide these ones they were after.

If one were to try and run out, the army would be there to stop anyone —and everyone—from escaping.

The chanting of the army was deafening and the Travelers covered their ears and trembled. That was all they could do now; they knew this would be their end. There was no chance of escaping.

"Look," Bella whispered and pointed toward something hovering in the tree beside them.

They all turned their heads to where Bella was pointing. As they did, the Travelers saw that the trees which surrounded them had filled with Trows. They were quiet all right, those miserable soul stealers, and the Travelers were horrified at the number of ghastly creatures that had snuck up and surrounded them.

Undoubtedly, the army was planning to kill the Travelers and had called for the Trows to come and be ready to steal their souls once their last breaths were breathed. If there had been any doubt of such a thing, it was swept away now and heaved into the River of Acheron. This would be their end.

Bella wailed uncontrollably.

Kaija Mae and Tahlia screamed at the sight of the Trows.

The boys tried to remain brave for the girls, but they could not withhold their anguish any longer. They too, let out miserable lamenting wails.

The Travelers looked from the Trows to the army and were surprised to see they'd stopped coming toward them … about twenty or so feet from the thicket of trees those Travelers were cowering in, the army had just stopped. The Travelers looked back to the Trows to find them gone.

"The wind," Sam whispered.

Indeed, the winds had stopped swirling around them, although they could see that the winds carried right on blowing just beyond the trees. They looked around, desperately searching for something that might give them a clue as to what was happening. They found nothing of the sort, of course.

They couldn't see above the trees, which is why they couldn't find what was descending from high above and was yet hidden by the clouds. They could hear a loud *whooooosh* sound, though, like a thousand kites flapping in the wind.

Whooooooosh …

Whooooooosh …

Whooooooosh …

Pierce knew what it was. He'd heard it before and immediately recognized the sound. It was a sound that once heard, would never be forgotten.

"Nehsher," he whispered to himself. Pierce smiled a peaceful smile and loosened up on the tablet. For the first time since being returned to the Travelers by this very eagle, Pierce felt a feeling that he welcomed quickly. Hope. Pierce had hope.

The others did not yet realize what had come to chase away the army, and they couldn't hear Pierce whisper his name, so they just stood trembling, oblivious to what had come but thankful that it did.

If it stopped the army and chased away the Trows, then whatever it was must be on their side.

In the blink of an eye, the army which was so close to the Travelers fell dead … every one of them and all at once, the army dropped to the ground. Many tumbled into the fractures and cracks in the ground, and others were pulled in by the dreadful raging fires below. The Travelers' eyes grew large, and their mouths fell open. They could neither believe, nor comprehend, what they were seeing.

With this vast number of the army dead on the ground, Nehsher came and stood before the Travelers—those ones were so flabbergasted that their breath left them and their bodies were paralyzed. In an instant, they understood why the army—which had only moments ago been coming right at them—had suddenly fallen dead.

"Come," Nehsher spoke in a booming voice.

The sound didn't seem to come from his voice but rather from inside of himself, although it was heard with the Travelers' ears. Regardless, without having to be asked twice or persuaded to go, they sprinted from their hiding place toward the one who'd beckoned them to come.

"Pierce," Bella called out. "You still have the tablet, right?"

"I do," Pierce called back and patted his jacket, which was still hiding the beautiful blue tablet. He had a glowing grin smeared across his face because he was sure that Nehsher would be taking them to a place he'd already been.

All together they scrambled upon Nehsher's back and gripped one another tightly. They assumed that from here, the Great Eagle would head to the twins, retrieving them also.

There was no way the twins would get left behind …

But as Nehsher stretched out his mighty wings and lifted the Travelers from the broken ground, they learned quickly that the twins were no longer on the ground. As the Travelers—perched safely on the back of the one known as Nehsher—ascended ever so gracefully above Trilleah, they saw the most horrific of sights. Jennifer was heavily bound and chained to the king's beast. The Travelers had no way of knowing what had happened to her since the army had blocked them, but they could see now that she'd been synched tightly to the back of this beast and now sat directly behind the king.

The Travelers scanned this way and that, looking, searching desperately for Judah, but they could find him nowhere.

Bella released a blood-curdling wail when her eyes fell upon her niece. Matt held her tightly, but there was nothing that would ease her pain or silence her screams. Bella went quite thoroughly crazy with sorrow and remorse for persuading Simeon to bring Jennifer to Trilleah. She still didn't understand that it was Simeon's choice to bring Jennifer—Bella could never have convinced the Shailma to do any such thing. After all, Shailmas do what Shailmas do without any input from mortals.

She was so positively overtaken with burdensome emotions that she could no longer hold on. If Matt hadn't been holding onto her, Bella would have slipped from the back of Nehsher and truthfully, she wouldn't have minded one bit if she was gobbled up by one of the many open pits in the ground.

It's what I deserve, after all, she told herself.

She had failed Molly and Theo. Bella had promised them that the twins would be safe and now, they were not safe. Not at all. Jennifer was in the very clutches of the evil one and Judah was …

"Where is Judah?" Kaija Mae whispered to Pierce. "I can't see him anywhere," she sobbed. Pierce scanned the ground. Matt scanned the ground. Everyone except Bella did the same, but Judah could not be found by any of them.

None of the Travelers had any idea what had happened to the twins. They had been blocked from seeing any of the happenings by the army that now lay lifeless and scattered across the broken land. Oh, what a horrible sight it was.

It became even worse as the black, rat-sized critters with the scorpion tails crawled all over the army, squeezing inside their helmets and burrowing beneath the breastplates. As those critters continued to scurry up from below the ground, the Travelers were completely horrified by what they were seeing. Kaija Mae began gagging and had to cover her mouth and look away.

Hundreds of thousands of those critters gathered around the army and one by one, they either gnawed at their flesh or carried them away, pulling them down into the pits below. Before very long at all there was very little of the army left scattered across the ground.

With each one that was dragged down to the Sea of Acheron by the black critters, a small explosion would erupt, spewing big clouds of black sulfur and smoke into the air.

As thousands of the critters continued to feast on whatever flesh of the army was exposed, their blood began flowing everywhere. The blood of the army mixed with the blood of the moon, and in an instant, the fires from below crawled up and lapped up every drop of blood. The smell was hideous. The Travelers had to cover their noses to block out as much of the smell as possible, even though they were so high above the horrendous happenings. Even then, it was overwhelmingly sickening.

With the Travelers circling so high above the ground, they could see clearly how little of the land remained intact. There was more of the Sea of Acheron peering through the ground now than there was ground to peer through.

The River of Acheron was wide. It was much wider now than when they had stood at its borders only hours earlier.

Still, no matter where they looked or what they saw, all the Travelers wanted their eyes to find … was Judah. Each one feared that he, too, had been swiped into one of the wide fractures in the ground and where those led to, none of them could let their minds even consider.

Certainly, Judah was somewhere. Surely his Shailma did not allow him to be swept to that unspeakable space below.

No matter how hard the Travelers looked, how greatly they strained their eyes, or how much they begged their Shailmas to let them find the boy, Judah was not to be found by any of them.

Unfortunately, Nehsher had not plucked Judah from the ground, but neither had King Shrailzhar been able to grab him. That wicked and dark king had been more interested in capturing his sister, so when he had to make a choice between Judah or Jennifer, he scooped up Jennifer and let Judah go free.

Chapter Twenty-Two

Seeds of Knowing

Judah was mortified.

He had run and run and run until he couldn't take another step. Now he found himself right back on the banks of the River of Acheron. He was overwhelmed with remorse. Heavy and unspeakable guilt burned his lungs, and he wished he could somehow shed his skin. The boy could not believe that he'd chosen to let go of his sister's hand. He was appalled and thoroughly disgusted with himself.

"How could you do such a thing?" he screamed into the atmosphere to himself. The wind mocked him viciously and carried his words right back to him, punching him in the face like a hard fist.

The choice didn't seem to be his alone, yet it must have been. After all, it was *his* hand that was holding so tightly to his sister's, and *his* hand that opened to release that small, fragile one belonging to Jennifer.

Even though she'd been screaming for him to "HANG ONTO ME, JUDAH," and all the while Jennifer had been gripping him so hard it had left cuts in his skin where her fingernails had dug in, he had to let go. He didn't know why but now Judah demanded answers from Shemaiah. Outrage overtook him, and he screamed at the top of his lungs.

"Why could I not go in her place?"

He was stamping his feet and ripping at his jacket. A button flung off before he finally let go and slumped to his knees. Oh, how he wanted to throw himself into the Sea of Acheron.

It was right in front of him, calling his name.

He pondered it for a time, off and on.

"I begged you to let the king take me instead! Why did it have to be her? Why Jennifer?"

He didn't dare look into the flames in case he saw his sister's face among them. He couldn't bear it! Judah was sure that King Shrailzhar would immediately take off her head and have the Trows drag her soul to the Sea of Acheron. If he had only known the deplorable beast-infested dungeon and the hideously evil plans that Shrailzhar did have for the girl, oh, Judah would have longed to find her face among the flames.

Of course, he had no way of knowing such things, but if he did …

Shemaiah didn't answer the boy … not yet. Judah had to scream and yell and holler and wail. He needed to flail about and let all that rage boiling in his heart drain out. One cannot keep such rage in their hearts, lest it destroys their very souls, so Shemaiah and the one dozen Shamars his Shailma had with him, stood by quietly, waiting for Judah to plummet in exhaustion.

They did not need to wait long. The boy had let such enormous and outrageous pain overtake his soul that it nearly did him in entirely. Just as he wobbled and was about to fall on his face, Shemaiah showed up in front of him—visible to Judah's eyes. His Shailma appeared and stood directly between the boy and Acheron.

There had only been one other time when Shemaiah had appeared to Judah's eyes and that was when the two of them had to outrun the Nakahs which the king had ordered to stand guard around the gates of Solstice to trap the Travelers. Because Shemaiah was the fastest of the Shamars, it was up to him to distract the Nakahs while the other Shailmas delivered their mortals to Asphelia's Hollow.

Judah had learned much during that time, and even now his mind flashed back to when he heard Shemaiah ask him the dreadful question.

"Do you trust me, Judah?"

Of course, he trusted his Shailma. The instant Judah said he did, Shemaiah turned and drove straight into the Nakahs—scattering them. Judah had often wondered what might have happened if he would not have trusted his Shailma. He wondered briefly now if he could still trust Shemaiah, despite such horror.

"Judah," Shemaiah spoke directly to the boy now. "It was necessary that you let her go and trust Simeon to look after her. I know it seems that King Shrailzhar has her, but you must trust what you know, not what you see; you must go by faith, not by sight. The Shailmas are so much more than you can understand, Judah. We get our orders from One much higher than ourselves … One you have not yet known."

Judah laid on the ground in a heap, unable to move, but he listened carefully. He was desperate to hear something that would make sense, something that might make any of this a bit less painful, but so far he heard what sounded like nonsense—pure gibberish.

Shemaiah could still hear the boy's thoughts even though the Shailma made himself visible to Judah's eyes. It made no difference whether Judah could see him or not, Shemaiah could hear what went on in his mind nonetheless. The Shailma didn't like what he was hearing, but such a heavy weight of doubt was to be expected, for Judah had indeed witnessed a deplorably heart-wrenching event.

"Judah," Shemaiah said firmly. "She was not yours to hold on to; she never was. A trade needed to be made—one soul for many;

Jennifer was that one soul. She was born to be that one, Judah. Everything that has ever been and will ever be, is not by mere coincidence or happenstance, but intricately planned out. It's like an orchestra playing a piece so perfectly that it sounds as if the entire song is played by only one."

This only served to anger Judah all the more, and he demanded that his Shailma stop talking. Now, Shailmas have no need to obey their mortals and so Shemaiah kept right on explaining the unexplainable. Judah covered his head trying to tune out the words, but one can only close off their ears, not their mind—Shemaiah could plant his words in either place. When Judah shut off his ears, the Shailma continued right on in the boy's mind.

You knew from the beginning that Jennifer was needed in Trilleah to break the curse, and you were completely aware that the clay tablets were only part of the requirement. What did you think she was needed for, exactly? Shemaiah asked.

"But I didn't realize that Jennifer would have to be THAT sacrifice. I didn't know that it would be one of us!" Judah shouted.

What did you assume it might be, then? Shemaiah asked earnestly, although he already knew the answer, as he always did before he asked any question. The questions needed to be asked nonetheless so that Judah would consider such things and find the answers for himself."

He did.

Judah thought and wondered and pondered while he continued to lay in a heap on the ground—with his head covered—right beside the ravaging Acheron. The land around him was terrible and growing worse by the minute, but Shemaiah had momentarily veiled the space around Judah so he would be undisturbed by the forces trying to persuade him to throw himself into the River of Acheron.

Those voices rang out, nonetheless, even though Judah could not hear them.

"Judah …" they called. "You can never live with such heartache … such regret …" they taunted. "Look at what you've done!" they accused. "You can never fix it, never change it, never reverse it." Judah's ears were burning, as though something sharp was biting at them, and he kept flicking them. Nothing was biting him at all; it was simply the barbs of those sharp words poking and prodding at his ears.

The dozen Shamar Shailmas had their work cut out for them. The king had sent many of his own Nakah Warriors to taunt and tempt Judah to throw himself into the Sea of Acheron.

That wicked king knew the Shamars would be there to protect the boy, so his only hope to end Judah was if he threw himself into the sea. Shrailzhar knew that his useless army would never be able to capture the boy. That was, of course, why there were a dozen Shamars there.

They battled on and on, the Shamar Shailmas swatting down every word the Nakahs threw toward Judah. If even one got through to his ears, it would be enough to cause the poor boy to toss himself into the sea.

"*Judah*," Shemaiah said. "*Get up, my boy.*"

Judah did not get up because his strength was long gone. The Travelers hadn't eaten in what seemed like days. He was so hungry but so much worse than that—he was broken. Inside, he was thoroughly, and altogether, destroyed.

"Judah, get up," Shemaiah said again, this time to his ears.

"I cannot," the boy muttered. "There is nothing to get up for," he wailed. "Mamma and Daddy are gone, and now my Jelly Bean is gone. I was supposed to protect her. I should have kept her safe and I didn't," he screamed. "I gave her to that wicked king! I handed her right over to him."

"One soul exchanged for many," Judah heard.

It was evident that Shemaiah was not going to get through to Judah, so he called upon someone who would.

"Judah," the boy heard and instantly, the boy sat up. His eyes were opened wide now, and he stared at the flames dancing in front of him.

"Judah, my son, she was not yours to keep. There is more for you to do, now get up and listen to Shemaiah."

"But Mamma," Judah wailed even harder now, hearing the voice of his mother and knowing she was aware of Judah's most brutal of failures. *How did she know?* Judah wondered. *Surely, Jennifer must be in there too, in the River of Acheron, if Mamma knows,* he thought. Her soul must already have been cursed to that wicked place.

Now things are never as they appear, and so that was not the case at all. Jennifer was not in the River of Acheron as her brother had assumed; not yet. Judah forgot for the time being just how much power the Shailmas had, so he never even considered that perhaps it was Shemaiah who had told his mother what he'd done.

Regardless of how she knew, Mamma did know, and she had told Judah to listen to Shemaiah. So that was what he would do. For once, he would listen to Mamma. With any hope left, it would not be too late.

Judah sniffled and wiped his eyes with the back of his torn and tattered sleeves. He wiped his nose with the back of his hands and that boy gathered all the courage he could find, and stood himself up. He had a glimmer of hope that perhaps if he did what Shemaiah required of him, that somehow Jennifer would be okay. Maybe he could trade places with her. He was going to try. If one soul had to be sacrificed for the freedom of the rest, then he would do all he could to make sure that one soul was his own or at least, not his sister's.

It was far too late, however, for any of that. This was just the way it was meant to be, which is why it was of such great importance that Jennifer was brought to Trilleah in the first place. While Judah assumed such things were in his power, he was wrong … so wrong.

Such things were never in his power, and never in Bella's power, either.

While Bella thought it was her gut urging her to bring Jennifer, it was far more than her gut. It was so much more than just a stirring in her belly; it was Shura. Shura had not said the words to her mind, as the Shailmas normally did, but instead, he had planted the idea way down deep in her belly a long time before it ever worked its way up to her mind.

When there was something of great importance that would be needed in the future, something that was going to be very difficult or take great courage, the Shailmas would plant the idea—like a tiny seed—in the belly of the one who needed to grow it.

After a time of growing and being watered by the Shailmas with other thoughts and wonderings and ideas, then the mortal would finally think to themselves, "I don't know why, but I feel that something or other must be done about such and such."

That was how it was with so many things that the mortals thought were their own ideas. Even though they couldn't explain the idea and often would admit they didn't know where it came from, they knew that it must take place. There was just that "knowing."

That was exactly what Bella had said time and time again about bringing Jennifer to Trilleah.

Each time she had mentioned it to Pierce or Matt … and especially to Judah … they would argue with her saying she was too fragile—just a brokenhearted orphaned girl—and remind Bella how useless Jennifer would be here in Trilleah. Bella listened the first few times carefully and agreed completely. But the "knowing" would not fade, so she began answering their arguments by saying, "I can't explain it but there's something, some reason she needs to be here. I just know it."

And indeed, there was, but it had never been Bella's idea. That was just how the Shailmas worked.

Keep in mind, it was never the Shailmas who came up with such ideas or laid out such plans or created such seeds of wisdom. It was the Nameless One. He was in charge of all things that went on. The Shailmas received their power and their instructions from that One.

When a new soul would come to the earth in the form of a baby, that Nameless One would choose the perfect Shailma and send him to watch over that new mortal.

That child would never take a breath … or think a thought … or have an idea … without their Shailma being there and knowing it fully. It would be the Shailma of that new mortal who'd plant the seeds from the Nameless One so that in due season, those seeds would grow into whatever they needed to be. So it was on the day that Judah and Jennifer took their first breaths. Shemaiah had been assigned to Judah and Simeon to Jennifer.

Jennifer's entire life had been for this very purpose, even though she did not know it. How could she? How could she have known that she would be required to sacrifice her own soul to buy the freedom of every other soul ever stolen by those dreadful Trows?

How was she to understand how high a price she'd need to pay for the freedom of the souls of those she loved dearly—and countless others whom she'd never even known?

Chapter Twenty-Three

Heights Above

The Travelers hung on to Nehsher, but they clung even more tightly to each other. They had no idea where there were going, if anywhere at all. All they had to go on was Pierce's recollection of where this same Great Eagle had taken him. However, at the time, Pierce had been so badly wounded—and frozen thoroughly with fear—that he hadn't paid attention to the path of this mighty flying rescuer.

Regardless, being on the back of Nehsher was far better than where they had just come from. The Travelers were certain that the army was going to remove their heads and order the Trows to toss their souls into Acheron. As they remembered such things, they were each deeply grateful for this monstrous eagle that had plucked them from their impending doom.

The ground was far below them now. The Travelers' eyes could no longer see any remains of the dead army or the black critters, and even King Shrailzhar and Jennifer had disappeared from their sight. All that remained visible at such great heights was the bright orange Lake of Acheron. Even the places where the ground had been badly fractured and the gurgling bits of fire from below spouted, were now covered over with sulfur and smoke.

The winds had died down considerably. Nehsher had finally risen above the hail, and even the lightning was now far below. It seemed eerily calm where they were, but above them, the War of the Firmament continued to rage. The Travelers were so close to the war now that they could feel the stirring in the air and smell the horrible scent of blood and death as the warriors continued to battle … and fall.

There were far less Shailmas fighting now, though, as countless numbers of the Nakah Warriors had been overtaken and were either captured or beheaded. Both the Nakah Warriors and Shamar Shailmas continued to plummet to the ground below, but fewer and fewer were falling as time marched on. The Shamars were doubling the numbers of Nakahs now, and it was looking like the war would soon be over. Nevertheless, the Travelers could see that they were about to be carried right through the middle of it all—unless this one called Nehsher changed directions quickly. There didn't seem to be anywhere else for him to go, however, so they dug down, held on, and prepared for the worst.

"It won't be long now," Pierce said and pointed above. Bella's eyes grew large, and she gripped Matt's arm tighter.

"We're going there?" she wailed.

"I have no idea," Matt replied. Pierce, of course, knew the way, and he spoke up.

"We will go straight through the war, yes," he answered, "because where we are going is beyond the firmament. Don't fret, though, Bella," he smiled. "Nehsher knows the way of safety, and he will carry us through."

Well, this jibber-jabbering made no sense to anyone else, but Pierce had come this way before, so it only seemed reasonable that if he was not afraid, then they need not be afraid either.

The eyes of the Travelers took in sights they could never imagine if they didn't see it for themselves. Even with their eyes drinking it all in, it was impossible to believe.

Many of the Shamar Shailmas pulled themselves away from the war and immediately surrounded Nehsher. They gracefully formed a type of funnel in the air for Nehsher to travel through. It was evident to every eye watching this graceful dance between the firmament and Nehsher, that the Shamars had done this many times before now. This was not the first time the Great Eagle had made this journey—that much was obvious.

There was no way even one Nakah could squeeze through such a wall of Shamars and for just a moment or two, the Travelers set their fears down and gawked at what was surrounding them. They were awestruck. Nobody whispered or uttered even a sound as they ascended through the tunnel of Shamars.

The light was pure in that tunnel. Not in all of Trilleah had the Travelers seen such light and even now when they did, they had to shield their eyes a bit as the brightness of it stung. Still, they managed to peek out a little, and when they did, they saw as they were on the back of Nehsher, the Shamars opened their mouths and were spewing forth great and unimaginably pure light.

The higher Nehsher flew, the more powerful the light became. Eventually, the Travelers were forced by the brightness to not only cover their eyes but shut them tightly *and* cover them firmly. There would be no more peeking until the light dimmed.

Nehsher swooped this way and that, up through the atmosphere. That magnificent creature rose passed where the stars had been hiding, and right by the moon—which was carefully balancing a full measure of blood. They spiraled straight up through the incredible light and finally ascended through the smallest of holes in the heavens. They hadn't even noticed the opening until they had passed through it.

Never had any of the Travelers—except Pierce and Kaija Mae, of course—even considered that there was so much more to Trilleah then they could imagine. But indeed there was. It went on and on endlessly. From this great height, their eyes could not find one end of Trilleah from another. It went beyond what they could see in every direction.

It felt to the Travelers, who were trying to hold onto Bella, that this was taking far too long. Their arms were getting tired from keeping her upright. Once in awhile, one Traveler or another would shake her a little to try and get her to hold some of her own weight. Nonetheless, they held onto her tightly.

"Maybe we're not going anywhere at all," Matt said.

"Maybe this is all one big joke," Sam added. "Maybe this eagle is going to take us to the highest of highs and throw us down!" Even though they'd all seen the tunnel of light they had just passed through, fear still trembled a little, deep down in their souls. They were battling the same thoughts that Pierce had wondered about when Nehsher had taken him through the tunnel of light earlier.

Now, Pierce smiled and nodded. He knew differently, but he also was aware that his words would never convince them; only seeing such things for themselves would make them believe. "You won't believe it even if I were to tell you," he whispered. There was no need for shouting or screaming or hand signals up here—so high above everything—because it was quiet … not an eery quiet like those six minutes in Trilleah, but a peaceful overwhelming sort of quiet.

The only sound heard was the *swooooosh* of Nehsher's wings as they occasionally rippled through the air, stirring it up. Every *swoooooosh* was followed by a long period of complete silence as the eagle's massive wings caught the air and drifted effortlessly upon it.

Pierce finally spoke up and broke through the hushed quiet. The boy was filling with excitement at knowing he was about to stand before the Nameless One again, and he couldn't keep it inside any longer. He felt thoroughly intoxicated with excitement for himself … but also for the others who had not yet experienced this One they were about to see.

"We are going THERE! You won't believe it even when you see it," he laughed. "It will overwhelm you more than you can imagine …" Nobody else was laughing, and none of the others caught even a glint of his excitement. Of course not. How could they? They had no idea what they were about to experience. They had no way of knowing that the One whom they were about to stand before would remove every ounce of pain or sliver of sorrow or shred of shame they'd ever felt.

They could not understand yet, how standing before the Nameless One would be a thousand times more peaceful than the Chamber of Rest. They had experienced that chamber and the pureness of its air and the peacefulness held in the brilliant walls, and they were thoroughly convinced that nothing—absolutely nothing—could compare to it, let alone outdo it by a thousand.

Those Travelers would find out soon enough, though, because Pierce caught a glimpse of something that felt familiar to him. He didn't remember it specifically, probably because of the state he was in the last time Nehsher had carried him to this place. Nevertheless, it felt like he'd seen it before and indeed, he had.

Just ahead of them, only a few feet now, was the veil. Not a veil that was unseen to the eye like earlier when the shelter was veiled in the atmosphere. Not a veil to cover the eyes of the king or his miserable army from finding the Travelers. No, nothing like those veils.

This veil was to keep the Nameless One from showing his power to all of Trilleah. This veil was created and suspended by the Nameless One Himself. If not for this veil that separated that One of all Light from the land and the king and his army, the sheer power and pureness from the Nameless One would have purified the entire land in one breath; and that was not to be.

You see, King Shrailzhar and his army and even the Nakah Warriors would never be allowed to enter the presence of the Nameless One. Not now … not ever again. That place—beyond the veil—was exactly from where the horrible king and his army had come.

There had been a day, long before any other day, where King Shrailzhar had dwelt with the Nameless One. The army which now marched with that dreadful king had once marched alongside the armies of the Nameless One and indeed, those armies were enormous. There was more than any eye could take in and their power was mighty—shadowed by only the Nameless One Himself.

The problem, of course, came when King Shrailzhar, who the Nameless One had made mighty in His kingdom, had become jealous and unsatisfied. He schemed instead to be greater than the One who had called him to be great in the first place. Of course, nobody is greater than their master and no created being better than their Creator, and so, the Nameless One could not allow such a thing to take place in His Kingdom.

That One who had existed before any other, that Uncreated Being of all power and authority both in His Kingdom and in Trilleah, would not give up, nor share His throne and so, King Shrailzhar was thrown down from his position of greatness and power that he'd been freely given.

Shrailzhar was banished from this place where he was second in command only to the Nameless One Himself, and sent to Trilleah for a time. Now that time had nearly run out. The sands had run through the hourglass, and only a few grains remained.

King Shrailzhar had convinced one-third of all the Shailmas to come with him to Trilleah, promising them they would set up their own kingdom. He deceived them into believing they would be far more powerful than the Shailmas who remained with the Nameless One.

That wretched king had other plans completely, with one goal in mind. He would make Trilleah his kingdom and steal the souls of those very ones whom the Nameless One had called as His own. King Shrailzhar would seize them as they were on their way to the Nameless One, and make sure they would never arrive.

Yes, that miserable Shrailzhar had one goal; to end the Kingdom of the Nameless One or, at least, make it as small as possible, which meant his own kingdom would be bigger. You see, that place where the Nameless One dwelt was filled with unimaginable beauty and unthought of colors. Its air was so pure that it could not be explained and even to this day, no words have been created to explain such things that are found there. Shrailzhar was livid about having to leave it. Trilleah had no color and the air was putrid. These were some of the reasons he was such a wretched and jealous king, so his entire focus became stealing all those who didn't belong to him so the One of whom he was jealous could not have them.

What a beast.

What a wretch.

What a fiend indeed.

Because of this very thing that Shrailzhar had done, the Nameless One suspended an impenetrable veil between His Kingdom and that of Shrailzhar to make sure that wretched Shrailzhar would never re-enter the very place where he once had full access.

Of course, by suspending such a veil to keep King Shrailzhar out, it also kept the others out—those whom the Nameless One longed to have enter into His Kingdom. Having the veil separate those souls whom the Nameless One loved so dearly, from Himself, broke his heart every second of every day. The Nameless One had to make a new way for all those who belonged to Him to have access to the other side of the veil.

Yes, that veil would have to be destroyed soon.

If that dreadful curse was ever broken—the one that was keeping the souls of the very ones the Nameless One longed to have in His Kingdom—the veil would come down. He would make sure of it because He would take His own hands and tear it in two.

That time was not yet, though, and the veil would remain firmly in place for a while longer—until that hideous curse was broken once and for all.

There was still much work to be done in Trilleah. A sacrifice was still needed—that was the only way to release the souls. The Travelers would soon be given the keys from the tablet, and they would successfully break the curse. Unfortunately, that would only release the souls from the curse. They would still need to be freed from the Rivers of Acheron which was surrounded by an impassible chasm. If the sacrifice was made—and oh what a wretched sacrifice it would be—then the chasm would not be too deep, and the souls could be saved.

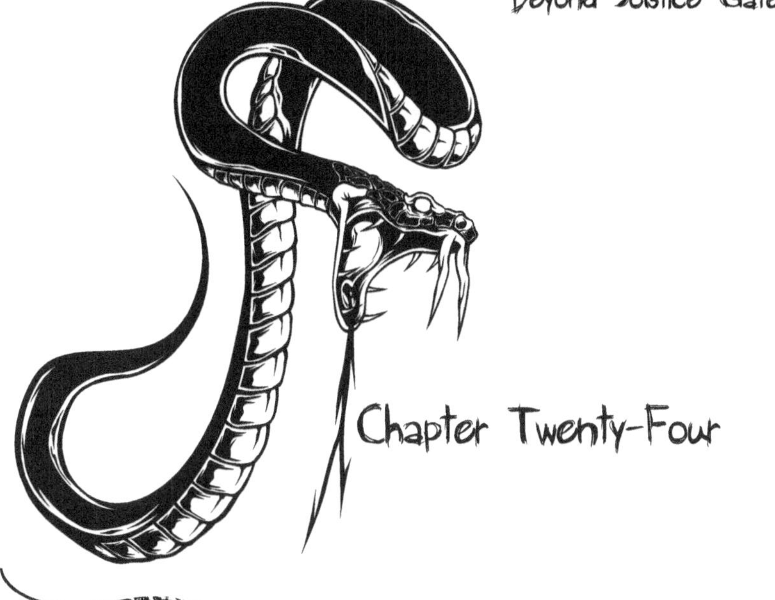

Chapter Twenty-Four

PrincessWarrior

Jennifer sat wide-eyed and trembling behind King Shrailzhar. She was so tiny compared to the huge king; she had not noticed his enormous size when she'd seen him in the adder's pit.

Her soul begged her eyes to close, but they refused. Nothing inside of her wanted to see what was going on, yet she could not force her eyes to close. It was doubtful if she was even blinking. Those big brown eyes watered fiercely, but she wasn't sure if it was because they were stuck open or if the sulfur and smoke from the Dark Land were burning them. Whatever the reason, it felt like a hundred razor blades were slicing them; even still, her eyes refused to close. Her wrists were throbbing and she could feel the chains cutting sharply into her skin.

Throw yourself down from the beast, she heard a dark voice whisper. There were so many voices in her head right at this moment that she couldn't tell which was which. *You will lose your head soon,* sang out another tune from the choir of dark voices pelting her mind, *then your soul will be one of many that are filling the River of Acheron.*

Just lean your weight over to the side and let your body topple down. Perhaps the beast or the army behind will trample you and put you out of your misery.

Oh, the voices pounded her mind so hard that she was tempted to do any one of those things they were suggesting … just to silence them.

They were driving her mad! If her body was to be beaten or severed from her head, or if her blood was to be poured out on the ground and her soul thrown into Acheron, at least she wanted to keep her mind quiet until that last moment. She had to find a way to silence the unharmonious evil voices that kept squawking off-key and ricocheting in her mind.

Jennifer couldn't deny that the king had finally got what he wanted. What he had wanted all this time was her. She understood that now … now that it was too late. As her mind wandered back through all the journeys; it seemed clear that what this dreadful and despicable king had wanted all this time, was Jennifer.

Well, you have me now you disgusting dog, she wanted to scream out, but of course, she didn't.

Instead, she searched for Simeon. He had never let her down before, even though it seemed many times as though he would. Every time Jennifer had thought her Shailma had abandoned her, he would show up right on time and rescue her. Surely this time would be no different. Surely he'd not leave her now, would he?

Then again, she'd never been in the clutches of King Shrailzhar before. Maybe this was the time, that one time when Simeon would fail her. Maybe he was supposed to have rescued her before the king could grab her but had failed somehow, and now it was too late. Could it be?

As much as Jennifer tried to stay calm, as much as she repeated to herself that Simeon would never leave her, never abandon her, maybe he had lied. He was after all, mostly unseen to her. Trusting something that one could rarely—if ever—see for such a time as dreadful as this one was a bit much to expect, was it not?

Where was Simeon now? Jennifer couldn't hear him, although she continued to call his name and search for him with furious desperation. There was no way to tell where this dreadful king was taking her or what horror waited for her once they arrived.

"Why me?" Jennifer sobbed. It was obvious that Shrailzhar wanted her specifically. She'd questioned it a few times before, but now, after what she had just seen, it was apparent that it was her blood he'd been after all this time. Now he was about to have it. He would take it from her; there was nothing she could do to stop him.

Jennifer didn't realize that she'd been wailing outside of her mind instead of inside the privacy of her head, but when the king suddenly stopped his beast and halted the army, Jennifer knew her voice had somehow found its way into the putrid air.

"Why you?" the king wailed. He unhooked the chains that kept Jennifer connected to him and jumped down from his beast. He turned to look at the terrified girl—face to face. He was so big that he could look straight into her eyes with his feet on the ground while she remained propped up on the beast.

Shrailzhar threw his head back and laughed heinously. He moved in close to her—so close that she could smell his breath and it made her gag violently. It reminded her very much of the smell of death she remembered from the adder's pit. Oh, he was such a snake indeed. He belonged in that pit and nowhere else. Without thinking, she spit in his face. Most of his gruesome face was covered by his helmet, but there was a space cut out for his mouth and another for his eyes, so she made good and sure to aim perfectly.

Thwack!

The ball of spit landed square in his eye, enraging the king a thousand times more than he was already enraged.

He thought this little one would be terrified of him—that she'd cower in his presence. The king was terribly wrong, for even though he knew *about* Jennifer, he did not *know* her. By the time the king realized what had hit him in the eye—what this very foolish girl had done—she'd tossed one leg over the enormous black beast and had hurled herself to the ground.

Her arms were still chained behind her back, and she hit her face in the dirt as she fell. She jumped up and ran nonetheless. There was no doubt in her mind that the king, or one of his foolish army idiots, would catch her in no time, but she was surely going to try.

You see, all the experiences she'd had in Trilleah up until this very moment had made her strong. Jennifer had first come to the Dark Land fearful and weak, but after so many journeys and so much trauma and tragedy and calamity, she was no longer that weak little girl. She was courageously strong, hopeful, and willfully determined.

Now Jennifer turned her fear into anger, and she ran—fast. She didn't look at the ground nor did she watch behind her, but kept her eyes straight ahead and let her feet carry her forward. If she were to step into a crevice in the ground and tumble into the sea gurgling below, at least she would not die at the hands of the king. If she could take that away from him, then so be it. Part of her wanted to fall into the fiery sea below, but her feet refused to take those steps. As if someone else entirely was controlling her feet, they continued choosing the stable pieces of ground—which were few and far between, even when she willed them to carry her into the chasm.

It had taken only a few seconds before she felt a sharp pain ripple through her body as she was lifted from the ground by her hair.

"Going somewhere, Jenniferrrrr?" She had heard that disgusting voice before—that one that made her blood curdle. She was not surprised when the soldiers who'd grabbed her swung her around and she found herself looking right into the face of the king. But it was not the king from whom she'd heard the voice come from before; it was the adders.

Jennifer hung, suspended between the two soldiers, and kicked her feet wildly, hoping to force the soldiers to drop her. Instead, she watched as the king stepped closer and snarled in her face like a rabid dog. Yellow slime flew from his mouth and hung from his blackened teeth. What the little one noticed as she was trying to get out of the way of whatever he was spewing, made her fill with terror … her blood curdled in her veins the same way it did the first time she'd ever heard that voice.

As Shrailzhar opened his mouth, her eyes caught sight of a black adder … it was slithering where his tongue should have been. It was thoroughly disgusting, but it explained the smell of his breath … and the voice. The black adder's voice had come right from the king's mouth for that, she now learned, was where the black adders came from.

Jennifer remembered the smell and it made her stomach turn viciously. Without expecting it or having any warning at all, she threw up. It seemed odd, since she'd not eaten in quite a while, that she had anything in her stomach to hurl out. But as the king screamed at the soldiers to throw her back on top of the beast and chain her there, it was evident that something had been hiding in her stomach. The king was not appreciating having it run down the inside of his helmet, and he cursed loudly.

In an instant, the chains around her wrists tightened, and she felt blood trickle down her hands and drip from the ends of her fingers. She was viciously hurled back to the top of the smelly black beast and felt shackles slap around her ankles. There was a chain that was strung from one ankle to the other under the belly of the beast. There would be no more jumping down and if she toppled over or slipped, she would be dragged under the belly of this beast and surely meet her death there. Jennifer suddenly regretted very much what she'd done to anger the king.

"Back to your question, Jenniferrrr Lilllllllian Elllllliot," King Shrailzhar sneered. "Why you, you ask? YOU are the one whose blood I have needed since the day you were born!"

"HOW DO YOU KNOW MY NAME AND HOW DO YOU KNOW ANYTHING ABOUT THE DAY I WAS BORN?" she screamed. Her rage outweighed her fear now, as she continued to scream at the king.

"You know nothing of what I know … or where I have been … or what I have seen," the king snarled right back. "I will tell you this; I know you … I always have!"

It must have been perfectly easy to be brave and snarl like an animal, she supposed, when he had his stupid army chain her wrists and shackle her feet. Oh, how she wanted to tell him what an inadequate excuse for a king he was and just how altogether pathetic he must be to have his army chain such a small girl, but she remained quiet. For one enormous king to need an entire army to capture and hold such a small, frail girl—a mere child—seemed outrageous and hideously unfair. Nonetheless, that was what it had taken for him to get what he needed, which was apparently her blood.

Well, he did not have her blood yet!

"I've had my eye on you since the day Molly spit you out of her despicable womb," the king roared with hideous laughter.

Jennifer's heart stopped beating. Her blood turned cold. Her skin began to sweat. The king had said her mamma's name. How did he know such things as her mamma's name? She was horrified and choked on her own breath.

"YOU DON'T KNOW MY MAMMA," Jennifer wailed.

"Oh, but I do." he smiled. That king was excited that he'd finally found an opportunity to tell this one how he'd seen her at her birth. How he'd waited for her as she took that first breath and how he knew she would be the one to come to Trilleah—to his kingdom—all in a useless attempt to free the souls of the Waiting Ones. He took delight in knowing he would be responsible for her last breath.

"Oh, but I could not let that happen now, could I?" he wailed again.

It was evident that he was enjoying this, mostly because the look on Jennifer's face was more terrified, more angry, more wretched than he'd even dreamed about … and he told her so.

"I sent one of my greatest Nakah Warriors to watch you, and that one has been watching you ever since. Not one breath has gone into—or come out of—your lungs that my Nakah has not seen." Now Jennifer was panicking greatly because it seemed that she had been mistaken all this time.

She thought only Simeon had been with her since that day she was given life, but now, if King Shrailzhar was telling the truth, Simeon was not the only one who'd been with her. She suddenly understood many things that she wished she had no understanding of at all. Jennifer searched for her Shailma again now, wanting to have him come and comfort her or give her truth or rescue her from such a beast as this one in front of her. She recalled how Simeon had grabbed her from the dragon's nest in the adder's pit and wondered if he'd do the same now … at any moment …

Maybe the king is lying. Of course, he's lying! How could he not be lying? But then again, how does he know Mamma? How does he know her name? How does he know mine?

Jennifer went back and forth on this one thing, praying he was lying but knowing in the deepest part of her belly that he wasn't.

Little One, came the sweetest of sounds to her soul. *He is speaking truth. You have never been weak or frail, like everyone—including yourself—had thought. Jennifer, from the very day you were born, there was a great purpose and a plan for you. You were born a princess and trained to be a warrior and the time has finally come for you to go to war.*

The souls in Trilleah were getting to be so many that someone had to come along to free them; that one is you. It has always been you, and the king knew it. All of your life, when I have been with you, there was also a Nakah with you.

Every time you heard lies, it was from that one. Each time horrible dreams would fill your sleep—or nightmares would overshadow your days—it was that one who was putting them in your mind. I've been battling that Nakah your entire life. Sometimes, when you've had to wait for an answer and would become angry with me for not answering when you thought I should, it was because I was battling that Nakah on your behalf.

That one wanted to fill your mind with such lies—and your heart with such fear—that you would never come to Trilleah. I had to constantly battle with him so you would hear truth, learn how to overcome fear, combat the lies that did slip through.

Jennifer, there is much you have never known and I have tried to keep you from ever needing to know them, but I see that the time has come for you to know all such things.

You will know the story of your being, and what really happened to your mamma and daddy, and the purpose of your being here in Trilleah. There is so much that has been covered from your eyes—hidden from your heart—but the time has come to open your eyes to see, and your ears to hear, and your heart to know all that I have kept from you, for your own good, until this very day.

Chapter Twenty-Five

Who Can Stand

From the moment Nehsher crossed the threshold of the veil that was suspended in the uppermost part of the heavens, the Travelers were awestruck. An overwhelming, consuming peace wrapped itself around them, and they had no idea they were about to meet the One they'd heard about as Nameless. These Travelers were about to find out that this one did indeed have a name—many names—unutterable names.

It was just as Pierce had described it, except he'd left out so much—likely was there was no way to describe such things. No one uttered a word; not even a sound escaped their lips. They were amazed—overwhelmed—by such greatness that they'd not even fully seen yet. They were only seeing in part for now, but the fullness of power they were about to experience would be without description; all the words ever uttered over all of time would not be enough to describe the indescribable One their eyes were about to look upon.

In moments, Nehsher settled down gently, and the Travelers found themselves standing before this One of all Light of whom they had heard. They tried to stand—really they did—but like Pierce had said, such heavy guilt and weights of shame overwhelmed them that as they tried to stand before that One, they were unable to. Instead, they found themselves on their knees with their faces in the … what was it their faces were in, exactly? All at once, they looked around, trying to drink in all they could.

There was no dirt here, no rubble or dust or ground whatsoever. Instead, they found themselves kneeling on something similar to what was in the Chamber of Rest. It was as clear as crystal and glimmered with unimaginable colors; colors that had no names because they'd never before been seen. Unlike the chamber back in Asphelia's Hollow, however, whatever they were kneeling on was not hard on their knees.

Whatever it was, the Travelers could see into it, but not through it—like a sea of perfect clarity yet unending depth. The unnamed colors sparkled and danced as they bounced off the light which penetrated the entire realm of space.

It felt like perfection—if anyone could describe what perfection might feel like. Without any explanation or description at all, the Travelers were experiencing perfection; there was no imperfection or flaw or blemish here. They bent over and put their faces down, nearly on top of their knees, and covered their heads.

They were not afraid—not at all. But like Pierce had said, every terrible thing they'd ever done, or thought, or wondered, flooded into their memory in one instant, and they covered their heads in shame. Every hateful thought or little white lie or the few candies they'd stolen from Mr. Kinyak's corner store, or the weird kid who they pushed down and treated poorly in second grade, suddenly filled their souls with burdensome sadness and shame and nauseating regret. It was heavy … it was deplorable … they wanted to hide.

It was as though every second of their lives had been put under this powerful microscope and when the switch was flipped on, everything was fully exposed. What a horribly painful thing it is to see one's own filth, fully exposed and on display.

Those flashes of their soiled past took no more than a second, although it seemed like a movie that rolled on for hours. Then, from nowhere yet from everywhere, a voice rang out. Pierce had tried to explain it to them, but he had said over and over again that there were no words to explain such a voice. Now that they heard it for themselves, they knew what he meant, and they knew to whom the voice belonged.

"Stand up," the voice said. It was loud and powerful but fully peaceful and altogether loving. "You have been redeemed."

They stood. Every one of those stooped down Travelers stood and immediately noticed that Pierce had been standing the entire time.

"How could you stand, Pierce?" Bella whispered to him. "Didn't you feel that filthy heaviness push you to your knees?"

Pierce chuckled. "Oh, Bella, not at all."

"Why not?" she asked. The others were listening intently to Pierce's answers, surprised that either of them could speak at all in the presence of this One who was before them.

"Because I have been redeemed," was his answer.

Now, one might not think that such conversations would be acceptable when standing before the One of all Light, but in fact, it was that very One who set up this exact conversation. It was that One who wanted the others to know that once they were redeemed, they could stand in His presence. It was that One who wanted the Travelers to understand that only one time was such a cleansing required. Once the Travelers were cleansed, once they'd been redeemed by this One of all Light, they were free—eternally pure—redeemed.

Each one was completely free to stand before Him and be welcomed and accepted in His presence. It only took one cleansing, and as Pierce had stood while the others felt pressured and weighted down, that lesson became clear to them all.

"The Nameless One has redeemed you," Pierce beamed. "You can stand before Him free of any shame or guilt. You can experience freedom from all of that and live the way we were meant to live!" The Shailmas began explaining to their mortals that they were no longer Travelers, for they had arrived at their destination.

They were now and forever to be called, "The Redeemed Ones."

It wasn't until Pierce explained this that they realized what had happened. They, like Pierce, were changed in the blink of an eye … different … totally transformed … purely clean. The burdensome and overwhelming brokenness that Bella had felt for the twins was gone in a flash. She still knew in her brain that they were not here with her. She was well aware that King Shrailzhar had captured Jennifer, and Judah was nowhere to be found. Somehow, in the presence of this One of all Light, peace rained upon her, covering her from the outside and a trust in this One filled her like a fountain from the depths of her belly and flooded her from the inside. The peace here was a thousand times fuller and truer and deeper and richer than what they'd ever experienced in the Chamber of Rest.

There was not a shadow of fear or a sliver of shame left in Bella—or the others—anywhere. Bella knew this One had His eye upon both Judah and Jennifer and that whatever was happening far below in Trilleah, was the way it needed to be for a time such as this.

All of the Redeemed Ones had a complete knowing that this Nameless One was in control of all things. No words were needed to explain such things—they were just known here—all things were.

Whatever the reason the twins were not here with them now, this One would be with the twins … wherever they were.

They were right, of course. The Nameless One had so many of his strongest and most powerful Shamar Shailmas surrounding both Judah and Jennifer, that whatever would come to them, they would be okay. The Nameless One had endowed those Shamars with an extra measure of strength and an additional portion of power and a double portion of courage to enable the twins to do exactly what it was they were brought to Trilleah to do—bring freedom to the souls that were so painfully waiting.

Judah, on the other hand, was having a very hard time knowing anything other than misery and regret. There was a full portion of remorse spread out before the boy, and he was having one helping after another, choking on its miserable bitterness.

Even though his mamma had come to him from the flames and had told him that Jennifer was never his to look after, and it was necessary he let go of her and let whatever needed to happen come, it was no easier for him … not even slightly. The boy was in such a wretched state of anguish that again he considered throwing himself into the River of Acheron.

Judah fell to the ground and began clawing at his skin with the sharp rocks. If he could not trade places with his sister, if he was supposed to just let her go and face the worst of all possible deaths on her own, then he did not want to live either. There was no way he should live if Jennifer had to die. He couldn't bear such a thing. What kind of ridiculous treachery was that? A string of terrible words tumbled from his mouth, and a few more slipped off his tongue.

One soul condemned for the freedom of many?

Shemaiah had said those exact words earlier, and he just now was realizing what it meant. That was complete rubbish and he'd have no part of it. How could he? Unless he was that one soul—unless he could free his sister—then *his* life was without meaning and he would end it himself.

Judah stood up and watched the blood from his slashed arms flow down. He took a step toward Acheron and lifted his foot to take a second step. There was no second step to be taken, however, for at that moment something so bright and powerful caught his eye that he was immediately thrown back down to the ground.

The brightness of whatever was in the sky and coming directly toward him overpowered him and threw him off his feet. He wasn't afraid, but rather curious, and he watched closely until the brightness was overwhelming and forced him to shield his eyes with his bloodied arms.

"Stand up," he heard a deep voice say right in front of him. His curiosity was gone and all that remained was fear. He'd heard the voice before but couldn't remember where. He didn't want to stand up; he could hear the great power that was carrying the words of this one and it terrified him. He didn't deserve to stand up; he deserved to be thrown into the River of Acheron.

"Stand up," he heard again and then, a familiar voice repeated it.

"Stand up, Judah," he heard Pierce say. Judah immediately stood up because suddenly he remembered where he'd heard the voice and knew it was the eagle who had returned Pierce to them earlier on the journey.

Now the boy stood and faced the mighty Nehsher even though he was trembling uncontrollably. Pierce was hunched high on the back of this one with the wings of an eagle and the face of a lion.

"Pierce," Judah wailed. "I was going to ..." but Pierce interrupted before Judah could finish his sentence.

"I know what you were about to do," he said with compassion. "It was the Nameless One who sent me here with Nehsher to stop you."

"But ... but I ..." Judah stammered and stumbled over his words. He did not wish to be stopped. He wanted to carry out his plan and end his life. Feeling nothing certainly had to be better than feeling the horrible anguish that was swallowing him up now. Nehsher must have heard his thoughts because it spoke. The power that carried his words nearly knocked Judah down to the ground again, but this time he stumbled and caught himself.

"Come," Nehsher commanded. Judah looked at Pierce.

"Why?" he asked, but nobody answered. Instead, the voice rang out again with more power and more authority.

"Come to the One who will take away your sorrow and give you rest," Nehsher said.

Judah came. He fought within his mind, though, because he felt like he deserved to feel this pain. He had, after all, abandoned his sister to let her take the punishment that was not hers to take. Judah did not know why the king was so adamant that he take Jennifer, but from the first journey until now, when he had finally captured her, it was clear that Jennifer was always the one Shrailzhar had wanted.

"Judah, trust me," Pierce said. He had his hands out to lift Judah up and finally, after a terrible battle between the voices in his mind that went back and forth, Judah clutched Pierce's hand and hovered on the back of that Great Eagle, right beside Pierce.

"Thank you," Pierce whispered. "Now hang on for the ride of your life. You will never experience again what is waiting for you on the other side of the veil."

Pierce was right.

The way up, under the canopy of the Shamars and through the tunnel of magnificent light, dodging the lightning and soaring around the hail, was unbelievable—truly inconceivable. But what was on the other side of the veil, nobody would believe even it was told to them. Only experiencing such awe, such wonderment, such splendor, would cause one to believe and even then, it seemed perfectly and believably unbelievable.

Judah saw the others—Kaija Mae, Bella, Sam, and everyone else; everyone except for Jennifer. But at that moment, it didn't overtake him. In the very instant that the One of all Light was before him, Judah fell to his knees like the others who had already faced the Nameless One. He went through the same feelings of guilt and regret and shame that the others had experienced, and then, the words of the Nameless One rang out loud to Judah's ears.

"Stand up," the light echoed, and Judah stood up.

He immediately looked to the others, and they hugged and danced and rejoiced. They spoke of how only one moment in the light of that Nameless One blotted out every hurt, mended every heartache, and healed every wound. The scars, of course, remained, but as Judah looked down to his self-inflicted injuries of only an hour earlier, he saw that the wounds had been healed up, leaving only the scars behind as a reminder.

Even the pain of knowing that Jennifer wasn't with them became bearable. It was a knowledge in the mind, not a wound in the soul. In the place where an unbearable pain had been only moments earlier, now stood peace which held hands with a *knowing* that something bigger was at work, something of power was going on and Jennifer had a role to play.

Somehow, these Redeemed Ones knew that her role was the key that would unlock all things that needed to come. This key would turn the lock to close all that was filthy and dark and open all that was true and just. This one key would turn the locks of both good and evil, and even though the Redeemed Ones did not understand it now, they realized that Jennifer was that key.

The *knowing* must have come from the Nameless One Himself, whose very presence brought a deep fullness of joy because that was all the Redeemed Ones could see or sense or feel now. They laughed and danced and spoke of how the other side of the veil was pure dark while this side was pure light.

"How can it be?" one would ask.

"It's the presence of the Nameless One," answered another.

"The One of all Light," squealed a third.

On and on and on the Redeemed Ones went, dancing around and shouting joyfully and singing perfectly in tune. There was nothing of any darkness here—no shadows, no regret, no sadness, no rejection, no fear. Only light—pure and sacred light.

"All things are as they must be," thundered the One of all Light.

Of course, the voice of this One caused them all to stand in motionless awe and face Him. As they did, they noticed that Nehsher had left and wondered if the Nameless One had spoken the words to them, or to the eagle as it disappeared back through the veil.

There was one more in need of rescuing before the ground gave way and Trilleah fell into the sea that was thirsty and tired of waiting.

Every Traveler crossed their fingers and hoped that when Nehsher returned, Jennifer would be perched high on his back.

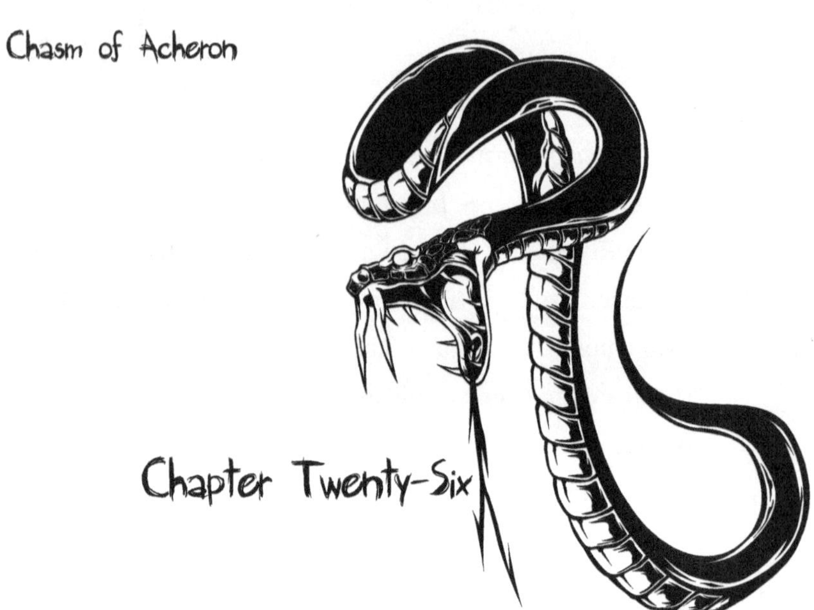

Chapter Twenty-Six

One Pure Soul

Jennifer hung her head, defeated, and let her chin bounce up and down, banging against her chest. It hurt her neck, but then everything hurt. Her wrists throbbed from the chains and her ankles ached from the shackles. Her head throbbed from earlier when the king had grabbed her by the hair as he rode between her and Judah when they were running for their lives.

That wretched brute of a king had cornered Jennifer earlier without even having to slow down. Judah was thrown to the right of the king's beast as Shrailzhar reached out and grabbed Jennifer. He lifted her up by the hair and slammed her down hard behind him. For a minute, Jennifer thought the king was going to double back and grab Judah too, but he didn't. He just kept riding, straight ahead, with the army marching behind him, chanting.

"Oh, Judah," she cried quietly now. Big, hot tears rolled down her cheeks and stung where her face had hit the back of this beast she now sat upon. Jennifer went right back in her memory to the moment the king had finally caught up to the twins.

Judah had been screaming at her to "MOVE FASTER," but she was already moving as fast as she could! Her feet were going much quicker than the rest of her, and she'd stumbled and fallen. Judah picked her up and was so patient; he never let go of her. Even when she kept stumbling, somehow her brother had hung on and kept her on her feet and moving at breakneck speed.

Then, her memory took her to an ugly place, one she didn't want to recall and hoped that she was remembering it completely wrong. She was not, though, and Jennifer knew it but had a hard time admitting to herself that Judah had, in the end, let her go.

There was no doubt that he had purposely let go of her hand. There was no reason for it, not at the moment when it happened. Jennifer could have understood it if she'd fallen or if Judah had stumbled and not wanted to pull her down with him. But in that one moment when her brother did let go of her hand, nothing was in the way. Neither of them tripped or stumbled or had to move in a different direction. There was no doubt about it; her brother had willingly let her go; he'd given her up to the king.

It didn't seem like he was particularly trying to save his own skin either, though, because the king was still a ways behind. Judah may have had to let go of her hand eventually; the king may have given them no choice … but not then … not at that moment. He could have gripped her hand for many more steps.

In the wretchedly pain-filled memory that was playing over and over in her mind, Jennifer glanced at Judah's face and saw a look that shattered her heart. It was the same look she'd seen on his face when the vines had pulled her into the adder's pit—that brief moment when she had looked up and had seen him gawking down at her. There was no good word that she could come up with to describe the look, but horror and dread and regret and even guilt … if all rolled up into one … might begin to describe the look she saw then—and the look she'd seen again now.

Jennifer understood it the first time when the vines had yanked her below, into the adder's pit. It was in an instant, and of course, both Judah and Matt who had her firmly by the hands were taken by complete surprise as she was ripped from their grip. The boys would have done anything to keep her tiny hands wrapped in their big ones. There was nothing they could have done to save her then; she'd understood that. But now?

This time was different.

Judah had the same look on his face, but he was not taken by surprise at all. Jennifer remembered feeling her brother let go of her hand and even though she reached out for him to take hold again, he didn't. The words he screamed to her as he slowed down noticeably, right before the king scooped her up, rattled in her mind now, as though it took all this time for his dreadful words to reach her ears.

"I'M SO SORRY, JELLY BEAN ... PLEASE ... PLEASE FORGIVE ME!"

It seemed that her brother had purposely given her up to King Shrailzhar—abandoned her to the enemy. Of course, that *was* exactly what he had done, but she'd never let herself believe such a thing. Jennifer had no way to understand that he didn't want to let her go, or that he had been fighting with his Shailma for so long over it. She had no way to see how broken he was about it, or how he'd nearly thrown himself into the River of Acheron because of it.

Neither of the twins could see beyond what was right in front of their own eyes and so they were unaware that things were exactly as they needed to be so that the Waiting Ones could be set free.

Jennifer's heart was completely shattered, not because King Shrailzhar had finally captured her, but because she knew in the depths of her soul, that her brother had abandoned her to the king. She sniffled louder than she meant to and the king sneered at her.

"What's the matter, Jenniferrrr?" he mocked. "Did everyone leave you? Where's your dear Simeon? Has even that one left you to me?" The king pretended to look to the right ... and then to the left.

He acted as though he was straining his eyes trying to find Judah or Simeon ... anyone at all. "I don't see anyone!" he taunted and mocked ferociously.

How badly she wanted to scratch his eyes out, and if her hands would not have been tightly bound behind her back, she would have tried to do just that.

Instead of screaming back at him, she searched for Simeon. She didn't know much about anything that was going on right now, yet she was confident that Simeon was still with her. She called loudly for him in her mind.

Simeon, she hollered. *I need you.* She was not the least bit surprised, and her tears slowed a little, as his voice came to her mind.

I am here, Little One, he said calmly.

Jennifer, the time has come for me to explain such things to you. She was not sure that she wanted "such things" explained to her, but it was better than listening to the grunting and growling of the king and his beast, she supposed, so she tuned her mind fully into the voice of Simeon and listened carefully.

The day you and Judah were born, I was there in the room with Molly and Theo, Simeon began. *Oh, how pleased your mamma and daddy were to have Judah, and then you.* She could not see Simeon, but in her mind, she knew he was smiling as he remembered back to those moments.

Your mamma and daddy thought you were both boys, so they had no name chosen for you, only a boy's name. Oh, Little One, you took them by surprise even on the day of your birth.

It took them a while before they could settle on a name, even though your name had been planned long before that moment you entered the world, Jennifer. It means White Spirit you know, Jennifer does.

No, she did not know that, nor did she know that her parents were expecting twin boys.

White is the color of purity, which is what is necessary to free the Waiting Ones. Furthermore, Simeon went on, *Lillian means pure, and so, from the minute you were born, you were a Pure White Spirit.*

Now Jennifer was so confused by all of this freeing the Waiting Ones' gobbledegook-poppycock, and so she asked Simeon about it.

I thought the tablets would break the curse, she said. *Why am I needed if the tablets are going to break the curse? Besides all of that, why is the curse not already broken, Simeon? We collected all of the clay tablets! How is it that the souls of the Waiting Ones are still trapped?* She waited impatiently for more understanding to these things of utmost importance.

Breaking the curse is twofold, Simeon explained. *Both the tablets and a Pure Soul is required. The words on the tablet will break the curse, but the Chasm of Acheron is too wide for them to get across. The souls will no longer be bound, but One Pure Soul is* required as an exchange to open the gates for them to be released from Acheron. Does that make sense, Jenny? Simeon asked.

I suppose it does, but what is a Pure Soul and who has one? She still had not made the connection that it was her soul that must be exchanged for all those waiting in Acheron to be released.

One soul to free many, she'd heard Simeon whispering the words repeatedly. He was somehow chanting that even while he explained other things.

Your name came from the One of all Light, Little One, Simeon continued. When you were born, the Nameless One sent me to your parents with the name. The Nakahs were already there, trying desperately to persuade your parents to use a different name. A great battle was waged right there, from the very beginning, Little One. Don't you see?

Your mamma and daddy finally did choose Jennifer Lillian, and the war was on to grow you up into exactly who you needed to be in order to free the Waiting Ones. You see, Little One, it's you. It's always been you.

Oh, Jennifer was confused indeed, but slightly less confused than before. Rather than waste any more time on understanding this, though, she asked another question.

Simeon, why me? There were probably hundreds of babies born in that same hospital, so why me? Why was I the one chosen to be the pure soul? I am nobody better than anybody else. I'm just me—small and frail and naive and insecure. I have no special powers or *magic in my hands.* Jennifer was so intrigued by all of these things of which Simeon was speaking, that she had forgotten where she was or who she was riding behind. She completely forgot, although only for a second, to be terrified about where the king might be taking her or what he might do once he got her there. Jennifer would remember soon enough, but for now, she needed whatever information the Shailma could give her.

That is a good question, Little One, one only the Nameless One knows the answer to. It is not me who chose you, but that One of all Light who chose you, he replied tenderly. *I do know, however, that He told me you were special; a one-of-a-kind soul because of your great ability to trust.*

You trust me, Jennifer. Before you ever saw me, you trusted me. When you heard me in your mind, you trusted that it was I who was speaking and you never doubted. You trust, Little One, and that is what the Nameless One requires. That trust is what makes you unique.

Furthermore, Simeon continued compassionately, *you are trustworthy. No matter how difficult something might be, if I ask you to do it, you obey. You can be trusted to do those things the others would never do. Jennifer, the Nameless One has not told me this, but I believe it is these two things that have caused you to be the one with the Pure Soul—the soul worthy of being exchanged.*

I cannot answer all your questions, Little One. Oh, how I wish I could. How I wish I could rescue you from everything, Simeon whispered with a voice so filled with softness, so overflowing with compassion, so altogether honest, that Jennifer knew he meant it.

These things, though you cannot see them now, you will know them then. In the blink of an eye, Jennifer Lillian Elliot, you will know all these things.

When? she wanted to scream but was very careful to keep every thought, every sigh, every argument, silently within the boundaries of her mind.

Very little of what Simeon was whispering to her heart was making any sense in her mind. She had learned, though, over the journeys and through the years, always to trust Simeon, even when she did not understand. Her understanding of such things, after all, was never required.

It was right now—here in this moment—that Jennifer purposed in her heart to do whatever was required of her, no matter the consequences, so long as Simeon promised to be with her.

Simeon heard her thoughts and answered her straightaway. *Jennifer ... Little One ... I will be with you to the very end,* and indeed she believed that he would be.

Chapter Twenty-Seven

A Broken Curse

"How are we going to figure this out?" Bella asked.

They looked at each other … and then to the tablet. Back and forth it went. There was something much different about the tablet now. The unrecognizable words which had been smoldering with a bright orange glow—like embers in a fire—had changed color. Now, here on the other side of the veil, the fire had died into nothing and what appeared to be blood had taken its place.

The words were etched so deep into the tablet that it looked at first glance like they might go right through. But when the Redeemed Ones flipped the tablet over earlier to see if the words did go all the way through, all they saw was the old clay tablets, all jammed together with the same symbols and jargon as before.

Judah touched the letters and looked at his finger. It was dry. What looked like blood was being held captive within the boundaries of the tablet.

"Unbelievable," he muttered.

"Unbelievable," the others echoed.

A loud thunderous crash was heard on the dark side of the veil and the tablet shook. Judah nearly dropped it.

The Redeemed Ones looked toward the veil; this was the first time since they'd climbed onto the great Nehsher's back that they had felt anything—or heard anything—like that. Now they were immediately taken back, in their minds, to what was going on below.

No fear gripped them, only curiosity and an understanding that something very final was happening in the Dark Land. They wanted to ask the Nameless One about it but didn't dare.

They didn't need to.

As the Redeemed Ones thought about what they wanted to ask and spoke to each other about what it could be—and where Jennifer might be—another great crash roared from somewhere on the dark side of the veil. Instantly, the Shailmas answered their questions —both the ones they'd been pondering and those they hadn't yet considered. Rather than in the privacy of their minds, though, the Shailmas spoke out loud to their ears.

"The War of the Firmament is about over," Shura answered. The Redeemed Ones all turned their heads to follow the voice of the Shailma. They recognized immediately that it was a Shailma who'd spoken.

"The sounds you hear are the final clashes and explosions of the remaining Nakah Warriors being hurled to the ground, for the War has been won. The Shamar Shailmas have defeated the Nakah Warriors." There was great rejoicing among the Shailmas, who the Redeemed Ones realized were all now visible to their eyes. They had never seen such a sight and were in utter amazement of it now.

"Will the Shamars take the rest of the Nakahs as prisoners then?" Kaija Mae asked. Now it was Shekinah who answered.

"Oh no, there will be no more to take as prisoners."

"What then?" Bella wondered. "Surely they won't be freed again to roam and attack and cause such trouble."

The Redeemed Ones heard a great laughter resounding around them. What a sound! It was loud and it was glorious; it was like a thousand trumpets playing in perfect harmony. Never had the ears of the ones listening heard such a powerful—yet magnificent— sound in all their lives.

"The Nakahs will never be freed again … no … not ever," Shekinah explained. "They are being gathered up this very moment and chained together, but not as prisoners. Along with the Nakahs being thrown to the ground is the deafening sound of the Shamar Shailmas pulling out the chains to bind those gathered Nakahs so they can be destroyed."

Now Shura joined into the explanation and was happy to do so. "We have waited for this day for thousands of years," Shura cried. The Shailmas laughed again, which caused the Redeemed Ones to begin dancing and singing and laughing as well.

"Why?" Sam asked. "What's going on this day that you have waited so long for it to come?"

"Oh, Samuel!" shouted Mishan. "This is the day the Nakah Warriors are thrown into the Sea."

"Hmm?" the Redeemed Ones all asked at once.

It was then, at that moment, the Shailmas began to tell the story of how Trilleah came to be, and how King Shrailzhar had once been a mighty Shailma. "The mightiest of them all, in fact, second in command only to the Nameless One Himself!" blurted out many of the Shailmas.

The Shailmas told the story—every detail—to the Redeemed Ones of how King Shrailzhar had been the most beautiful of all the Shailmas but that he had become jealous of the Nameless One and wanted to rule over even that One of all Light.

Of course, this simply could not be, for the Nameless One was the only uncreated being. It was that very One who had created the Shailmas—all of them—even the king of the Shailmas, whose name was called Shrailzhar.

Shura told how Shrailzhar had convinced one-third of all the Shailmas to come with him and they would go and rule Trilleah. He would be the king, and they would have great rule and authority over everything in the land.

"They were all lies because after all, Shrailzhar was known by this time as 'the lying one.' He chose the weakest of all the Shamars to follow him because he knew they were weak in their minds and would believe his lies," Shura explained. Again they laughed and the joyful uproar was beautiful music to their ears.

"The Nameless One allowed Shrailzhar to rule Trilleah, but soon the foolish king became unsatisfied even with that. Oh, he is a jealous one, that stupid, ungrateful king," Shura continued. "What he did then, was he began to steal the souls of those who belonged here, with the Nameless One. He chose to crown himself, King of the Dead, and stole as many souls as he could from the One of all Light.

"Because the Nameless One would never give up the souls of those who belonged to Himself—not even one—He spread out a great and horrible sea of fire beneath Trilleah and put a limit on how long Shrailzhar could remain on the land.

"Trilleah used to be filled with such beautiful colors cascading and flowing off of every corner, but when the One of all Light banished King Shrailzhar to the land, He removed its beauty and called every fleck of color back to Himself.

"Every ounce of light was driven out of the land, which is why it is referred to as the 'Dark Land' and all that was once alive and beautiful was now dead and … well … exactly how you saw it." Shemaiah explained. "When the Nameless One suspended the veil, it was a promise that all light and beauty and color would never return to Trilleah. Furthermore, a great and horrible sea was laid out just beneath the crust of Trilleah's ground, ready to swallow Shrailzhar and all those who had followed him. It's been thirsty, waiting all this time."

The explanation was going fantastically well … until this point. The Shailmas had been wildly excited at all they had been speaking … until this moment. At this moment in the story, though, every Shailma hushed and only Shekinah spoke.

It was clear to those who were listening intently to the story, that something horrible was about to be told.

"The Nameless One brought His mighty arm back down and said, 'The land I have banished you to shall be destroyed by your very own hand. When you have become so greedy and selfish that you send out even those Shailmas you've taken from here to fight against my Shamars there, and when their breath has been beaten from them, they will be gathered up and thrown into the eternal Sea of Acheron.'

"When that is complete, Shrailzhar, that Sea of Acheron will swallow up everything that sits upon it. It shall drink up the land and inhale each tree and every branch; it will leap into the heavens and lick up even the stars and the moon and the sun. Nothing shall remain.

"Finally, you pathetic one who calls yourself a king, that very Sea of Acheron will lay its hands upon you, and you shall be no more.

Every moment, for all of eternity, you shall remain at the very bottom of that sea, for once inside its clutches, you shall never escape.

"Let this be the punishment for you … and all who you take with you … and all who follow you."

Shekinah still spoke, although much quieter, and for this moment there was no laughter to be heard and no whispers from the other Shailmas. Only the hushed voice of Shekinah lingered in the air.

"In that moment," and here, Shekinah lowered his voice to merely a whisper, "there was silence here on this side of the veil as the decree was made by the One of all Light. It was not good, and we thought it could get no worse. Nevertheless, the Nameless One said to us, there will be one moment where it will be worse—and on that day I will bind Shrailzhar and throw him into the Sea Acheron which I have created specifically for him."

There was a time of great and perfect silence then; even Shekinah stopped making any sound, and the Redeemed Ones stood silent. The only noises heard were the roars of the Nakah Warriors as the Shamars gathered up those last ones and chained them together to be tossed into that Sea of Acheron they were now hearing about from Shekinah.

When the sounds of the clanking chains stopped being heard, and the Nameless One roared out a sound much louder than even the laughter of the Shailmas (and sounded like perfect trumpets blasting in unison), there was another roar on this side of the veil. It was a sound of valiant jubilation as every Shailma—and there were thousands and hundreds of thousands of Shailmas—jumped and laughed and rejoiced and danced and sang.

"Let us sing as we have triumphed victoriously for the Nakahs and their riders have been thrown into the sea."

Oh, the Shailmas sang this over and over and over again. Bright colors such as the Redeemed Ones had never before seen, were splashing here and pooling there and within moments, the light that was being cast from the Nameless One exploded with all the colors of the rainbow and even more than that. The Redeemed Ones joined in with the Shailmas and together, all around the Nameless One, they danced and sang with great jubilation.

Kaija Mae noticed something at her feet, like she was suddenly standing in a pool of color. She bent down to pick up the tablet and as she looked at it one last time, words she'd never said before fell from her lips. She knew they did not come from her, since she didn't know the language of the tablets, but as they rolled off her lips, she and the others knew undoubtedly that this was what was transcribed on the tablets.

"I have gone before you, I have fought against your enemies, I have won; it is finished—the curse has lost its power," she said with boldness. As she said the words and held the tablet in her hands, it turned to liquid and flowed all around the feet of the Redeemed Ones.

She squealed a delighted squeal, and in seconds the others joined her.

"What happened?" they began asking.

"Why did the tablet turn to liquid?" Bella asked loudly.

"You broke the curse, of course!" the Shailmas began squealing. Oh, how excited those Shailmas were. How very intoxicated the Redeemed Ones felt.

"But how?" Sam cried out.

The loudness and the dancing and the singing continued, but Shura spoke loud enough for the Redeemed Ones' ears to hear his voice.

"You broke the curse … You broke the curse!" he repeated on and on and on until all the Shailmas were singing the same song, chanting the same words of "You broke the curse."

Finally, Shura explained to the very confused, but over-the-moon excited Redeemed Ones, that the curse of the tablets could not be broken until after the Nakahs were finally gathered and thrown into the Sea of Acheron. Once that was complete, the curse could be broken but only by redeemed souls, and only when one of those souls said the words, "It is finished," as Kaija Mae had done. Then, those redeemed souls, together with the Shailmas from the light side of the veil sang together these very specific words:

"Let us sing together as we have triumphed victoriously, for the Nakahs and their riders have been thrown into the sea.

"You see, the tablets held the blood from one dozen Nakahs and one ounce of fire from the Sea of Acheron," Shekinah explained.

"That's why there were one dozen tablets and why, when you laid them together in the proper pattern beneath Nehsher's veil, the blood began to bubble up. Then, you were able to see it through the words etched into the clay. That clay was thirsty for the blood of the Nakahs," Shura wailed excitedly.

Shekinah continued since Shura was too excited to do so.

"After the War of the Firmament was won—but before the Shamars could gather the remaining Nakahs and chain them—the fire in the tablets turned to blood. You see, the clay knew that all the Nakahs' blood was about to be fed into the fire and was forced to give up even the drops that had been hidden in the clay tablets."

Now Matt's Shailma jumped in and told more of how the curse was broken. It seemed as each Shailma would speak out a piece, they would become so excited that they'd become unable to speak and another Shailma would have to take over.

"The moment we joined together and sang those words, the ones that would break the curse King Shrailzhar had put on the souls of the Waiting Ones to hold them from coming to this side of the veil, that dreadful curse was broken and the tablets turned to liquid."

"You broke the curse," the Shailmas began chanting once more. "The Redeemed Ones have broken the curse of the blood and the fire … The Redeemed Ones have broken the curse of the blood and the fire … The Redeemed Ones have broken the curse of the blood and the fire."

The Redeemed Ones began to look around, expecting the souls of all those who'd been trapped beneath that curse for so long to suddenly be here, with them, on this side of the veil. That did not seem to be happening and the Shailmas, of course, understood what they were looking for.

"Oh dears, the souls of the Waiting Ones cannot yet be released, we're afraid," Shura said.

"But the curse has been broken!" Bella squealed, still outrageously excited and looking everywhere for Molly. "We broke the curse of the blood and the fire! You said it yourselves," she cried happily.

"Yes, the curse has indeed been broken, and the River of Acheron can no longer hold the souls," Mishan explained. "However," he continued, "the chasm is far too wide, and One Pure Soul must be exchanged for those still locked behind the chasm. These souls are no longer cursed, but they need one to take their place so they can go free. That One must get the key and open the gates."

Nobody needed to explain anything else. The Redeemed Ones knew without even one Shailma having to tell them, who that One Pure Soul was.

They knew, even though no one spoke of it, that Jennifer was that one.

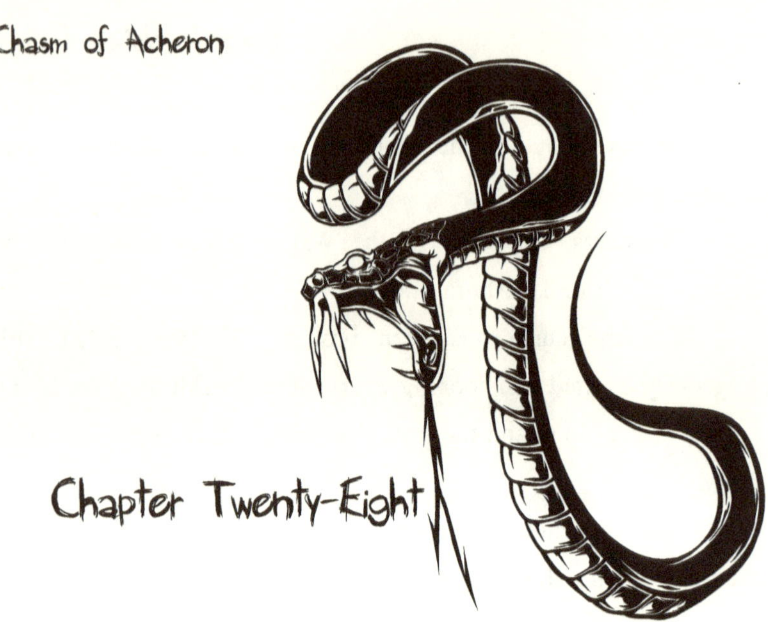

Chapter Twenty-Eight

Shackled

"Ahhh … HERE WE ARE!" King Shrailzhar bellowed from the very bottom of his belly. Oh, how he laughed, making his entire grotesque self, shake. That miserable king threw his head back and laughed the most disgusting laugh ever and commanded his army to do the same.

Jennifer shuttered from head to toe. If she had even a morsel of anything left in her belly, it would have come up, and really, she wished that she had. She would have thoroughly enjoyed the opportunity to spew all over this pathetic beast of a filthy king, one last time.

"Bring her down," that wretched one shouted to his army.

He seems to be in a desperate hurry suddenly, Jennifer thought. Of course, he was in a hurry. He had heard the same clanging of chains and thunderous roars that the Redeemed Ones had heard on the other side of the veil. The king did not need any explanations of such sounds, however. He knew what they were from and he knew his time was short.

Shrailzhar knew that all the remaining Nakahs—the ones who had not been beheaded or thrown to the crumbling crust of Trilleah—had been gathered and chained by the Shamar Shailmas. King Shrailzhar had a full understanding of what the Nameless One had promised to him, and now, with the clanging of those chains and the trumpet blast and the Shamars' laughter, the king knew his time was nearly gone. He could almost hear the last grains of sand drop through the hourglass, counting down to the final moments of his destruction.

Yes, that would explain his hurry if Jennifer had any idea about all these things that the king knew of, which of course, she did not. Jennifer didn't know anything about the Nameless One, or the other side of the veil, or that there was a veil at all. She had no knowledge that the curse had been broken and all that was needed now to close the chasm of Acheron and release those no-longer-cursed souls was the blood of One Pure Soul.

All she did know, was that Shrailzhar was suddenly in a very big hurry.

The army generals were not gentle with Jennifer. While one was unshackling her feet, another was yanking her from the top of that miserable beast to which she had been tied. She wanted to scream out, "Wait until I'm undone, will you?" but she did not. In fact, Jennifer kept her mouth completely shut. She had decided to seal her lips and say nothing to anyone no matter what happened or what questions were asked of her or how deplorable the anguish from the taunting king became. She had nothing to say, after all, so she decided to stay quiet.

Simeon was with her. Jennifer needed not open her mouth for her Shailma to hear her … or for her ears to hear from him. Even though her mouth was sealed, her soul was not, and she talked much with Simeon. Great amounts of wisdom, strength, and courage were passed between the Shailma and Jennifer during this time of such anguish.

Jennifer remembered the songs that Mamma had sung to her before the accident and she let them run through her mind now. Simeon joined in and together they sang in the silent places of her mind … those places where nobody else got to see.

Jennifer had no idea what would happen to her, but she had resolved that whatever was to come, her soul would remain steadfast. She would keep her lips sealed, her eyes focused on Simeon, and her thoughts on Mamma.

Yes, that will be enough, she reasoned.

As Jennifer pondered these things in her heart, she remembered that Simeon had mentioned something about telling her what had truthfully happened to Mamma and Daddy. She asked him about it now, confused by his words.

They were in a terrible accident, she whined to her Shailma. *They went out for an evening and never came back,* she recalled with great sadness. As those brutish army guards were prodding her to "get moving," to wherever it was they were taking her, she stopped singing and instead let the memory of that night replay for the thousandth—and possibly last—time in her mind.

Jennifer watched as Mamma fixed her hair up in that way that Jennifer would never have the opportunity to learn to do herself; she saw herself kiss Daddy just before he went out to get the car. Jennifer was sad now, at remembering how her daddy had smelled so perfectly handsome and strong—like all good daddies should. But even more so, Jennifer was sad because she knew that she would never get to kiss any boys or hold the strong hand of one that loved her like Daddy had loved Mamma. So many things Jennifer said goodbye to in her shattered heart as she thought of countless dreams she would never get to experience.

Jennifer had secretly pretended to kiss Sam, many times, for he was indeed a handsomely funny looking boy, which was just the way she preferred them. But now, wherever Sam might be, his first kiss would be with someone else and her's would never come.

That small girl with the courage of a warrior and the beauty of a princess began thinking of all the things she would never have or adventures she'd never experience. She began to wonder about Judah and all the things he might miss about her. She felt broken about having to leave him and forgave him for leaving her.

Oh, what a deeply courageous girl this one was.

If it is my soul that will pay the price owed for all the other souls to go free, then so be it. I will cover the cost. Anything for Mamma, she cried silently to Simeon. *Find your courage, Jennifer. Find your courage,* she repeated to herself over and over and over again.

But even as she pictured her mamma, who always brought her such strength, it was the others who marched through her mind that gave her the strength to keep going now. It wasn't as if she had any choice in the matter, for if she had, she most certainly would choose something different … anything else.

In her mind, Jennifer saw little Justice and Tom and Peter and, of course, Mamma was there in the parade of souls. Jennifer thought it was only in her mind that she saw such a thing; like she was making things up in her imagination to bring any amount of peace since she was in the most unpeaceful place that ever existed.

BOOOOM!

She was tossed headlong into a cold, small, dark, and terribly smelly pit that had been dug down deep into the ground. At least, it felt like it was under the ground. Jennifer couldn't tell since her eyes were fuzzy and one was badly swollen. The chains on her feet rattled and clanged together.

King Shrailzhar instructed two of his most gigantic soldiers to push a large boulder in front of the hole in the ground and stand guard outside the pit. Those imbeciles did exactly as the filthy king instructed and any amount of dirty, mist-filled light that had been sneaking into that pit faded to blackness as the boulder was put in position. She could hear the guards standing just outside but finally, she was alone in what would surely become her grave.

"Simeon," she whispered.

It was so black in this pit that even the corners of her mind were dark. Those places where she could usually find Simeon were too dark for even the eyes of her imagination to see into.

"I am here," came his voice to her ears.

She felt him beside her and asked, through unstoppable tears, to tell her what really happened to her mamma and daddy that night they went out and never returned. Part of her didn't want to know the truth, but the other part of her, that part that always ended up getting its way, would not do without it.

The truth is a funny thing. Once it is known, it can never be unknown. Sometimes, it's easier to believe a lie because sometimes, a lie hurts less than the truth. Nevertheless, Jennifer asked for the truth now, even though she wasn't sure she wanted to know it.

"Oh, Little One," Simeon said, and for just a moment, Jennifer thought she heard a rasp in her Shailma's voice—like one would expect from a grown man trying to hold back tears.

"That was a terrible night, I'm afraid," he began. "Your mamma and daddy had planned to go out for a celebration and then to return home; it was to be just that simple. They had picked up wonderful gifts for you and Judah while they were out because even though the celebration was just between the two of them, you and Judah were always on the forefronts of their minds."

Jennifer sniffed and sobbed almost silently as Simeon continued with the story.

"There was a vicious battle between the Nakah Warriors and the Shamar Shailmas that night—it was not meant to be your parents' last one. They were meant to live a long, healthy, wonderfully, joyful life together. That time, so long before—when your daddy was sick, that was another time the Nakah Warriors had come and tried to steal him away.

"But the lady down the street, that one who gave him the red blanket which is in your pocket even now, had prayed for your daddy and had asked the Nameless One to take away Theo's sickness. The doctors could make no sense of it, Jennifer, because it was not a human illness. Sicknesses given by the Nakahs are senseless as was your daddy's sickness. Only the Nameless One could remove it, and He did. It had nothing to do with the red blanket, per se, except for the tassels did hold the requests the neighbor had made—the ones the

Nameless One heard. It was because she'd asked so many times—as many times as there are tassels on that blanket—that the Nameless One finally sent the answer and removed your daddy's sickness.

Jennifer had forgotten about the tattered red blanket shoved so deep in her pocket and wished she could get to it now. But her hands had remained chained tightly behind her back, so instead, she pretended she had it in her hands … she pretended to wind the tassels around her fingers just like when she was little. Now, though, she put her own requests into each tassel, hoping this Nameless One, whoever that might be, would hear those requests and answer.

"Jenny," Simeon continued, "those wicked Nakahs came that night your parents died and fought with the Shailmas about the car wreck. You see, Little One, the Nakahs mistakenly thought that if they could lure you to Trilleah, the king could capture you because you were the one with the Pure Soul. Shrailzhar reasoned that if he could lure you to his Dark Land with the soul of your mamma, and imprison you before you could grow up and become wise and strong and oh-so-courageous, that Trilleah—and the souls he'd already stolen—wouldn't be able to be taken from him.

"The Shamars did fight for a long while, but then the Nameless One called them back and assured us all that you were already strong enough to defeat King Shrailzhar. He told us that you were born with the seeds of strength and wisdom—to do what needed to be done—already planted inside of you. The One of all Light told us that He'd put His light in you the moment you were born and so, even if the Nakah Warriors lured you to Trilleah that very night, it would be okay.

"Even that night of your parents' death, Jennifer, you were stronger than any of the Nakah Warriors and, in fact, you had the authority to defeat the king even then. You just didn't realize it yet. Even still, you don't realize it."

"But …" Jennifer was about to ask Simeon how she was to defeat the king when he had such a tremendously large army, but she had no time. The boulder was suddenly pushed aside, and King Shrailzhar stood before her, large and far more hideously evil than ever before. That wicked, wretched king had vengeance in his eyes and hatred in his hands.

He opened his mouth to say something to her … to mock her … to ask where her friends were now … or her Shailma … or the Shamars. The entire time he was sneering and taunting her, that black adder with the blood-red eyes snapped and hissed from Shrailzhar's mouth.

That thing probably comes straight from his heart, thought Jennifer, *if he even has a heart.*

With the smell of his stench making her stomach heave, and the darkness becoming even more so, she heard a voice—faint but certain—whisper to her mind. It was Simeon, of course. He was bringing her the answer to her question from moments ago … the one she never got to ask.

You will know, Little One; you will know.

Chapter Twenty-Nine

Blood Stained

Oh, how that miserable, no-good, wretched, evil king taunted her.

He ordered the guards he'd posted just outside the prison door to shackle her feet tightly to the post that he'd had inserted into the floor the very day Jennifer was born. Her arms had already been chained to the rock wall that she'd been hurled against earlier.

Shrailzhar was giddy with excitement; he'd waited so long for this day—for this moment. He could hardly contain himself now that it was finally here.

So there she was, with her feet shackled to a post and her outstretched arms hitched firmly to the rocks beside her. She was bleeding from countless places by now, and her face had a large gash just above her right cheekbone. Her eye was swollen, her stomach—though empty—was heaving, and the blood in her veins had turned cold.

She was not alone, though. Sure, the Travelers had been separated from her and Judah had let her go, surrendering her to the king. Nevertheless, Jennifer was not alone.

Simeon was with her. He had touched her eyes so she could see him right to the bitter end. Her faithful Shailma empowered her eyes to see many things, things that she'd never imagined—wonderful things, beautiful things. There were countless Shailmas jammed into that pitted prison cell, and it was those ones who Jennifer kept her eyes on. They certainly were keeping their eyes on her.

It was clear that while Jennifer's eyes were opened and could see what was hovering and battling in the unseen atmosphere, Shrailzhar either could not see into that atmosphere or he was choosing to ignore the beings that were there.

That dreadful king rubbed his hands together with gleeful anticipation. He could hardly believe that finally, after all the snares he'd set … after Jennifer had escaped him so many times before … after those stupid Travelers had hidden in their hollow time and time again … and how they'd been covered by a veil from Nehsher, that now, FINALLY, he was about to take her head as a trophy of his victory.

The king had spent a good amount of time over the last year, personally collecting thousands of critters and millions of cradle bugs and all kinds of adders and poisonous vipers. He had been excited to finally have the opportunity to unlatch the doors to those numberless cages that held all those deadly critters just so that he could watch this one suffer. But now … oh, now that she was here in his grip, King Shrailzhar became far too anxious to waste any more time with such trivial things. That despicable king could wait no longer.

With Trilleah crumbling in on itself quickly, his time was limited. The deplorable king knew his fate, but he still believed that if he could just spill out the blood of the One Pure Soul, somehow his own ending might be revoked and his land could be saved.

Yes, Shrailzhar would take her head and let her blood drain out immediately. He'd let all those critters in later to finish off her flesh and lap up her blood.

That king had planned to gather his army as witnesses to her approaching death. Of course, he had killed one-third of his army because they enraged him so, and another one-third had been killed by other means, but there was still one-third remaining. That would be enough to witness his actions. It would have to be …

He had hoped to have the Nakah Warriors join him and the army to guard the prison that he'd made just to hold this one, this

Pure Soul, but they too, were gone. Those Nakahs had failed miserably to win the War of the Firmament.

"What a pathetic bunch of weasily weaklings they were," King Shrailzhar barked to the guards at the prison door.

The king knew that the remaining Nakahs—those who'd made it through the War with both their riders and their heads—had been chained, because he had heard the chains clanging and rattling. He knew what that sound meant. It had shaken the entire land—everything below it and everything above it—clear beyond to the other side of the veil.

He was well aware that when that particular sound echoed throughout his Dark Land, that it was the end of his Nakahs. Those sounds meant that all those Shailmas which he'd been allowed to take with him when he was forced to leave the light side of the veil were useless to him now. Those Nakah Warriors would indeed be thrown into the Sea of Acheron sooner than later.

"INCOMPETENT IDIOTS," he screamed. Yes, he would have to finish this work himself. The king went out of the prison to gather his army, or what was left of them, at least.

"Do NOT let her out of your sight," he wailed to those who were guarding Jennifer.

All this time, Jennifer kept her eyes fastened firmly to the eyes of Simeon. Oh his eyes, how much power and compassion and great love she saw there, in the deepness that pooled just behind his red eyelids. Her mind wandered back to when she was so young; to a time, a better day, when she and Judah had gone swimming.

Just days before Mamma and Daddy had been in the accident —which now she knew was set up by the Nakah Warriors—their aunt Bella had taken the twins swimming. It had been such a lovely day, but too chilly to swim outside. Bella instead took them to the local pool where they had the place nearly to themselves. It was so quiet that day … they never figured out why but it didn't matter. They were happy to be able to spend the day diving into the deep, clear water at the pool.

That's exactly what Simeon's eyes reminded Jennifer of now, and she spent a good while there, beneath the deep waters of her Shailma's eyes.

One memory after another waded through Jennifer's tired mind. Some stayed longer than others, but each one was happy. Not one hint of an unhappy time found its way into her memory.

Suddenly Jennifer was thirsty. She was so thirsty and wondered if she dared to ask the guards for a drink. It was so dark here in this pitted dungeon that she didn't notice the few rats that were gathered in the corner drinking something that was gurgling up from a broken rock.

She tried to clear her throat or find enough saliva hiding in the crevices of her mouth to swallow and wet her mouth a little, but she found nothing.

Simeon, I'm so thirsty, she cried in the confines of her soul.

Hold on, Little One, she heard come back to her. *Hold on.*

There was no time to hold on. In the same moment that Simeon's words came to her mind, the small door—which was nothing more than a broken piece of a boulder really—again slid from its place one more time. Oh, what a wretched sound it made as it was pushed away.

The king was back with his army right behind him. They couldn't see inside the prison because there was no room. There was barely room for the king and the two guards he'd planted just inside the chiseled-out door. Nonetheless, the king gave some ridiculous speech about how the blood of this One Pure Soul would give him back his land and he'd be the greatest king ever and would reign for all time and what-not and so-forth.

He went on and on really, but Simeon graciously plugged Jennifer's ears so that she was deafened to all the ruckus and hogwash that the king was spewing.

Finally, the moment came when that one thing Jennifer had feared most since her very first trip to Trilleah was upon her. Fear did fill her to an overflowing measure and made her dizzy. She began to heave, and her stomach hurled. Her throat was so dry that she began choking.

She watched in great horror as the king put his left hand on the sheath that hung from his side. He reached over with his right hand and slowly and painstakingly wrapped his fingers around the metal handle of his sword. With one swift movement, King Shrailzhar drew out that gigantic, razor-sharp sword, and held it high over his head. Jennifer did not wish to look, but suddenly she couldn't control herself, and her eyes would look nowhere else.

She was sure there would be a glimmer from the blade, which was already so stained with innocent blood that no glimmer could possibly be seen.

Jennifer, she heard Simeon calling her. She could not look away from the sword. She sucked in her breath quickly and tucked it away into her lungs, forcing it to remain there.

Jennifer, look at me. Keep your eyes on me, Little One, she heard come from her Shailma. This time, she did. That fear ravaged girl with her hands chained and her feet shackled, forced the breath from her lungs and her eyes back to Simeon.

Please help me, she begged. Jennifer pleaded with Simeon to overpower the king, to make him so fearful that his own heart would fail. She knew Simeon could do such a thing, she just knew he could.

Little One, I am with you 'till the end, but dear one, the end must come. I want to rescue you. I want to take that wicked king's head off, but the Nameless One has forbidden me to interfere. I cannot help you, I cannot rescue you, I can only stay beside you and give you the courage you require to go through to the end. You must purchase the redemption of the souls with the blood of your life.

Jennifer thought she saw tears falling from Simeon's eyes and indeed, she had. There truly is nothing worse for a Shailma than to have to watch as their mortal suffers, but there is much to gain in suffering. Even though Simeon knew what was to be gained by Jennifer's suffering, it was deeply painful for the Shailma, and he wept openly, without shame. As he stood silently beside this one that he loved so dearly, Simeon wept hard. His tears fell to the dirty ground, and Jennifer thought she could feel them splashing up onto her feet. Never, though, did they look away from one another—not even for a moment.

The king grabbed Jennifer by the hair one last time. He forced her head toward his own face which, for the first time, was not hidden by his helmet. She saw nothing except pure evil in his hateful eyes and perhaps a small bit of fear but then again, probably not.

The black adder snapped at her and was only inches from her face as the king shrieked.

"For Trilleah," he whispered and spit in her face.

The king raised his arm. "FOR TRILLEAH," he screamed. As he did, the Dark Land shuttered for fear of what was about to come.

With one swift motion, Jennifer watched his arm slice through the air, and she felt the sharpness of the blood-stained blade rip through her flesh. She saw blood—her blood—pour out, and as her legs disappeared beneath the pools of bright red blood that flowed freely from her severed throat, Jennifer's world went black.

She would never know it, but at the moment this One Pure Soul gave up her life, the exact second the last breath slipped from her lungs, a deafening *CRAAAAAACK* rang through Trilleah and the land divided itself in two.

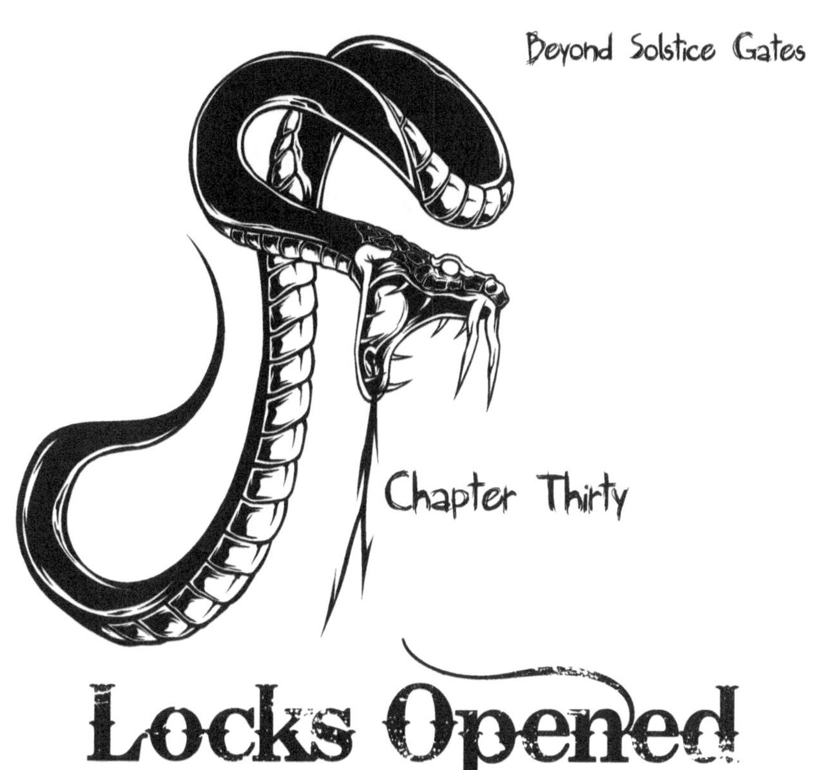

Chapter Thirty

Locks Opened

The Redeemed Ones, who'd been hushed since hearing the clanging of the chains that had been used to bind up the remaining Nakahs, looked at each other with wide eyes and racing hearts. They had heard the echoing CRAAACK that had just reverberated through Trilleah … and they waited in deafening silence.

Nobody had told them to be silent, but a knowing from deep inside their hearts made them aware that something unspeakable had just occurred in Trilleah. No one made a peep or a quibble or even a stutter. They turned immediately toward the Nameless One, who burned brightly, regardless of what may have been happening in the Dark Land below.

In the blackness of that pit—now a tomb—carved into the belly of the land, the king threw his head back and laughed horribly. The guards who had watched what this miserable king had just done, were silent. There was nothing to say, so nothing was said.

Shrailzhar watched with gleeful satisfaction as the deep red blood of this One Pure Soul ran down to cover his boots. He stomped his feet in it, making it splash everywhere. The smell was nauseating, but the king didn't notice. It was a victory for him, and he was not going to let the sick joy he found in this moment, pass him by without enjoying his final overpowering of the One Pure Soul.

He moved to the opening of the prison, which would now be Jennifer's grave. The king tipped his head toward the sky, pointed his blood-smeared sword into the air, and screamed. "THE BLOOD OF YOUR PURE ONE RUNS ALONG THE GROUND AND SEEPS INTO THE DIRT... MY DIRT. SHE IS NO LONGER FREE, FOR I HAVE DRAINED HER OF HER BLOOD AND TAKEN HER LIFE." Shrailzhar laughed and sneered and sneered and laughed. He was intoxicated with his self-proclaimed victory and enjoyed thoroughly screaming in the face of the Nameless One. Shrailzhar couldn't see Him, but he knew that the One of all Light would know of Jennifer's demise.

Oh, how Shrailzhar truly believed that was all which was required. That stupid king thought that without the Pure One, Trilleah would be his. He stepped out and called the guards out of the tomb. Shrailzhar instructed them to move the boulder in front of the hole and stand guard at the tomb just in case someone came to steal her morbid and broken body.

The guards did as they were ordered and the darkest of all darkness filled the tomb completely. Not a crack of light could push its way inside. Even the rats scattered, scared of that much darkness.

Trilleah continued to fall apart, only quicker now. Monstrous chunks of the ground began to give way and fall into the Sea of Acheron, which was beginning to lap the shores as the ground fell away. From one side of the Dark Land to the other, the shores were being revealed, and the sulfur that was rising from the sea was overtaking the air, filling it completely.

The Chasm of Acheron grew quickly, pulling more and more of the gnarled and twisted trees which had held the souls of the Waiting Ones into itself. Like a hungry lion finding food, the Lake of Acheron quickly expanded and began feeding its hunger with whatever it could pull into itself.

On the other side of the veil, the Redeemed Ones had no idea what was happening below, but they knew that something horrific was indeed happening. The Nameless One disappeared for a time, although there was so much light that remained where they were that His absence wasn't noticeable. The colors continued to dance and the air was singing sweet, delicious melodies.

Bella breathed in deeply.

"Never have I smelled such beautiful air," she said. The others gulped in big amounts of the air and nodded their heads, agreeing with Bella's words. It was thick with lighted purity.

"There aren't words to describe how a smell can be beautiful but indeed, it is!" Kaija Mae said.

"It's like a million flowers releasing their scent all at the same time," Bella replied. "As though they are opening their petals for the first time, sending out all that has been held in."

The Redeemed Ones wandered this way and that, free to go anywhere they chose as long as they stayed on this side of the veil. After all, they'd been on the other side and knew well that there was nothing on that side that was desirable or tempting.

Those ones could not have been more right, even though what had just happened down on the land was more heinous than any of their minds could consider. Some things in the Dark Land were so dark, so deplorable, so disgusting, that the mortal mind is without an ability to comprehend it. Likewise, some things on the other side of the veil are so breathtaking, so perfect, so pure, that the mortal mind can come up with no words to explain it.

A rattling loud SPLASH was heard. The Redeemed Ones looked toward the veil, knowing the sound came from the other side of it, far below them. Now even one of them inquired as to what caused the sound; they knew, without having to question it. Those Redeemed Ones were perfectly aware that the splash came from the Shamar Shailmas tossing the Nakah Warriors into the Sea of Acheron.

The Nakahs were no more; not even one remained.   Whether the Shailmas threw in the living Nakahs or the sea had lapped up the dead ones, it was clear that none remained.

Judah wondered about his sister and asked Shemaiah about her. He kept expecting Jennifer to appear through the veil and nothing that he would hear or smell or see would convince him of anything different. She would be coming soon, he knew it. She had to come, didn't she?

Where the Nameless One had gone to, none of the Redeemed Ones would know. Where that One had journeyed to was for the very purpose of redeeming one more. Before Jennifer's tomb filled with blindingly radiant light, the Nameless One went first to Shrailzhar.

"STAND UP," he commanded firmly to Shrailzhar. The king knew that he had to do what this Nameless One commanded, for whether they were on this side of the veil or the other side, the Nameless One ruled over both.

That Nameless One bound Shrailzhar with the skin of his own Nakah Warriors and weighted him down with the bones of his army. With one last violent assault, the Nameless One dragged Shrailzhar across his dilapidated kingdom of Trilleah, to the very edge of the Chasm of Acheron, where the hungry fire was jumping and dancing and begging to be fed. In one motion, the Nameless One fed the King of Trilleah to the sea and just like the promise had been made, Shrailzhar was indeed, taken to his death by his own land.

With King Shrailzhar finally at the bottom of the Sea of Acheron, and the dark kingdom of Trilleah destroying itself at a very rapid speed, the Nameless One took a few long strides toward the tomb that held the One Pure Soul.

Jennifer had no blood remaining. Every drop that only recently had run through her veins was now drained out completely and had soaked the ground that held her lifeless body.

Suddenly—quite suddenly indeed—a light so bright that if an eye had been opened to see it, that eye would have never seen anything again for the light would have blinded it, appeared where Jennifer was. Without moving the boulder, the Nameless One stepped through the walls and stood before the one soul who had purchased the redemption of many.

The tomb that held the body of the One Pure Soul was so permeated with light that the darkness hid completely. Not a shadow could be found anywhere, and nobody was inside to witness what would take place next. None would ever know what happened next, except for those who were inside.

The Nameless One stepped out of the light that encased Him. He stepped toward Jennifer and knelt beside her, taking her cold, lifeless hand into his own.

"Jennifer Lillian," the voice of this One whispered. His words were carried to her on the wings of peace and nearly before He'd finished whispering them, they reached her heart and began breathing life back into it. He lifted her head and laid His free hand over her throat, sealing it up completely, leaving only a scar.

"Get up," he said gently. He bent toward her and breathed His own breath into her nostrils.

In an instant, Jennifer's eyes opened, and she was able to look directly into the face of this One who was looking into hers. She was able to look at that One because she was the One Pure Soul, now resurrected from death. Where she had been to while she was yet dead, gave her the power to be able to look straight into the eyes of this One of all Light.

Oh, she did. There was nothing that could have forced Jennifer's eyes away from the Ones she was looking into now. There was fire in those eyes, and it raged wildly … yet at the same time, they were filled with a powerful gentleness that she'd not experienced before and would never be able to explain to anyone else.

"Stand up," He said again and lifted her gently to her feet.

Jennifer felt no pain. She glanced down at her feet, which were terribly scarred but held no wounds. She rubbed her wrists, which were the same. Both wrists held deep scars, but there was not a wound on either one of them.

The girl looked down at herself and was so utterly amazed to see that her filthy, bloodied clothes had been replaced with a spotless, seamless, glowing white robe. It flowed down and was held at her waist with a golden buckle-less belt. She had no words but saw that this One of all Light who stood before her, had gathered up every drop of her blood and had poured it into the most beautifully pure, crystal flask. There was no trace of her blood left on the ground or on the rocks where she had been chained.

As she was looking at her new garments, spotless and without even a wrinkle, she noticed something hanging on that golden belt which hung perfectly around her waist. She ran her fingers along what turned out to be one large, solid gold key.

"What is this?" she asked. Certainly, Jennifer did not expect this One who was before her to answer, but that is exactly what happened. This One with the eyes of fire and a voice as smooth as oil but as powerful as the wind opened His mouth and spoke to her.

"Pure One," He said, "when you were without breath or blood, Simeon took you to the deepest parts of Acheron. While you were there, you looked Shrailzhar right in his eyes. You spoke words of a warrior, full of power and authority. You defeated him completely and you took this key from him."

Now, while the Redeemed Ones who remained on the other side of the veil in the most heavenly places had been far too unsure to speak directly to this Nameless One, Jennifer was not. She had no uncertainty about exactly who this One was, nor was she too timid to speak directly to Him. She knew that this was who had returned life to her and who'd replaced her bloodied clothes with this pure and spotless robe. He was the One who had forced the ground to return her blood and now held it firmly in that crystal flask.

"What is the key for?" Jennifer asked, even though she already had a fairly good idea that she already knew.

This Nameless One just smiled brightly at her, His eyes of fire danced with joy, and He took her by the hand. He was the most gentle being that Jennifer had ever experienced. Her heart was filled with perfect peace merely from standing in His presence.

"Roll the stone away," that Nameless One spoke, and without anyone to hear Him, Jennifer wondered if He was speaking to her. She looked up to Him, but before she could think a thought, the stone rolled itself away.

Even the rocks obey His voice, Jennifer thought to herself.

Hand in hand, the Nameless One, and Jennifer—the One Pure Soul—exited the tomb and moved to the edge of Acheron, although their feet never touched the ground because the ground no longer existed. It had been swallowed up by the Sea of Acheron.

The chasm was so wide now that Jennifer's eyes could not see from where she stood, to the other side. She had no fear, though, even when Nehsher came from somewhere high in the smoky-ash-filled sky, and hovered effortlessly before her.

Swoooooosh ... Swoooooosh ... Swoooooosh ... she heard.

With no words being spoken, the Nameless One picked Jennifer up gently and set her in the same manner onto the strong back of Nehsher. It had the same lion's face as when it had returned Pierce, and Jennifer was confident this was the same being.

"Go now," the Nameless One said simply to Nehsher. The beast spread out his immense wings and with one brisk sway, the Great Eagle rose up and carried Jennifer over the chasm. Once the chasm was crossed, that mighty Nehsher landed and pointed Jennifer toward a lock. She hadn't noticed it before, but somehow she knew that this was the very reason that all of those things which had happened before were for … all of it was for this exact moment.

Jennifer was indeed the One who had to give up her life so that her Pure Soul could go to the depths of Acheron. It was there, and there alone, where King Shrailzhar would be defeated. There, at the bottom of the sea, as she defeated Shrailzhar, her pure soul retrieved the key—this very key that would now open the Gates of Acheron and close the Chasm, releasing all those souls of the ones who'd been waiting for so long to be free.

That was the exchange that had been spoken of.

"One Pure Soul in exchange for many."

That was exactly what Jennifer had done.

With one big breath breathed in, and a nod toward Simeon who still stood by her—who had always stood by her—and with the powerful Nehsher hovering above her—Jennifer put the key into the lock and watched it fall open.

Chapter Thirty-One

Risen Souls

In one instant … one moment … one breath … every soul that had been locked inside Malleana Forest for so many years, and then trapped inside the Chasm of Acheron for far too long, were free. Jennifer watched as hundreds of thousands of souls ascended toward the heavens and disappeared beyond the other side of the veil.

Next, every soul that had fallen into the River of Acheron, which Jennifer was sure would be unsavable, suddenly began ascending from the flames. It looked to her eyes like the flames were opening up like hatch doors and releasing the souls they'd been holding onto so desperately. She watched with joy as those souls rose higher and higher until her eyes lost sight of them.

Of course, Jennifer had not yet been on the other side of the veil, but she knew that after the last soul was raised, she too would be. What she did not know, was that once her own soul was safely on the other side of that veil, she would be robed in splendor and greatness as that One Pure Soul who'd been required for such a great exchange to be made and the curse to be broken.

The Great Nehsher stood, in honor of those souls that continued to rise from the flames. Jennifer was so proud that she had turned the key and released these ones, yet so completely humbled that she was somehow found acceptable to be the One Pure Soul.

In this very moment of such unmatchable and unimaginable peace, as she saw the souls of Tom and Peter and baby Justice rise in front of her, she knew deep in her knower, that she'd done nothing to earn such a position. Jennifer had been born to regular parents whom she did not choose, and lived a few years in a life which she did not request.

The great pain that had overwhelmed Jennifer when her parents were taken and the rejection she felt as Judah had to let her go suddenly all made sense. Even though she chose none of it, she was thankful that it had chosen her.

Then it happened.

Her mamma.

There was Mamma … and as the soul of that most beautiful one ascended toward the heavens, Jennifer heard the most incredibly beautiful sound that had ever danced in her ears.

"All is as it must be, Little One," Mamma whispered to her, and indeed, it was so.

Epilogue

With the last soul freed from the curse and safely on the other side of the veil, Nehsher scooped up Jennifer and the Nameless One stepped back into His glorious light.

Together, Nehsher, Simeon, and Jennifer ascended into the heavenlies, passing through to the other side of the veil. Judah saw his sister and screamed.

Bella cried out.

The Redeemed Ones spun around and together they ran to her and lifted her up. They would never believe all she'd been through or all that she had seen and so she decided not to tell them. There was no need to, unless of course, they would notice the large scar that crossed her throat from one side clear to the other. That might need some explaining … but not right now.

With one final blast that resounded like an orchestra of ten thousand instruments—playing in a harmony so perfect, so excellent, so pure, that it sounded as though it was one—the Nameless One stood large before the freed souls and the Redeemed Ones. The space was full, because all those ones who'd been entrapped in the curse for so long now stood redeemed before the One of all Light.

Clothed in blinding light, He spoke. His voice rang out from the light like a mighty rushing wind.

First, He spoke to Jennifer. "Well done, Faithful Warrior Princess."

Next, He spoke to all of the Redeemed Ones and all of the redeemed souls now on this side of the veil.

"I AM," he announced. "Both the beginning and the end of all things.

"I have many names and shall forever be called Elyon, Adonai, Elohim. Come to Me all you who are weary and tired and broken and rejected and ashamed, and I will give you perfect rest. I AM your Redeemer who takes your pain and gives you peace in its place. I conquered death, and now I give you life without end.

"I AM the King of the Great Exchange," He roared.

"I AM," He bellowed from the all-encompassing light.

And as He thundered out His countless names—for indeed He never was a Nameless One—He raised His hands and took hold of the heavy veil.

With one great cry and in one strong, swift motion, He tore that veil in two—from the very top to the very bottom. Not even a thread remained to keep one side of the veil fastened to the other, and with that, I AM opened the way for all of the redeemed souls to enter in forevermore.

Chasm of Acheron

The Beyond Solstice Gates Series:

1. Casting Shadows

> Where truth exists ... even if no one believes it.

2. The Fowler's Snare

> Strength is found when the eye sees what the heart already knows.

3. Perfidy of Labyrinth

> Where the only way forward is all the way back.

4. Veiled Sun ✧ Blood Moon

> Where the sun gives no light and the moon throws great
> drops of blood ... singing of both a great and terrible day.

5. Mist Over Leviathan

> Where wickedness of the heart is revealed and
> thrown into the depths of the sea.

6. War of the Firmament

> Where what lies above and what lies beneath,
> is nothing compared to what lies within.

7. Chasm of Acheron

> Where no eye has seen and no ear has heard all that may be,
> when one truly believes.

Page 331

Chasm of Acheron